DAVID LEE HOLCOMB

Strange News

This is a work of fiction. Similarities to real people, places,events, or crows are entirely coincidental.

STRANGE NEWS

CHAPTER ONE

Selby Coates died on his birthday. A remarkable coincidence, he thought, looking back.

When Selby first signed on with the Buckley Herald-Star, boys on bicycles still lobbed the early news against suburban front doors every morning. Orange boxes on every downtown corner dispensed the late edition for fifty cents. Wednesday's paper was fat with coupons and grocery store inserts. Every Friday, the Herald-Star's entertainment section told its readers what movies to see, what restaurants to sample, and what concerts to attend.

The daily paper was part of the landscape, a way of life, as much as the river, the downtown freeway flyover, and the brass statue of Zeus brandishing thunderbolts atop the Pautasquot Power & Light building.

That had been more than thirty years ago. The Herald-Star —now Herald-Star Media—still produced a print newspaper on Sundays for the people who drank craft beer and brewed their morning coffee in a French press, but these days, the real news arrived via a slick website and a flock of email newsletters. All very modern. Clean and efficient.

Selby Coates could read the writing on the wall. Paperboys on bikes were not essential to the new way of doing things. Nor were aging entertainment critics obsessed with vintage drive-in movies.

On the premise that it was better to jump than be pushed, Selby gave notice that September fourteenth—his sixty-fifth birthday—would be his last day with the company.

Management accepted his resignation with relief packaged as regret. Selby spent the next four weeks training the young woman who would be replacing him. The new media critic was a pleasant twenty-something blonde with an undergraduate degree in marketing and a well-heeled husband fifteen years her senior. Times had changed. *Evolve or die*, Selby thought.

When the big day finally arrived, there was, of course, a party. The company laid out cupcakes and cheap champagne in the third-floor conference room at five o'clock. Selby's colleagues and co-workers shook his hand and wished him well. There were even a few tears. Many of those he was leaving behind assumed he would soon drift untethered into senility and death.

Little did they know.

Around a quarter to six, as the festivities dragged to a close, DeQuinn Pitts walked up holding a small box.

"This is for you, Mr. Coates," he said.

"What? For me? Oh. I'm … Thank you, DeQuinn."

DeQuinn was the lobby security guard during regular business hours, Monday through Friday. He had been on the job for three years, and in all that time, Selby had never been able to speak to him without blushing and stammering.

DeQuinn smiled. "I knew they'd get crappy cupcakes—they always do—so Jenny made some last night, and we wrapped one up for you."

Selby opened the gilded cardboard box. Inside, nested in orange tissue and swirls of icing, he glimpsed chocolate cake, rich and dark as tar. DeQuinn grinned and reached over to poke a candle into the elaborately fluted orange-pink crown.

"The cupcake is for your last day, and the candle is for your birthday. I've enjoyed working with you, sir."

Selby had been swilling champagne for almost an hour. He looked at the cupcake and then at DeQuinn and couldn't think of a thing to say. He hoped he wasn't going to embarrass himself.

"You said once that you liked devil's food cake," DeQuinn went on, overlooking Selby's paralysis. "I remembered because it's my favorite, too."

"Please thank Jenny for me. This is sweet."

DeQuinn laughed. "Well, yeah. Cake. Tends to be."

Selby's ears grew warm. "Oh, right. I meant—"

The security guard patted him on the shoulder. "I know, Mr. Coates. I'm just messing with you." He looked around the conference room, littered with half-eaten cupcakes and empty plastic cups. "Speaking of Jenny, I'd better get moving. She'll think I've been run over by a bus or something." They shook hands, and DeQuinn made his departure. The door eased shut behind him, and Selby found himself looking at his own face reflected in the glass, the face of a man who wasn't young anymore, a small man with big ears and a gray buzz-cut, his eyes round and owlish behind horn-rimmed glasses. Selby Coates, alone, a little drunk, holding a cupcake in a box. *Happy birthday, sir.*

He shook his head and looked away.

Selby had taken all his personal possessions home during the preceding two or three days. The entire second half of his life, boxed up neatly and hauled away to be buried in storage. *Might as well go ahead and shovel in the dirt*, he thought.

Champagne and strong emotions: Selby was unaccustomed to either of those things. He rode the elevator down to the deserted lobby, then walked carefully out the front door.

On the sidewalk outside, Selby opened the box to check on the cupcake as if it were a kitten or a bomb, something to be handled with great care. The intoxicating scent of chocolate and sugar rose from the box. Selby stepped off the curb to cross Centennial Avenue, clutching his prize and thinking about De-

Quinn. Thinking about the last thirty years. Wondering about the next thirty.

Somebody shouted, and something happened.

Something *sudden*.

Something *huge*.

Pain blossomed, a riotous jungle of pain, and the world slammed into him, wild and hot, full of noise and glistening chrome teeth.

As he fell, his cupcake flying out of his hands, a voice spoke in his ear, a woman's voice, husky and intimate, plunging him into stillness. "Sleep, dear Selby. Rest. Everything is under control."

Barbara Shelley in The Gorgon, *playing opposite Peter Cushing*, Selby thought. Why was Barbara Shelley talking to him in the middle of the street in front of the Herald-Star? Cushing had worn a beard in that film. Selby always hated that beard. He was able to turn his head just enough to glimpse the gorgon's face, lovely and dark, smiling.

"Sleep, now."

Like I have a choice, he thought, as he turned to stone.

Selby awoke from vast, windy dreams filled with whispers. In those dreams, people told him things he knew were of vital importance, but everybody spoke a language he couldn't understand. He opened his eyes—no commitment, just a peek—and found himself in a hospital bed, surrounded by an assortment of tubes, hoses, and electronic devices. A few of the tubes actually entered his body, which disturbed him, while others seemed to snake around the room for no good reason at all, which irritated him. Selby wanted to get up and tidy the mess away, but he was tired.

Maybe later, he thought.

A handsome, dark-haired woman sat next to his bed, wearing an elegant gray wool suit and a faintly amused expression.

The eyes of the visitor were a peculiar shade of greenish hazel. The color of fallen willow leaves in autumn, dusted by afternoon sunlight. There had been a tree with leaves that color at his Aunt Martha's house when she still lived out in the suburbs. Little Selby had always wanted to climb the willow tree, but he was concerned about the man-eating snakes that haunted the up per reaches, disguised as branches to trap the unwary. He'd seen enough afternoon Shock Theatre features on his mother's fuzzy black-and-white TV to know where danger lurked.

"How do you feel?" The stranger's voice was husky, soothing. When she leaned forward to look down at him, Selby caught the scent of cloves, tea, cedar ... perhaps a hint of beeswax?

Selby took a breath, collecting himself. Everything was a blank from the moment he walked out the door at the Herald-Star.

"All right, I suppose. What happened?"

"You stepped in front of a bus on Centennial Avenue. A little too much champagne, I suspect. How much do you remember?"

"Not a thing."

"Traumatic brain injury will do that."

"Oh. I see. Hence, all these wires and things. Are they necessary? I feel much better now, and one does hear stories of staph infections transmitted by the needles."

The visitor smiled. She had lovely teeth, Selby noted with approval.

"The effort to stave off death may often involve more pain and indignity than death itself," she said. Selby felt this to be a profound and possibly controversial statement for a healthcare worker to make at a patient's bedside.

"Are you my doctor?"

The visitor laughed. "Oh, no, dear. Call me Laylah."

"Is that a first name or a last name?"

"Just Laylah."

"I see. Like Cher. Or Lassie. I'm pleased to meet you. If you're not my doctor, who are you?"

The woman calling herself Laylah had none of the harassed look that ER doctors always had in the movies. She would never be the nurse who falls in love with the broodingly handsome stranger brought in from the desert with peculiar animal bites, or the physical therapist who discovers that her patient is a brain-devouring alien.

The Wasp Woman, Selby decided. *Janice Starlin.* The actress in that role, he recalled, had ultimately been beaten to death with a barbell by her son, a dwarf bodybuilder.

This is not the time, Selby chided himself. "Why are you here?" he asked, refocusing.

"To ease the pain."

"That's rather ambiguous."

Laylah shook her head. "You have nothing to fear from me, Selby. Whatever bad thing could happen already has. Now, you and I can have a little chat."

Selby frowned—or at least he thought he did, although he wasn't sure what his face was actually doing. Things seemed … disconnected. "Can I go home?"

"Can you sit up?"

He tried, failed to move, tried again. "No," he admitted.

"Well, there you go."

Laylah directed his attention toward one of the devices flanking the bed. Selby was able to turn to look at it even though his eyes were staring at the ugly acoustic tile of the ceiling, which was convenient but disturbing.

"That machine displays your heartbeat as a waveform. Humans do so love to measure everything."

Humans. Selby filed that remark away to think about later. "Not much happening."

Laylah smiled. "Exactly. That's your diastole that you see

there, all the way over on the end, but the systole, the other half of your heartbeat, hasn't happened yet."

Selby thought about the buzzer that would summon a nurse or somebody, but his head wouldn't turn, and his hands were a million miles away. Could he shout for help?

"Won't work, dear. They're all out there, those other people, out there where time is, and death. We're here, snug and safe inside your final heartbeat." Her voice was low, her delivery calm and assured.

"Snug and safe. Wait—did you say *final*?"

"Dear, *dear* Selby. You were hit by a bus. Literally. You tied up traffic for almost forty minutes. They brought you here brain-dead, and you died in that bed. Or you're about to, I should say."

This was a bit much. "You have an unusual bedside manner, Laylah."

The woman's skin was lightly tanned, the color of pale honey. Her hands were strong, with neatly trimmed nails, unpainted. The hands of an artist, or a gardener, or perhaps a serial killer. Practical hands. Useful. Selby admired hands like those. In the abstract, at least.

"Thank you," Laylah said. She pulled her chair a little closer to the bed. "Let's be clear about things. You've been killed in an unfortunate accident, brought on by overindulging in fake champagne and cheap sweets on your birthday. Your brain slammed into the front of your skull, then it bounced and hit the back. The double impact pulped your white matter, and the torque tore a large number of long nerve fibers."

Selby felt remarkably clear-headed for someone whose brain had gone through all that, and he wondered how much of what she was telling him was true.

"I would never lie to you, Selby," Laylah assured him. "Surely you realize that things are not as they should be. You're lying in the ICU hooked up to massive life support, and yet here we are, chatting away quite comfortably."

She was right, of course. In the sadly underappreciated *Carnival of Souls*, from 1962, the central character is dead but doesn't realize it. Was that the case here? Could Selby be dead and not have a clue? He wondered if there was a busload of zombies in the waiting room, staring into infinity with hollow eyes.

"So I'm ... *dead*?"

"You're half a heartbeat away from dead," Laylah clarified. "You have some scrapes and bruises but no broken bones. In fact, aside from the terminal brain damage, you're in pretty good shape for a man your age. If we could restore the mess inside your skull somehow, you'd be walking out of here in a couple of days. Well, perhaps limping—you're going to have to do something about that knee sooner or later—but you get my point."

"We're talking about my brain. It's not as though you can fix that with a few stitches. Are you about to propose some exotic, untested treatment? Radioactive bat blood? Kryptonite injections? Nine tana leaves burned at midnight?"

She laughed, a deep, plummy laugh that made Selby want to laugh with her. "Nothing so outlandish," she said. She gestured at the hardware all around them. "You hover at the threshold between worlds. Here, the dream is all that exists. Here, we are outside life and death, and I can do all sorts of interesting things."

"But there's a price, isn't there? Healthcare in America. There's always a price."

She leaned forward, exhaling a scent of incense. Selby thought about candles burning through endless dusty afternoons in dim desert shrines, the hum of voices wandering ancient byways of ritual.

"I will return you to your life. The life you've known. In exchange, you will do something for me."

"What? What can I possibly do for whoever or whatever you are?"

She reached out but didn't touch him. "You will know what to do when the time comes. Do you accept my terms?"

"Can I take some time to think about it first?"

She smiled gently. "There *is* no time, not here, here in this dream. You must choose. Will you accept the peace death is offering you? Or will you take *my* bargain instead and live on? Flawed and frail and human, for another decade, maybe even two or three? Suffering and struggling as the years pile up, and your body slowly gives way under their weight?"

He hated being old and weak, knowing that DeQuinn Pitts looked at him and saw something sexless and withered. He was tired of aching joints and scratchy eyes, of having to get up to pee every twenty minutes, every single night. Selby Coates was tired of being tired.

But *death*?

"I'll do whatever you want."

Laylah stood, smiling, the tips of her fingers not quite touching the bed rail. "I'm glad. Rest now. The day after tomorrow, you'll go home."

Laylah's voice, her scent, and her willow-green eyes brought sleep to Selby's bedside and spread it over him like a blanket. He struggled, clinging to awareness.

"Such a shame about my cupcake," he murmured, his voice slurring, slowing. "It was special. A gift."

The strange visitor looked down at him with a fond smile.

"There will be other gifts."

Sad but comforted, Selby sank back into sleep. He didn't hang on to consciousness long enough to ask what kind of gifts.

The confusion among the hospital staff and administrators was considerable.

A parade of specialists in lab coats and lawyers in tasteful suits marched in and out of his room, speaking gently but firmly, holding out clipboards full of incomprehensible documents for him to sign, offering him pens with the names of pharmaceutical companies printed on them. At first, Selby just blinked foolishly at these people and their papers. Later, he made snappish comments that he knew made him sound like somebody's cranky old virgin aunt but were, he felt, entirely justified by the circumstances.

In the end, the patient agreed to some of the things they told him while ignoring others, and everybody involved decided to attribute the entire episode to equipment malfunctions and over worked ER staff.

As he prepared to check out and go home, he felt that some sort of fanfare would have been appropriate—seeing as how he had just died and all—but he had only been in the hospital for a couple of days, so nobody who hadn't actually witnessed the accident would have even noticed the interruption in his routine. Selby signed the last stack of waivers and NDAs and asked the nurse at the reception desk to call him a taxi.

The cab dropped him at the River City Grocery, a couple of blocks short of his apartment, so he could buy some fancy canned food for his scruffy, one-eyed cat, Pancake, who had been sitting next to an empty food dish for two days. Since there was a bakery right next door, he picked up some cupcakes while he was at it.

As he exited the elevator on the tenth floor of his building, his neighbor stepped from her apartment, glancing up and down the hallway as though there might be wild beasts hiding behind the plastic palm trees next to the elevator doors.

"Hello, Mr. Coates."

"Hello, Rita. How are you?" Selby held up the bag. "Please come in. I have cupcakes. Chocolate with cherry icing. And sprinkles. They were baked yesterday, but they'll still be good."

Selby and Rita Okorie had been inside each other's apartments but did not simply drop by for a visit. Rita was a pretty woman, not small, but graceful as falling leaves. She always covered her hair with a scarf: yellow and green, brown and white, blue and tan. Today's scarf was gray and orange with delicate black markings like the tracks of birds. Rita had moved in with her husband and two children three years ago, and she and Selby were friendly but not friends.

"I can't visit, Mr. Coates," she said in her pillowy Senegalese accent. "I wanted to tell you someone was in your apartment while you were gone."

"In *my* apartment?"

"You didn't know?" She pronounced *didn't* as *diddun*, which Selby found captivating.

"No, I didn't. What did he look like? Or was he a she?"

"A man. Short, maybe a little taller than you." Selby winced at this observation about his height, but she continued without noticing. "Sort of heavy, you know?" She held her arms out from her sides as if pantomiming a gorilla. "A worker. Blue jeans, work boots. Gray hair. He looked suspicious to me, so I knocked on your door after he went inside and then ran back to my place and watched from there, with my door open only a crack. The man rushed out and got on the elevator."

Selby frowned, looking up the hall toward the elevator doors. "I'll call the security people. I've noticed residents propping the back door open when they bring in groceries. Maybe somebody left it open. That would have allowed him into the building."

"Did you leave your door unlocked?"

Selby turned the knob and gave the door a push. It swung open. "I must have. I do sometimes forget to do things."

They exchanged a few more remarks, mere filler, and then Rita returned to her own apartment.

Inside, Selby stood in the middle of the floor, looking

around. The entire apartment consisted of one fair-sized room with a galley kitchen to the side, plus a bathroom and a walk-in closet, so an inventory took only seconds. What was missing?

"Pancake? Where are you, boy?"

He was answered by a falsetto growl from under the bed. Selby released a long breath he hadn't realized he was holding. That sound was Pancake's standard response to strangers. The cat would come back out when he had determined to his satisfaction that Selby was alone.

Selby checked the bathroom and walk-in closet and found no sign of an intruder. He returned to the main room.

Nothing had been stolen, and the only thing the visitor had damaged was a photograph that hung on the wall between his big window and the corner of the room, where it watched over Selby as he slept.

In the picture, eight-year-old Selby was in a park. Old-fashioned deathtrap playground equipment, all steel pipes and protruding rivets, loomed in the background. He was standing in front of his beaming father, whose hands rested on the boy's shoulders. Shrimpy little Selby looked uncomfortable, squinting into the light, his smile strained and unconvincing, but Sullivan Coates was handsome and relaxed. Even in black and white, his charisma was unmistakable.

The mysterious visitor had broken the glass, leaving the fragments on the floor beneath the picture, then attacked the photo itself, clawing at the surface of the image. Selby speculated that he might have been trying to pull the photo out of the frame but was interrupted by Rita's knock at the door. His father's face was damaged, the eyes torn across. Selby stood the picture against the wall. He studied it for a time, something dense and spiky stirring in his chest, then went to get the dustpan and brush.

It was the only photograph of his father Selby owned. As far as he knew, it was the only one in existence.

That night, Selby woke up at every creak or groan from the plumbing and appliances, expecting to find marauders roaming the apartment. Only when the early sunlight was gilding the thunderbolts of the statue of Zeus atop the Pautasquot Power and Light building did he finally slip into a deep and dreamless sleep.

CHAPTER TWO

Morning traffic on Central Boulevard was brisk but orderly, its exuberance restrained by the Tower Circle roundabout. Selby negotiated the pedestrian crosswalks and strolled up the hill toward the 29th Avenue bus stop. His uneasy sleep had left him feeling more tired and bruised than his encounter with the bus.

It's as if it never happened, he thought. He touched the scrape on his cheekbone, virtually the only evidence that he had been in an accident.

He stepped under the awning of the bus stop and surveyed the familiar street, the people passing by, the buildings across the way that he had looked at every day for years. Routines, rituals, familiar byways of thought. Movies about forty-foot praying mantises or women from Mars. The occasional cupcake. His cat Pancake. These were the things that kept Selby's demons at bay.

Except when the demons show up next to my hospital bed looking for a chat, he thought.

"I beg your pardon?"

He looked over, his eyes round behind his glasses. "I'm sorry, was I thinking out loud?"

The woman produced a smile, an October smile, slightly faded, crisped by frost. "We all do it."

The smile added personality to the woman's face, providing a glimpse of past beauty. Her green velveteen jacket, her coloring, and the shape of her face reminded Selby of Hazel Court, vamping both Vincent Price and Boris Karloff in *The Raven*. When did that one come out? Sixty-two? Sixty-three? He wondered whether this woman had ever been a *femme fatale*. He hoped she wouldn't end her days by having a sorcerer's castle fall on her in the third reel.

The woman seemed to sense something of the flavor of Selby's thoughts, and when the bus arrived, she hastened aboard and sat well away from him, avoiding further contact.

The weather was pleasant, and Selby's doctor was always encouraging him to get more exercise, so he chose to walk the mile or so to his destination from the central terminal. He walked down to the pedestrian walkway leading out onto Centennial Avenue and turned east.

The sidewalks here in the heart of the financial district were never crowded. Selby assumed that bankers and brokers preferred not to walk around outside any more than necessary. Perhaps the sunlight was deadly to them. Did they develop physical adaptations for their lives in the cubicles that would startle and dismay people on the street? LCD eyes? Ethernet ports set into their skulls? Were-brokers. Zombie loan officers. Mutant investment consultants. *Not that much of a stretch, really*, Selby thought.

The main headquarters of Herald-Star Media, the building in which Selby had spent most of his working life, was a WPA-era pile occupying half a city block. The facade was covered with a pale pinkish-yellow limestone, carved with stylized bas-relief images of eager photographers with cameras sporting flash attachments as big as dinner plates, men in fedoras hunched over typewriters, and muscular, shirtless laborers sweating and straining over titanic rolls of paper. Selby had visited the pressrooms many times, but the men were always fully clothed and rarely all that muscular. In fact, the pressroom staff as a whole tended toward flabbiness. The digital revolution had a lot to answer for.

"Hi, Mr. Coates!" DeQuinn said, coming around from behind his kiosk to shake Selby's hand. "Glad to see you back on your feet! You looked like you were out cold when the ambulance took you away. Nobody could tell us anything."

DeQuinn Pitts was not in the least flabby. Looking at him gave Selby an ache under his sternum, as though he had swallowed something hard without chewing it first. He had been that young once.

"Just a bump," Selby said. "After a couple of days, the doctor accused me of milking the accident for sympathy and made me go home."

DeQuinn grinned. "Mean suckers, those doctors. What brings you back to the scene of the crime?"

"I'd like to spend some time in the archives. I'm thinking of writing a book."

"I'm sure it'll be a bestseller. Will I be in it?"

"Of course."

The young guard pecked at a keyboard and handed Selby a badge on a red lanyard. He grinned again, his teeth irregular but snowy white, his mouth curving higher on one side than the other.

"Well, then it's bound to be a winner, right?"

Selby chuckled and pulled the lanyard over his head, his ears hot. "Can't miss." He stumbled through his thanks, then crossed the lobby to the elevators and punched the button for "Basement 2."

A minute later, the elevator delivered him to the subterranean region known to all and sundry as Mosley's Mausoleum.

Immaculately clean, dimly lit, rigidly climate-controlled, the basement archives housed almost a century's worth of Herald-Star content preserved on reels of microfilm or sheets of microfiche, on solid-state hard drives, and even, in some cases, on ancient newsprint stored reverently in airless darkness.

Selby knocked on the open door of Owen Mosley's tiny office.

"Hello, Owen. Everything quiet?"

The gnome in a white lab coat ignored him as he finished typing something on a computer keyboard. He pressed a sequence of buttons on an impressive-looking machine and a reel of film behind a narrow window in the front of the device advanced by tiny increments. Click-ka*chunk*. Click-ka*chunk*.

The little man turned his wedge-shaped head, and Selby wondered whether Owen Mosley had ever climbed a mountain, broken a heart, or witnessed a crime.

"Hello, Coates. I thought you had moved on."

You have no idea.

"I did, but I'm back. I need to consult the archives."

Mosley nodded. "That's what they're here for."

Selby gestured toward the empty hallway. "Quiet."

Mosley made a face that Selby chose to interpret as a caricature of polite agreement. "Yes. It is."

Selby Coates and Owen Mosley had worked together for longer than many of the people currently in the building had been alive, and they were even friends in an abstract way. They had never visited each other's homes or had a drink together, yet they had both served for decades as cogs in the same machine. Selby thought Mosley was wasted in the Herald-Star basement. The archivist might have been Leo G. Carroll's mad scientist in the film *Tarantula*. He needed to be in a laboratory in the Nevada desert surrounded by cages of mutated lab animals, assisted by a young female scientist whose strapping blond boyfriend was a big-city journalist, an Army officer, or the local sheriff.

"You know the drill," Mosley said. "Put all materials on the cart when you're done with them. I'm on my way to lunch, but I'll be back in an hour."

"Thanks." Selby imagined giant spiders roaming the Herald-Star basements, held at bay by the boyfriend, his shirt in tatters.

Mosley nodded, oblivious to the clashing mandibles, the dripping fangs, and the hero's sweat-sheened chest. "Have fun."

"Thanks, Owen. I'll let you get to your lunch."

Selby settled into the tiny viewing room and wiggled the mouse to dismiss the screensaver. His login and password were still good—a retirement perk for former employees—and the Herald-Star welcome screen came up.

Somebody had gone to a lot of trouble to deface the only photograph of Selby's father in existence. Why? Who was Sullivan Coates that somebody would go to such lengths?

Selby's life had intersected with his father's for no more than a decade. Sullivan existed—had existed, might well still exist—for a long time outside that relationship. Maybe his name had found its way into the public eye at one time or another?

Selby called up the comprehensive index and started searching. If his father had made enemies during his life—his life apart from the ten years he had spent with Selby and his mother—perhaps there were traces somewhere in the archives. A police incident, a court proceeding, a barroom brawl … anything was possible.

Selby started well but soon began tumbling down rabbit holes. The archives covered an enormous span of local history, and there were shiny things buried everywhere, distracting him from his objective. A couple of hours went by—enjoyably, although not productively—before something startled him out of his rambles.

What on earth …?

He moved his head, tugging at his earlobes. He blew his nose, he yawned, but nothing changed. "Hello, hello. La, la, la…"

Something was terribly wrong. He climbed out of the chair,

shaking his head back and forth as though bothered by a persistent mosquito.

Selby had gone *deaf*. Absolutely, impenetrably deaf. He looked up and down the hall outside, his heart racing.

Everything looked normal, but the basement felt as though the air had been replaced with sand. The whirring of the air conditioners, the faint hum of the lights overhead, even the constant running-water sound of the fans in the server room at the end of the hall ... everything had gone dead silent. *No. More than silent*, he thought. This silence was not merely the absence of sound but a positive presence that filled all the available space, granular and dense, making his jaws ache. He knocked on the wall hard enough to hurt, but there was not the slightest trace of noise.

The silence of the tomb, he thought, his skin crawling, then caught himself. *Stop that! This is creepy enough as it is.*

He caught a brief glimpse of someone slipping past the end of the hall, where the corridor made a T. A tall person, maybe two, moving quickly in the deathly silence.

"Are you looking for Owen?" Selby called out. "I think he's gone to lunch." As he said the words, he could feel the breath passing through his throat, the vibrations in his vocal cords, but the silence swallowed up every syllable. Selby waited for some response, some sign that those people down the hall had heard him. He wanted reassurance that whatever was wrong was all in his head, nothing more than a temporary hearing problem, something a shot could cure, maybe some drops in each ear twice a day. Maybe just a delayed side effect of the accident.

There was no answer.

Selby took a deep breath, then let it out slowly. *Breathe. In and out. In and out.* He had watched far too many movies set in windowless industrial basements. Laboratories, hospitals, military installations. Abandoned lunatic asylums.

"You! You down the hall! What's going on?" Selby

squinted against the painful pressure in his ears. This wasn't just an attack of deafness. Something was objectively, externally wrong.

He thought about all the times he had shouted at the people in horror movies when they insisted on opening the basement door, climbing the stairs to the attic, or going out to the barn to investigate a ruckus among the horses. Stupid to run the risk when all you have to do is lock yourself in and wait for the closing credits.

Desperate times call for desperate measures, he thought.

He took a deep breath, then stomped out the door and down the hall.

Mosley was out, a *SpongeBob SquarePants* screen saver cycling on one of his monitors. His office was the last door before the intersection. The left-hand turn led to the elevator. The right-hand turn would take him to the fire stairs.

Definitely left. Head for the elevator and get out of here. Somebody else can be brave after I'm upstairs.

Selby rounded the corner but immediately skidded to a stop, dancing back awkwardly, having barely avoided running into two men standing in the middle of the narrow hallway. He froze, his heart pounding, his hands icy. He was almost glad there was no sound because he was reasonably sure he had just screamed like a girl.

Selby's first impression was that the intruders were tall and thin, and their clothes smelled like a thrift store. When he saw that they weren't coming after him, he stopped and looked at them more carefully.

Two men, both young, tall and skinny, one a bit taller than the other. Both wore dark blue knit slacks and white short-sleeved dress shirts. One had on a blue tie, the other dark gray. White sneakers, black belts. The taller one had a pen in his shirt pocket, while his partner wore horn-rimmed glasses. Aside from one glaring distinction, they looked remarkably generic, as though someone had ordered them from an online service.

They look like Mormon missionaries. Selby squinted at their faces in morbid fascination. *Except for* that.

Someone had stitched shut the lips of both men, neat stitches, done with a thick white thread that might almost have been dental floss. The punctures were red and crusty, sensitive-looking.

"Owen! Are you still down here? Call security!" Selby shouted. The smothering silence swallowed his words, and panic flexed its wings inside his chest.

Both men were blonde, although the shorter one had dark roots and brown eyes. Selby guessed their ages as somewhere in the mid- to late twenties. Their expressions were calm and focused; they did not look as though they were drugged or crazy. Over the years, he had dealt with many young men from the Herald-Star's IT department who looked and dressed a lot like this. Alert. Reasonably intelligent. More or less normal.

Selby made eye contact with one of the men and mouthed. "Are you protesters of some kind? You need to be upstairs for that. That's where all the photographers and reporters are." He gestured. "The elevator is right back there. If you go up to the lobby, someone can give you directions."

The blue-eyed man smiled slightly, the gesture dragging at the stitches binding his mouth, distorting some of the holes. A drop of blood oozed out onto his lip.

Selby stepped back another pace.

The brown-eyed man raised his right hand as if to swear an oath, his face taking on an expression of intense concentration. The silence rippled, and Selby felt a throb in his head as though he were descending in a fast elevator. The man narrowed his eyes and stepped forward, and the sensation became painful. The taller man made a similar gesture, and Selby gasped as the effect intensified. His jaws ached, and the pressure in his ears felt like someone was thumping the sides of his head with sacks of flour in time to his heartbeat. His vision shimmered, and he couldn't breathe.

The two men struck poses that smacked of the next step in some ritual observance. Selby didn't wait to see if they were about to offer communion. Taking a cue from Mantan Moreland facing Dr. Sangre's undead henchmen in *King of the Zombies*, he lurched forward, gibbering like a maniac, startling both men out of their preparations.

I'll be damned. It worked. I'll never make fun of that awful movie again.

Taking advantage of the momentary confusion, Selby spun around and headed for the fire door.

"Warning! This door is alarmed!" read the sign on the door.

That makes two of us, Selby thought half-hysterically as he crashed against the bar.

He fell through, bracing for the noise of the fire alarm, but there was no sound until he entered the stairwell and slammed the door behind him. Then, the caterwauling of the alarm poured in, and he slumped onto the steps in relief. He had never been so glad to hear such an unpleasant sound. His heart was pounding, and his knee hurt, but he hadn't tripped over his shoelaces.

He stared at the door, counting his breaths. There was no reason the strangers couldn't follow him into the stairwell, but he needed a moment to regroup. Maybe several moments. *Breathe.*

At breath number fifty-seven, the sound of the alarm ceased. Selby climbed to his feet with a groan and prepared to bolt—or at least stagger away—but everything else was still normal. It wasn't the unnatural silence this time; somebody had simply turned off the alarm.

"Testing. Testing. One, two, three …" he said, glad to hear the sound of his own voice. "Testing, testing …"

At that moment, the door popped open to reveal a tall,

abrupt woman Selby recognized from the pressroom one floor up. He waved away her questions; it wasn't as though he had any answers. A man stood behind her, a big man, also from the pressroom, an oily, insinuating person that Selby knew and had always disliked.

"Did you see anybody in the hall by the elevator?" Selby asked the woman.

"No. There's nobody down here but you."

"Fuckin' grampa's gone off his meds," the man muttered, just loud enough to be sure to be heard.

All things considered, Selby wasn't going to be intimidated by a fat guy who lived in his mother's basement and made sexist comments about the women in Accounts Receivable to anyone who would listen. "Koslo," he said. "Buddy Koslo. I remember you. At the Christmas party year before last, you got drunk and passed out in the lobby. You were there all night, lying in a puddle of your own vomit. Good to see you back on your feet."

Feeling somewhat restored by this exchange, Selby pushed past his rescuers and limped back to the viewing room to collect his possessions.

CHAPTER THREE

"Eight minutes late, Coates! We were about to send out a search party."

Roy Freeborn's husky, wry voice was much like that of Suzanne Pleshette in her role as doomed schoolmistress Annie Hayworth in *The Birds*. That film was Selby's favorite Hitchcock movie, and Hayworth was Selby's favorite character. In their suburban backyard, Roy and her wife Régine cared for five crows, all rescues: one missing a leg, one with part of a wing removed, one with most of its upper beak gone, and two blind. If there was any justice in the universe, the gruesome fate of the Bodega Bay schoolteacher would never be Roy's.

"Crazy morning," Selby said as he slipped onto a stool.

He was already distancing himself from what had happened an hour before. His head still ached, but otherwise, he was none the worse for wear. The encounter in Mosley's Mausoleum might have been something that happened to a character in a movie, not to him.

Roy slid a mug of beer across the bar, a bitter IPA that was brewed in a warehouse on the edge of downtown, a place even older than Zeus and his thunderbolts. She punched in Selby's lunch order, which never varied. A predictable, comfortable routine.

Here, in this refuge, the stresses of the morning unwound a little. Selby partitioned away the strange incident in the Herald-Star basement and the stranger men at the heart of it. He would think about it later, after he had regrouped. Or maybe never. He had been expecting something to happen from the moment he left the hospital, and now it had. *Be careful what you wish for*, his mother used to say.

Circle Tavern opened for lunch at eleven thirty, and it was eleven forty now, so Selby was still the only customer in the place. This was his favorite time, with the space illuminated by the indirect light pouring in from the broad front windows, everything clean and tidy, the bright citrus smell of cleaning liquid overlaid on the darker aromas of new bread and old plumbing. No babble of voices or clatter of silverware, just the methodical clink of glass as Roy got the bar organized, the faint thump of the cook's Daddy Yankee playlist in the kitchen, and the intermittent whir of the fridge under the bar.

Taller than Selby and lean as a ferret, today Roy was decked out in a lime-green jumpsuit, floppy below the knees but tight along her narrow hips and her long, flat torso, fastened up the front by an oversized white plastic zipper. She had tucked a hothouse gardenia into her dense afro, and its scent came and went across the bar as she worked.

Not "afro," Selby reminded himself. *She prefers the term "natural."* So much had changed during his lifetime, and he prided himself on keeping up. *Evolve or die.*

"So what happened this morning that's thrown you off schedule?" Roy asked, laying out a place mat and napkin and a bundle of silverware. "You do look a little discombobulated."

Selby hesitated. So much had happened over the last few days, and so much of it was unbelievable. Dead and back again. Even he wondered how much had been real and how much had been some sort of psychotic episode. How much did he dare tell Roy?

"I've had a very busy week," he said carefully.

Roy ran water onto a bar towel and began tidying up a tray of condiments, wiping the gluey dribbles off the hot sauce bottles. "That's a non-answer if ever I heard one. You're super freaked out about something."

"What makes you think I'm freaked out?"

She made a face, her chartreuse eye shadow flashing. "Don't fuck with me, Coates. I know you too well. Are you okay? Health-wise, I mean? You haven't had bad news from a doctor or anything like that?"

Roy, at a vigorous thirty-four years of age, assumed that Selby's life was an obstacle course of age-related health concerns. He looked at her for a long moment, then he laughed. "You wouldn't believe it if I told you."

"Don't make me rough you up," Roy warned. "What's going on?"

Selby needed to talk to somebody about what had been happening, but he didn't want to be viewed as a crackpot. He could see how the two things might go together. Roy waited, wiping her hands with the damp towel.

If not Roy, then who? Selby thought.

"All right. Don't say I didn't warn you."

In terse newspaperman prose, Selby brought his friend up to date on everything that had happened over the last four days.

The bell rang at the service window, and Roy turned to collect Selby's sandwich. She put the plate in front of him and stood back with a deep scowl.

"You can't lie worth shit," she said. "You're not lying now. I'd know if you were. But if you're crazy, you might believe what you're saying. I might not know if you were crazy."

"I won't rule out my being crazy," Selby said, squaring his place mat to the edge of the bar and putting his beer mug in the correct place relative to his plate. "Even I don't believe the whole story."

Roy stared at him, measuring, calculating. After an uncomfortable minute, she shrugged. "Never mind. Whatever you believe, I believe. Reggie's into all this crazy spiritual stuff, and I just nod and smile. That woman, the one in the hospital: What did you say her name was?"

"Laylah."

"Nice name. What is she, exactly? Angel, devil, goddess, witch? "

Selby chewed a bite of his sandwich, thinking this over.

"I have no idea," he said finally. "She's just Laylah. No horns or wings or magic wands or anything. She looked like a character in one of my old movies."

"Shit. That doesn't reassure me. She could be from Mars, or maybe next time you see her she'll be forty feet tall. You got some weird-ass taste in movies."

Customers arrived, noisy and cheerful, three men from the architectural firm that occupied the Tower, the skinny five-story Art Deco oddity directly across the roundabout from the Tavern, an artifact of the same Roosevelt-era urban hyperbole that spawned the PP&L building and its big brass god. Roy slipped out from behind the bar to deal with them, and Selby turned his attention to his lunch.

He ate his sandwich and then his onion rings, stopping periodically to sweep up any crumbs that fell on the bar, brushing them into his hand, and then onto a bar napkin. He preferred fries, which generated no crumbs, but on any given day, the Circle Tavern would have one or the other, never both at once. The week had been messy enough already. Selby wondered how the men with their lips stitched up fed themselves. Everything through a straw, he supposed. No wonder they were so thin. What would induce someone to do such a thing? Or allow it to be done to them?

One of the architects laughed, and Selby glanced back, a handful of crumbs suspended over the napkin. The laugh was over-loud, artificial, attempting to convey a delight the young man did not actually feel. The men were talking about their fear and disdain for a woman they called "the Duchess," a level above them in the office hierarchy. Selby had seen them in the tavern on several occasions, and their conversations never drifted far from a few basic themes: Their sex lives, real or imaginary. The Duchess and her excesses. The lack of a professional sports franchise in Buckley.

Selby labeled them as Number One (the loud one, attractive but nervous, a follower), Number Two (an aggressively cheerful man, a backslapper), and Number Three (solid, quiet, and poised, with the wide, squashed face of a Russian hit man).

"Are you eavesdropping again?"

Selby looked up to find Roy grinning over the bar at him as she started rolling silverware into paper napkins, binding each neat little bundle with a piece of white tape and setting it aside.

"Eavesdropping?"

She indicated the architects with a thrust of her chin. "The boys. Listening. Eavesdropping, Coates. You do it all the time. By now, I bet you know what their favorite colors are and what nicknames they've given to their willies."

"No, but I know the quiet one's wife is called Letty, short for Letitia," he told her somewhat primly. "An old-fashioned name. It's the name of Boris Karloff's wife in *Die, Monster, Die*."

"What happens to her?"

"Letitia? She disintegrates, a little at a time. Goes crazy. Exotic radiation from a meteorite her husband is experimenting with down in the basement."

"Damn good thing you don't have a basement."

Should I have kept my mouth shut? Selby thought, glancing up at Roy, then away. He finished his lunch and stacked everything carefully on the plate.

As Roy reached across the bar to take it from him, she caught his eye.

"Coates, I know you're thinking you shouldn't have told me about Bride of Dracula at the hospital or about those jokers at the Herald-Star. Before you get all tangled up with that, remember that I would have known just by looking at you that you had a secret, and I'd have gotten it out of you sooner rather than later. It's done. You told me. Quit picking at the scab."

Selby made a face. "I know. Thanks, Roy."

"De nada."

Roy held out the card reader, and Selby tapped it with his card and signed with his finger. *Magic*.

"See you, Coates."

"Until next time, Roy."

Selby stepped out into the hazy autumn sunshine, feeling somewhat revived. The headache he had carried away from the Herald-Star basement was still with him, but by now it barely rose above the general background discomfort of being sixty-plus years old.

He knew he'd be second-guessing himself for the next week or so, but he also knew that coming clean with Roy made him feel better. It had been the right thing to do. Roy was his friend, and he needed friends.

Selby's apartment was less than a mile from the Tower Circle roundabout, and the River City Grocery was midway between those two points. He would stop in and pick up something interesting to prepare for dinner, maybe a treat for Pancake—*And bleach! The coffee mugs are getting dingy*—then go home and make sure he had remembered to save all his notes from the morning's interrupted research in Mosley's Mausoleum.

The most direct route to the grocery store was up Tower Lane. This narrow, tree-hung alley used to be Battle Creek Street before the Seventh Day Adventist church moved to the suburbs back in the 1970s, leaving their unusual octagonal building to be repurposed as the headquarters of a social service agency. There was a chain supermarket only two blocks south of the Tavern with lower prices, but Selby had been shopping at

River City for almost twenty years. The opportunity to save a few dollars a week on groceries was not enough to divert him from a long-established habit.

Tower Lane was barely wide enough for two vehicles to pass each other, serving merely as a quarter-mile shortcut from the Tower Circle to the point at which 29th Avenue looped around to begin the smooth curves that led past Selby's building and into the semi-trendy Trinity Park neighborhood. Apart from the former church, the only other address on Tower Lane was an odd little house, all mildewed stucco and wrought iron and stained glass, shrouded by ivy and a rank thicket of privet and hackberry. The man who inhabited this place was not that much older than Selby, but his manner suggested that he had arrived with Columbus and didn't much like the way things had gone since. Selby had found the squat, frog-faced gentleman every-one referred to as "the Colonel" impenetrably strange on the few occasions when he had spoken to him at the grocery store or out on the sidewalk with his dog, an insectile Chihuahua named Bolívar.

Selby negotiated the two crosswalks that brought him half-way around the Circle and tramped up the Lane's cracked side-walk. He passed the entrance to the small parking lot of the old church, then the gate to the Colonel's house.

"What are you doing out there, you little bastard!"

Selby stumbled, turning toward the voice. The door to the Colonel's house was ajar, and the old man's bulbous face pressed against the crack. "Come here! Right now!"

Before Selby could react, the dog Bolívar shot out of the shrubbery across the street, clutching what Selby thought might have been a dead chipmunk in its jaws. The nasty little creature dashed up the steps and into the house with its prize. The door closed quickly and firmly.

Selby blinked, shook himself, and continued up the hill to the store. He did his shopping and then went straight home.

Selby filled the kitchen sink with water, added some bleach, and left the coffee mugs to soak.

Strip away the stains of time, Selby thought, giving the cups a poke to make sure they were all completely immersed. *Make everything new again. Turn back the clock to when things were the way they were supposed to be. Before bus accidents and ghostly women and creepy blond boys in basements.*

Selby wiped his hands on a towel and then smoothed the towel over the handle of the oven. He walked to the window and stood staring out at the world beyond the glass.

From his vantage atop the PP&L building across the way, Zeus glowered down at the city, the watery gold sunlight bringing his thunderbolts to flashing life. The big brass god would have had little patience for the kind of people who would sew their mouths shut and stalk retirees through downtown basements, Selby thought.

Selby turned from the window and lay down on his bed—carefully, so as not to ruck up the bedspread—replaying the morning's excitement. Pancake hopped up beside him and butted his hand until he scratched him behind the ears, then the cat curled up against Selby's side, purring.

Was that whole episode some kind of message? Selby wondered. *If so, it was a mighty poor one, since it didn't convey a damned thing to me.*

Were the mute men telling him to do something? To *not* do something? More to the point, what—if anything—did they have to do with Laylah?

No, there was no "if anything" about it. Coincidences were one thing, but to believe that Selby might have two such unbelievable events take place in his life mere days apart, purely by happenstance, was stretching it. Did those men work for Laylah? Did they represent her in some way?

There again, it didn't make sense. Whatever her intentions

for Selby, whatever it was she expected him to do for her, he couldn't imagine Laylah sending someone like Tweedledum and Tweedledee to convey her messages. Men who couldn't even talk.

But if not Laylah, then who? After a lifetime of relentless ordinariness, was Selby suddenly to find himself the center of all sorts of weird happenings?

Frustrated, Selby closed his eyes and tried to clear his head. Pancake emitted a falsetto sigh and worked his forepaws.

Stuff like this just doesn't happen to people like me, Selby thought, drifting into sleep.

. . .

The withered little woman is heavily burdened with age and cheap jewelry. A brocade scarf conceals her hair, and she wears a tatty gray shawl around her shoulders. She peers at Selby Coates from beneath a forehead that has been creased by the weight of too much knowledge. The light of kerosene lamps illuminates her face in high relief, a rugged landscape of bright peaks and lightless valleys.

Selby is asleep and dreaming. He knows this—or rather, his dream-self does, a younger man with better knees. The fact that he *knows* it's a dream is almost the strangest thing about it.

He is sitting across the table from Maleva, the old gypsy woman in *The Wolf Man*, the 1941 version. Selby has always enjoyed this film, although he thinks big, lumpy, Oklahoma City native Lon Chaney Jr. is less than convincing in the role of the prodigal son of a dapper English nobleman. Maria Ouspenskaya's portrayal of the gypsy, on the other hand, is worth the price of admission.

He returns Maleva's gaze for a long moment, then looks down at the table. Dream or no dream, he feels foolish and exposed under her stare. The entire scene is in shades of gray, except for her eyes, which are a distinctive light hazel.

The old woman takes the lid off a flat cardboard box, the sort of thing an expensive piece of lingerie might come in—although Selby can't imagine that Maleva has unpacked a lot of expensive lingerie in her time. (*Don't judge,* Selby reminds himself. *Who knows what she was like in her salad days? We were all young once.*) The box contains a couple of dozen cardboard rectangles. With arthritic fingers, the gypsy extracts three from the box and lays them out on the table, facing Selby.

The objects are playing cards—or, more properly, tarot cards, although of a type Selby has never seen before. The old woman pulls the lantern closer, and he examines the ones she has selected for him.

On the first card, he sees a tall, pale woman standing on a low pedestal. Her hair is white, but her oval face is smooth and youthful, utterly impassive. Her eyes are a luminous gray. She wears a white robe, and a length of white fabric is tied across her mouth, the ends trailing. At her feet crouch a man and a woman, both wearing similar gags. Mist shrouds the entire tableau. Across the bottom of the card is written the word "Doma."

The second card depicts a dark-haired, strong-featured woman in a black robe like a nun's habit, standing in a rocky, barren landscape dominated by a dark sky spangled with seven-pointed stars. She holds a candle in one hand, and a crow is sitting on her shoulder. A man sleeps at her feet. Selby doesn't even have to look at the bottom of the card to know that it reads, "Laylah."

The third card almost jars him awake. Here, a handsome, fair-haired man sprawls naked on a throne, smiling, one leg hooked over the arm of the chair, the other extended. A piece of drapery loops up over the side of the chair to strategically cover his crotch. Two women—one fair and one dark—caress his outstretched foot with expressions of rapture on their faces. The bottom of this card has been torn away, so Selby doesn't know what name belongs there.

Even without the name, he knows the naked man, although he hasn't laid eyes on him in over half a century.

Sullivan Coates. My father. Dad.

Selby looks up at the gypsy, and she shakes her head at him. "Even a man who is pure in heart and says his prayers by night," she intones gravely, "may walk in front of a bus when his attention wanders. Who is your father, Selby?"

. . .

Fiona's Baby Diary:
We're in the new house, with the new baby. The company has taken care of everything. It's like we're the prince and princess in a fairy tale, after the kiss, living happily ever after. I've sent a "thank you" note to Bongo's partner. I'd like to invite her and Mitch out for dinner one night, but she works the most awful hours. The baby is the most beautiful baby there ever was. Bongo called him Bingo yesterday and has been singing that silly song five times a day. B-I-N-G-O. My poor baby is going to grow up thinking he's the farmer's dog.

CHAPTER FOUR

Tuesday dawned misty and damp, a preview of winter. Zeus was visible in the shadowless light, but shreds of mist covered his defiant nakedness and robbed him of his potency. Selby stood looking out the window in his baggy sweatpants, drinking his coffee, thinking about yesterday's dream.

A strange way to communicate, he thought. He felt certain that the old gypsy Maleva was simply Laylah in disguise, but why? And what was the purpose of those cards? Laylah, a masked woman called Doma, and his father.

Selby sipped coffee and watched the fog swirl around the king of the gods. Questions cycled below the surface of Selby's thoughts, like koi in a winter pond, waiting to break the surface, to be noticed, to be fed.

This is getting me nowhere.

Selby cleaned his coffee things and took a shower. He dressed in warm clothes, an extra sweater, a scarf that his mother had bought for him years ago, the exact blue of his eyes, and left the apartment.

The buildings lining the streets on the way to the 29th Avenue bus stop appeared furtive, hiding their secrets, permitting only brief glimpses of the people inside, snapshots of activity. Passing traffic ripped the fog with headlights and wind, and the occasional pedestrians walked with shoulders hunched and condensation glittering on their eyelashes. The bus stop was deserted, as though the last bus had come and gone years ago.

When the Number Two Red bus finally pulled in and opened its doors, Selby was almost surprised to see it.

Selby's fellow passengers were a dispirited and uninteresting group, and he gazed out the window as the bus worked its tortuous way across the South Side. There was something strangely familiar about the journey through the misty streets in the silent bus. When one of his fellow passengers, a hatchet-faced woman sitting behind the driver, turned and looked at him with protruding eyes and an expression of distaste, he saw what it was and laughed out loud. The woman whipped back around in her seat.

It's "The Shadow Over Innsmouth," he thought, chuckling to himself. *I'm on the bus ride from Newburyport.*

Here, there were no swamps, no "sand, sedge-grass, and stunted shrubbery," only an affluent urban neighborhood—and none of the bus passengers looked as though they were on the verge of turning into barking, gabbling fish-creatures—but the gray light and the silent and self-contained riders were right in character.

In due course, the bus deposited Selby at a stop on the corner of Park Road and the access road that paralleled Old Highway 117, only a hundred yards from the Josiah Redmon Botanic Garden's main entrance. At the gate, Selby tapped his senior citizen's pass on the reader, and the turnstile unlocked with an impatient clack, urging him onto a small flagstone plaza. This little courtyard belonged to the neat brick mini-mansion that had once been the home of Redmon's mother, the reclusive and absurdly wealthy Alice Whitney Redmon. Now, as the Welcome Center, the structure housed the administrative offices, a gift shop, an art gallery, and a tiny snack bar that was always closed, regardless of what the posted hours might say. Beyond the Welcome Center stood several rows of pine trees, spaced so that the scaly trunks obscured the view beyond. Several pathways led from the plaza through the screening trees. Selby ambled out into the ragged fog of the courtyard. Crows called back and forth somewhere among the trees. A strange, looming figure startled him briefly but turned out to be nothing more sinister than a gardener in his green coveralls and cap hauling a bale of straw.

There wasn't much to see in the garden this late in the season. Nothing showed in the flowerbeds but rosebushes, pruned to stumpy skeletons, standing naked in their beds of bark mulch. Although a number of trees still managed to hang on to their leaves, these were rumpled and disconsolate, not long for this world. The evergreens—pines and junipers, a few firs, a titanic magnolia in the distance—loomed black in the gray landscape. The mist gave everything a sense of atmospheric perspective that distorted distances. Selby found the melancholy emptiness soothing.

Several trails wound gently around the park, providing varied views of the grassy meadows and the plantings of flowering shrubs in their season and wildflowers in theirs. Selby's favorite walk was the Two-Mile Trail, a meandering path whose halfway point was a grassy knoll on the far side of the property. At the summit of the little hill rose an outcropping of gray sandstone so weathered that it looked like giant children had built it out of marshmallows. The monumental effect was diminished somewhat by a self-consciously rustic bench at the foot of the rockpile. Selby always enjoyed the view from this modest elevation and considered it worth the effort of clambering up the side of the hill despite the complaints from his knees.

The top of the knoll was a favored hangout for crows. Regular visitors brought snacks for them: dog biscuits, potato chips, cookies, maybe a half-eaten sandwich. Several of the chunky black birds strutted and flapped around the base of the rock outcropping as Selby approached. A few beady eyes turned to peer at him as he puffed and groaned his way to the bench, but they saw his empty hands and returned to their posing and squabbling.

The view over the park from the small hill was enchanting—what Selby imagined the English countryside might look like. A small pond spread around the far side of the knoll, stocked with enormous orange carp, torpid and heavy in the cold weather. Beyond the pond, a trio of maple trees stood watch. Beyond the maples, fields and woods undulated back toward the city.

Midwich, in Village of the Damned. *Such a lovely landscape, at least to look at. The perfect place for an alien invasion.*

A commotion from the crows caught his attention, and he looked around to see a woman climbing the hill. He waved a greeting and went back to admiring the landscape, enjoying the quiet. Anyone coming up to this spot on such a gloomy day was probably not looking for conversation, which suited him fine.

One of the crows flapped onto the end of the bench and stood peering at him sideways for a long moment. This was a handsome bird, larger than the others, its glossy black plumage reflecting an oily iridescence in the directionless white light. When the walker reached the crest of the knoll, the crow made a harsh clacking noise and sprang into the air and flapped out of sight.

Selby opened his mouth to say something pithy to the visitor about the weather or the crows, but the words froze on his tongue before he could deliver them.

The woman had the bland oval face of Botticelli's Venus, but instead of rising nude from a scallop shell, she was standing in the wet grass in a pair of white mukluks and a quilted Patagonia ski suit of the palest possible blue. Her hair was paper-white, long and slightly wavy, pinned back from her equally white face but allowed to cascade down her back. Her beautiful gray eyes were totally devoid of expression.

Her lips were sewn shut with thick black thread.

The woman gazed at Selby in a disinterested way as though

he were a species of shrubbery she might be thinking of planting in her own garden. Or uprooting from this one.

Selby stared back, hypnotized by her luminous regard.

He stirred uneasily, about to speak, and silence slammed onto him like a truckload of sand falling from the sky. Selby fell to one knee, gasping as lightning ran through the brittle joint. His glasses fell off onto the wet grass.

The woman stared at him, her expression unchanging, timeless and calm. The silence spiraled out from her to flood the hill top, muting the crows, blunting the rain, displacing the air.

Panting, Selby collected his glasses and forced himself back to his feet. He met the woman's blank stare, his vision gray around the edges as if he were looking the wrong way through a telescope. He shook his head. The unnatural silence seemed to force itself inside his skull, making his teeth ache, muddying his thoughts. He made a frustrated noise and took a step forward.

In Mosley's Mausoleum, he had been terrified. He was terrified now, as well, but he was also *affronted*. The whole scene was so theatrical, so overdone. Barbara Steele in *Black Sunday*, all bulging eyes and body horror, aiming for atmosphere but achieving only absurdity. If somebody wanted to revoke his resurrection, there were easier ways. This was like the villain in a movie contriving some Rube Goldberg mechanism to kill the hero when it would be so much more efficient just to whack him over the head with a pipe. What was the *point*?

She's terrorizing me. A bully. I'm a weakling and a coward, and she knows it.

The large crow swooped past the woman's head, snatching at a stray wisp of hair as it passed. She didn't flinch, merely turned her head to look at the bird, unblinking, as though she had never seen a crow before. Her attacker flew away clumsily into the trees a hundred yards away, cackling wildly.

A realization pushed its way through Selby's confusion.

"You're Doma. From the card in my dream. Those nerdy

boys in the basement were yours. What do you want with me?" His words made no sound, but he knew she heard them. The woman narrowed her silver-gray eyes almost imperceptibly.

The pressure increased, gripping Selby's body, oozing into his skull, massaging his eyeballs from behind. *Searching* ...

He could see well enough to watch the crow make another pass. The woman turned from Selby to face the bird, her gaze as bland and pale as milk. The crow came back a second time, then a third, the last time carrying away a few strands of silky white hair. The other crows did not join the attack but hopped and flapped at a safe distance, disturbed and uncertain, debating among themselves.

The sky had grown dark during this altercation, a flat, featureless slate gray. There was no wind, not even a slight breeze, but the uncertain mists and fog turned first to a spitting rain, then to a sudden downpour. The rain didn't touch the pale woman, but the silence eased slightly as the rain drew a curtain between her and her victim.

The ghost-white woman turned back toward Selby, her face utterly remote, detached. Assessing him. Studying him. Selby remembered a high school biology class in which the teacher had expected the students to dissect a frog. He now knew what it felt like to be the frog.

The crow flew to the top of the rock outcropping and stood in the pouring rain with its wings outspread and its beak gaping in a posture of ribald defiance. Selby was reminded of Zeus and his thunderbolts atop the PP&L building, laughing at time and the elements.

Selby's bruised knee wobbled, but he kept to his feet. The pressure eased slightly.

"You have something to do with Laylah. And with my father." His voice was audible now but thin, like an AM radio broadcast from halfway across the country at three o'clock in the morning.

He limped toward her, plowing through the gelatinous silence, a frustrated little man who hated loose ends and unanswered questions. The crow screamed, and the pressure in Selby's head lessened still further. He stopped out of arm's reach.

"Stay out of my home. Leave my things alone. Rita has enough on her plate, what with that lowlife crypto-scammer husband of hers; she doesn't need your ghouls hanging around."

The woman's strangeness was even more noticeable up close. Her gray eyes, slightly protuberant, reflected a metallic gleam, and her skin was translucent, like milk glass. In the dim light, her face seemed almost as if it were illuminated from within. The rain poured over her without touching her, sheathing her in a quicksilver skin of water. The stitching that bound her lips looked as if it had grown out of the substance of her flesh, not thread but sinew.

"What *are* you?" Selby asked, shouting to push his voice through the silence and over the tumult of the rain. "Are you a hallucination that I'm having? An after-effect of my head injury? Tell me what you want. Say it. Write it down. Whatever it takes."

The woman raised one delicate white hand, and the invisible giant grabbed Selby again and *squeezed*. He struggled, unable to breathe, sure that he was about to be crushed, but after only a moment, the grip relaxed. He fell to the grass, losing his glasses once again. A trickle of blood ran down from his nose, mixing with the rain, bringing a taste of rust and salt, washing down onto the front of his shirt. The woman turned to look at the crow. Gritting his teeth against the pain in his knee, Selby followed her gaze to find the bird staring down at him, turning first one eye, then the other, its beady gaze intent, full of significance. A heartbeat later, his ears popped, and when he looked around, he discovered that there was nobody on the knoll but half a dozen perfectly ordinary crows and one bruised and frightened man soaked to the skin.

Selby took a long, hot shower and climbed into his gray tracksuit. He had missed lunch in all the confusion, riding home on the bus in a daze, ignoring the stares of his fellow passengers. For dinner, he made grilled cheese sandwiches and tomato soup, his favorite crisis meal, soft and crusty, bright and mellow, full of lovely warm colors. The soup was the last of a batch he had prepared and frozen during the summer when fresh tomatoes were plentiful. It was a reminder of sunshine and bird song, blurring the outlines of today's experience. *No more local tomatoes for a while*, he thought sadly. If he experienced any more craziness that required comfort food, he would have to fall back on macaroni and cheese.

The woman today was not like the two men in the Herald-Star basement. The boys in their double-knit slacks and computer-nerd shirts were underlings, acolytes. There was something makeshift about them, rehearsed. Needy. People like that were a dime a dozen at evangelical rallies and on conspiracy theory mailing lists. The woman in the park was … She was what? No mere convert, certainly. Not someone seduced by a bizarre philosophical or religious construct. Her strangeness was inherent, part of her. She was no more human than Pancake or the brass statue of Zeus.

Laylah and Doma. Two women, both *other*, not human beings, as he defined the term. Messing around with him, with his life. With his *death*, even. *Why?*

His gaze fell on the photograph of himself with his father, still leaning against the wall in its warped and shattered frame. A stranger had come into his home and mistreated that picture. That specific picture, not one of the dozen others scattered across his walls.

Selby finished dinner and cleaned up. So many questions. Unanswered, perhaps unanswerable. His head still hurt, and his knee was swollen and stiff.

Enough. I need to relax for a little while.

Selby settled into his comfortable chair with his leg up, Pancake on his lap, a cupcake at his elbow, and the remote close at hand. Tomorrow, he would go back to Mosley's Mausoleum and make a more disciplined search for answers. Tonight, Richard Denning and Mara Corday, armed with Denning's manly scowl and Corday's improbable bosom, would battle prehistoric arachnids in *The Black Scorpion*.

Just what the doctor ordered, Selby thought with a contented sigh as the volcano erupted, and primordial terror crawled out into the Mexican sun.

· · ·

Fiona's Baby Diary:
Bingo has taken to imitating his father ALL THE TIME. It's hysterical. The baby watches Bongo like a hawk, and he tries to make all the same faces and clap and laugh every time his father does. Ruth and Mitch came by last night, and I'm afraid I went on and on about how adorable my boys are. I must have sounded like a lunatic, but I don't care. I guess this is what they mean by "deliriously happy." I should clarify that it's not always a bowl of cherries. Bingo is a machine that takes in vast amounts of food and converts it directly to poop and vomit. Meanwhile, every time the baby is well and truly asleep, Bongo comes running into the kitchen naked as a jaybird, demanding what he has taken to calling SNUGGLEBUNNIES(!) I'm living in an insane asylum, but I love every minute of it.

CHAPTER FIVE

"Owen, I'm trying to find a cult."

Mosley's eyes narrowed. "Having trouble staying busy?"

Selby blinked, startled, his eyes round. "Was that humor, Owen? I've never heard you make a joke before."

Mosley's lips twisted in something that an observer might, in dim light, have interpreted as a smile. "Life is full of surprises," he said. "So what sort of cult are you looking for, exactly?"

"One where the members sew their mouths shut."

Mosley turned back to his computer. "Might be just the thing for you. Let me see what we have. Come back in twenty minutes."

Selby nodded and returned to the viewing room.

There was no shortage of cults in the Herald-Star's area of primary interest—Port Sebastian, Buckley, and the towns and rural areas to the immediate north, west, and south—but none were of any great distinction. The Neo-Christians huddled in their fortified compounds while neo-Buddhists went grocery shopping in saffron robes. Pagans danced naked around Ogalacat Spike on May Eve and Halloween, and the Daughters of Hecate (Mid-Atlantic Chapter) met for two weeks every summer at the Rookery to swap recipes and stick pins in dolls. Not only John Kennedy but John Lennon, John Coltrane, and John Belushi all had their share of unhinged followers.

None of these were sewing their mouths shut. Selby

climbed out of the chair with a grunt and hobbled down the hall.

"Anything?"

"I said twenty minutes."

"It's been eighteen. I'll give you an extra two minutes next time, I promise."

Mosley rubbed his eyes, then nodded at his computer screens. "Not much, to be honest. I have stories of mouth-sewing protesters in Russia, Serbia, Venezuela, and Missouri, but these were political statements, not expressions of religious fervor. Locally, there's almost nothing."

"'Almost?'."

Mosley squinted up at him. "There's one that … No, I'll give you what I have and let you sort it out for yourself." He peered back down at his notepad.

"Six years ago, police and paramedics showed up for a three-car accident on the Maryville Road a few miles north of Vale and discovered that one of the drivers, a forty-six-year-old woman, had her lips stitched together. She was taken to the ER, interviewed by the authorities, and released. Mutilating yourself, while strange, is not illegal, and the accident had not been entirely her fault. There was heavy fog and possibly ice on the road." Mosley paused, then continued before Selby could jump in. "The name the woman gave the authorities at the time was Ruth Sullivan Coates."

Selby stared. "Sullivan Coates was my father's name."

Mosley nodded. "You told me that once. What's your mother's name?"

"Naomi. Her maiden name is Goodwin."

"Naomi. Like in the Bible?"

"Yes, the story of—"

"Naomi and Ruth. Quite the nest of coincidences, Coates."

Selby sagged back against the doorframe. *My mother is almost ninety*, he thought. *She doesn't even know how to drive a car.*

"Owen, after working together for more than thirty years, I'm only now learning that you have a sense of humor. If this is a joke, please tell me now."

"Not a joke, Coates. At least, not mine."

Selby looked down at him; Mosley met his gaze. His face, so like that of a well-intentioned mad scientist, was sober and intrigued.

"All right. The accident. Was there any follow-up?"

Mosley nodded. "The reporter went looking for Ruth Coates, expecting something nice and lurid to go on with, but her few inept attempts to track Coates down went nowhere, and she abandoned the story. Her notes are remarkably disjointed."

"Kids these days. No appreciation for proper journalistic procedures."

"It's scandalous. Did your father have relatives in the area? Everybody's got cousins."

Selby shook his head. "As far as I know, Dad was an only child, an orphan. No relatives, no past."

"That seems suspicious in and of itself."

"I was a child," Selby said. "I didn't learn to be suspicious until after he left."

"Is your mother still living?"

"More or less. She's in a retirement village in Florida with her sister. It's all very *Whatever Happened to Baby Jane*."

"Since this is you talking, I assume that's the name of a creepy movie."

Selby laughed, his ears turning pink. "Yes, it is." He held out his hand. "Thank you, Owen."

Mosley stared at the proffered appendage for a long moment, then shook it. His grip was dry and strangely brittle. Selby thought about mutated tarantulas.

"Will you pursue this further?" Owen asked.

"That's a good question."

"I'll email you these articles. Let me know if there's anything else I can do."

"I will."

Selby spent the rest of the day at his laptop with Pancake snoring in his lap, scavenging the internet for any reference to Ruth Coates or the names on the playing cards.

The card names popped up here and there, but the information was contradictory or absurd. The name "Laylah" appeared often, in a number of different spellings. "Doma" was likewise ubiquitous, but usually as a name for a trendy company or as an acronym for something.

Ruth Coates was a tougher nut to crack. She had a Facebook page that dated back to 2014, but she had never gotten around to posting anything but a profile photo and several pictures of cows. Selby studied the hard, quiet face, framed by short gray-blonde hair. Her eyes were blue, like Selby's, but narrow, suspicious. Her mouth was perfectly ordinary, her thin lips bent in a smile that Selby guessed she had brought out of mothballs for the photo and returned to storage immediately afterward. There was no trace of stitching. She had provided no personal information on her profile.

I wonder who took that picture, Selby thought. *Ruth looks like a person who doesn't have a lot of close friends.*

Pancake stretched and jumped down, and Selby moved to his comfortable chair to think about everything that had happened, was currently happening, and was likely to happen.

He was relying on a dream for his information. A dream based on an old Universal Pictures werewolf movie, no less. So much for credible sources, but what else did he have? An encounter in the hospital that might or might not even have happened, an intruder in his apartment, the incidents with the missionary geeks, and then the White Lady. Not to mention the fact of his continued survival, which could be explained as a massive clerical snafu at the hospital. Only the vandalism of his father's photograph had any objective reality.

Who was Sullivan Coates? It was remarkable how little Selby knew about his father and how little he had tried to learn in all the decades since Sullivan walked out of his life. Time to address that. But how?

Ruth Coates, as elusive as she was, was not a figure on a playing card. She was an actual human being with, presumably, a life, a job, a home, all the usual connections that human beings had. Could her name be a coincidence? Or could she be some previously unsuspected relative of Selby's? How and why was she connected to Doma? These were all questions that Selby could only answer by tracking her down and asking her.

If Ruth Coates was Selby's sister, that means Sullivan had started over with a new family somewhere locally not that long after he disappeared. Selby's parents had spent roughly a decade together. What changed after that time? Did Sullivan Coates get tired of being a husband? A father? No, that made no sense. Ruth's existence suggested that Sullivan had immediately segued into a new family, a new child.

Was it Naomi? Or was it me? Did he tire of having me as a son?

Toward midnight, Selby finally crawled into bed, feeling scattered and confused. His apartment seemed stuffy and claustrophobic, and his past crowded around the bed, jeering at him as sleep rose over his head and drowned him.

. . .

Selby is six. He has just started school, and he has trouble sleeping. He has learned to overcome his persistent bed-wetting by sleeping only lightly and waking up frequently, thereby giving him the opportunity to hurry to the bathroom before he has any accidents. The child now wakes up for every sound, every breath, from the gurgling of the pipes when the old man in the apartment next door flushes his toilet to the clunk of the refrigerator downstairs when the compressor goes on or off. He never gets enough sleep, but he no longer wets the bed. He has become convinced that children who wet the bed are eaten by the giant ants, as big as cars, that live in the drainage pipe at the far end of the backyard, so he has been diligent in addressing the problem.

It's Friday, and there's no school tomorrow to think about, so Selby sleeps a little, but something wakes him up. Voices. A voice. His father's.

It's intolerably hot in the apartment, stuffy and damp. Sweat has glued his cowboy pajamas to his back. His bed smells like the bread that sometimes gets lost behind other things in the cabinet, emerging weeks later green and dusty. He keeps hearing his father's voice coming from downstairs, thick and soft, as if it's the muggy air talking. Selby climbs out of bed carefully, alert to any sudden moves by the hideously scarred Ivan Igor, who has been crouching under the bed ever since the child saw *The Mystery of the Wax Museum* on the Dialing for Dollars Afternoon Thriller. Clutching Daisy, his stuffed monkey, Selby sets out to investigate.

His parents' room is quiet. He peeks inside and sees his mother, sprawled awkwardly, her nightgown rucked up, breathing through her mouth—not snoring, exactly, but making a rattling noise with each inhalation. She has begun taking a new medicine every evening—for her nerves—and nothing will awaken her. The smell of her powder hangs in the heavy air. His father's side of the bed is empty.

Selby has a scar under his chin from a too-quick trip down the stairs two years ago that ended abruptly on the landing, so he is more careful now. He holds Daisy under his left arm and reaches up to grip the handrail with his right. One step at a time.

His father is having a conversation. He's laughing, murmuring, whispering … His voice is like pancake batter, thick and gluey, nothing at all like his usual speech. For a moment, Selby wonders whether it really is his father, but he decides that it doesn't matter. He would have to check it out in any event; what you don't know will creep up the stairs and grab you while you sleep. (Selby Coates checks his closet every night; he doesn't bother to check under the bed because the terrible Ivan Igor presumably keeps all the other monsters out.) If it's an imposter down there, then maybe Selby's father needs rescuing. *Nobody* hurts Selby's father while Selby's on the job.

At the bottom of the stairs, he finds he has two shadows. One is cast by the streetlight outside, and the other by a dim glow coming from the kitchen. Selby's never heard of someone having two shadows before. For a moment, he pauses, thinking about the implications of this, and then he and Daisy step into the light.

He stares, standing in the kitchen doorway, shocked and fascinated.

The refrigerator door is halfway open. Sullivan Coates is standing in front of it, occasionally taking hold of the door and swinging it back and forth. He has pulled the telephone over to the counter next to the fridge, and he's talking to someone, sometimes playing with the curly cord with one hand, sometimes playing with himself, down there where Selby's mother has always told the child *never* to put his hands.

Selby's father is naked and sweating. His *thing* is swollen to an absurd size. Sullivan Coates is a snappy dresser, vain about his appearance. Selby has never seen his father like this.

"You know exactly what I like," his father says into the phone, laughing.

Little Selby makes a noise, and his father looks up, his eyes refracting green and brown and topaz in the light from the refrigerator.

"Who's your father, Selby?" the naked man asks.

. . .

Selby stood shaking in the middle of his apartment, shocked out of sleep and onto his feet.

Pancake, as addicted to reliable schedules and accustomed routines as his master, yawned at Selby's agitation and snuggled back down into the blankets.

I remember that incident, Selby thought, as he struggled to organize himself, to calm the pounding of his heart. *I remember coming downstairs and finding him like that. I was so horrified. That townhouse in Fair Park, freezing in winter, an oven of misery in the summer. My father jerking off in front of the refrigerator while he talks trash with one of his girlfriends over the phone. So Freudian, it's almost a joke. The dream was accurate in every detail. Except ... he didn't speak to me then. He never knew I was there. I ran back upstairs and hid under the covers with Daisy.*

Selby turned on the electric kettle and pulled an envelope of instant hot chocolate out of the box in the cabinet.

Sullivan Coates disappeared when Selby was ten, and Naomi had not mentioned him nor allowed him to be mentioned at any time since. *Who was my father? My father was Sullivan Coates. Who was Sullivan Coates? He was my father.* Selby's thoughts chased each other around and around as he poured boiling water on top of the gray-brown powder in his cup. His hands were shaking as he stirred the mixture, and he splashed hot chocolate onto the counter and down the side of the mug. With a hiss of irritation, he wet a dishcloth and wiped the counter and his cup, careful to clear away every drop, every smear.

I loved him so much, he thought. *I knew he wasn't like other kids' fathers, but that didn't matter. His smile made everything right.*

Selby hung up the towel and moved to his comfortable chair, holding the hot mug in his cold fingers, listening to his heart beating.

If my father was not who or what he seemed, then who am I?
A scent of cedar and warm beeswax hung in the air.

CHAPTER SIX

Despite her age, Selby's ninety-three-year-old aunt was an en-thusiastic consumer of high-tech gadgetry. Martha Goodwin Van Bever always had to have the latest smartphone, the most powerful laptop, the most sophisticated doorbell: the thinnest, the fastest, the newest. Selby suspected that this was her way of compensating for the walker she needed to cross a room and for the wheelchair she had to use every time she left the house.

When Selby called her on the morning after he dreamed of his father, she insisted on setting up a face-to-face, and Selby found himself parked in front of his desk with his aunt's distinc-tive visage peering out at him from his laptop screen.

"Your mother's not here, Selby," she told him by way of greeting. "She's at a mindfulness session down at the club-house. Every other Thursday. They sit around all day drinking wine spritzers and talking about whose fault it is their lives are so fucked up."

"That's okay, Aunt Martha. It's you I wanted to talk to."

She blinked. "You called at this hour of the morning to talk to *me*? You're shitting me."

"Nope. How have you been?"

Selby thought she looked like death warmed over, but she had looked like that for at least thirty years. He had concluded long ago that her appearance was a fashion choice rather than an indication of her mental and physical health. Black-rimmed eyes stared out of a face that was uniformly, aggressively flesh-colored, every pore carefully spackled over. His aunt's lips and cheekbones glowed unnaturally pink; her hair was of a purplish-black color that might have been more appropriate on a bruise. Today, Martha's coiffure rested slightly off-center, giving her a roguish look.

"I'm fine, for a fucking fossil," she snapped. "You look a bit like you've been rode hard and put up wet, yourself. Retirement not working out for you?"

"It's working out fine. I wanted to ask you something."

The mask perked up. "There's a first. What do you need to know?"

"Tell me about Sullivan Coates."

Martha's enthusiasm evaporated.

"Well, shit. Somebody finally asks me for my opinion about something, and they want to talk about that fucking loser."

Selby steeled himself. "Where did Naomi meet him?"

Martha reached off-camera to fetch a cigarette and a lighter. The lighter was the same color as her lipstick. Selby knew that Blue Spring Village was smoke-free, but Martha had never let that bother her.

"Port Sebastian. She was working as a secretary for some brokerage, and he was banging her bosom pal, one of the other secretaries." She blew a cloud of smoke off to one side. "She met him one day at the office when he came down to pick up the girlfriend. Sullivan and Naomi exchanged pleasantries, then phone numbers, then bodily fluids, all over the span of about four days."

"That … That doesn't sound like my mother."

Martha scoffed. "It's not like she'd have ever told you any-thing. Who talks about shit like that with their kids? She jumped in and out of bed with him so fast that first weekend the sheets didn't have time to wrinkle."

Selby digested this. With anything Martha said, he would have to filter out the bile to get to the facts, but she sounded almost proud of her sister's impetuosity.

"And then they got married."

"She got pregnant, and *then* they got married. Sullivan was charming and solicitous and seemed genuinely delighted that you were on the way, but all the time Naomi was pregnant, he was out screwing anything in a skirt." She thrust her face closer to the camera, a ghastly leer wrinkling her cheeks. Flamingo-pink lipstick smeared her front teeth. "He screwed a few things in a suit and tie while he was at it. Sullivan was into diversity and inclusion before there even was such a thing. That's probably where you got your … proclivities."

Selby remembered his father's charisma. To know Sullivan Coates was to love him. Did Martha ever succumb to that charm? Selby considered asking her, but only for a moment. *Sometimes it's best to leave the worms in their can.*

"What about family? He didn't just fall out of the sky."

Martha frowned. "Funny about that. We always assumed he was an orphan because he never mentioned his parents, and he'd dodge any questions about family. He was damned good at that kind of misdirection. You'd ask him a bunch of questions, and he'd talk for a while, and then you'd go away thinking you got what you came for when, really, all you got was smoke." She blew out smoke by way of illustration, holding up a finger to hold the floor while she sorted her thoughts. Her nails were painted a magenta so intense it vibrated. "I think he did have some siblings. There was a woman, evasive and charming like him. Cool as a cucumber. Naomi would have a little party. The woman and Sullivan didn't look anything alike, but you knew they were blood."

"Do you remember any names?"

"Nope. Nothing I could remember a day later."

"And he ran a bookstore."

"Yep. Made enough to keep the three of you alive, but only just. I don't know where he got all the money to entertain girlfriends on the side. I wouldn't be surprised if he had an old biddy somewhere slipping him a few bucks every time he slipped her the wiener."

"Nice."

"Yep. Your mother only had the one great love in her, and she invested it in a two-bit man-whore."

Selby flinched, then continued. "How did it end? The marriage, I mean. All I remember is one day, I had a father, and the next, I didn't."

"That's about the way it happened. Naomi dropped by the bookstore to see Sullivan about something, and she found the place closed up tight. She never saw him again. He left money in the joint bank account but no letter, no explanations. Naomi stewed for a year until the money started running out, then she called me up. I paid the rent, maybe some of the other bills. Naomi couldn't work, not with a child in the house. My Marty wasn't as pretty or as charming as Sullivan Coates, but he was up to his hemorrhoids in money, so we didn't have a problem with helping out. When you moved away, she came to live with us. After Marty died and I bought into this place, she came down here with me."

"Was there ever any question about Sullivan being my father? I mean, were there any other candidates?"

Martha laughed. "What a delightful way of putting it. No, Naomi didn't get around much before she met Sullivan and not at all after you came along. She wasn't a virgin when they met —I won't go into *that*—but she was pretty standoffish with men. That's why it was such a surprise when she jumped into the sack with her best friend's guy."

"What did Martin think of my father?"

"Not much. Thought he was too pretty, too slippery. Marty was all about having the right great-great-grandparents and going to the right schools. Sullivan was running the bookstore when Naomi met him, but before that, who knows what he was doing and where? No pedigree, no resume. They got along okay, but Marty never invited Sullivan to play golf or meet his rich friends for drinks."

Selby took in a deep breath and then let it out slowly. "You know Naomi's never told me anything at all about Sullivan."

The old woman shrugged. "She wouldn't. She doesn't like to talk about him now. As far as she's concerned, Sullivan Coates came into existence the day they met and was erased from the universe the day he went to work and didn't come back." She paused, then added, "She still loves him, though. She never stopped."

Northside Books had been around since the Great Depression, passing seamlessly from one owner to the next without anyone ever getting around to leveling the bookcases or putting in light fixtures that matched. Though the neighborhood had been gentrified in recent years, the bookstore resisted any attempt at improvement.

Sullivan Coates had operated the place for just about a decade, from the late 1960s through the late 70s, earning just enough to support his wife and child in genteel poverty.

The woman behind the cash register smiled as Selby limped up to the counter. "May I help you, sir?"

"I'm not sure. My name is Selby Coates."

She hesitated a moment before nodding. "From the Herald-Star."

Selby smiled, pleased. "Recently retired. I'm surprised you recognized my name."

"I'm a fan, actually," she said. "I've always liked your writing style. Correct, even courtly. Kind of old-fashioned. No trendy abbreviations. 'Who' and 'whom' used in the proper places. You never gave in to laziness."

Courtly? Selby's smile faltered. *Old-fashioned*?

"Thank you, Ms. ..."

"No honorifics, please. I'm just Alice."

Selby guessed that Just Alice was in her mid-thirties. She had the tousled hair and wary eyes of Pamela Duncan battling telepathic giant crustaceans in *Attack of the Crab Monsters.* Hers was the look of a survivor. Alice would always be the one still standing when the sun came up, or the rescue helicopters arrived, or the Professor's experimental gas finally took down the giant whatsit.

"Are you the owner here?"

"Co-owner, along with my brother. We inherited the place from our grandfather when I was all of two years old. I've spent my entire life in this shop. Are you interested in buying a bookstore?"

Selby chuckled. "As a matter of fact, no, but my father used to run this one."

"Of course! Coates. Samuel? Sylvester?"

"Sullivan."

"Sullivan Coates. My grandfather bought the shop back in the sixties. Your dad was the manager back then. Sullivan Coates. I haven't heard that name in forever." Just Alice started to say more, then hesitated. A pair of older women were giggling over a table of discounted romance novels right inside the door, but otherwise, the shop was deserted. Alice reached a decision and stepped out from behind the counter and pointed toward a doorway through which a narrow flight of stairs was visible.

"This is kind of crazy, but I think I have something up here that belongs to you."

"To me?"

"To your dad, anyway."

The stairs led directly into an apartment even smaller than Selby's own tenth-floor efficiency. A single room, crowded with boxes and disassembled furniture and smelling of dry rot, faced the alley behind the shop. Through an open door, Selby could see a tiny bathroom. Alice opened another door and shifted some things around in a shallow closet, finally pulling down a flat box bound with twine, the sort of container that might have held a nice silk scarf or a lace nightie. A romantic gift for a woman. A yellowed index card taped to the lid read "S. Coates" in black marker. The ink had faded to a tired plum color.

Maleva's box.

"I don't actually know what's in here," Alice said, "but my grandfather found this under a bunch of old magazines in a dresser full of junk that was up here. He taped it up, tied it, and put the label on it. He was kind of OCD sometimes. The rest of the stuff was trash, so he didn't keep it, but he thought what was in there might be of value to Mr. Coates or the family. He tried to get hold of Mr. Coates's wife—your mother?—but she wasn't interested."

"No, I don't suppose she would have been." Selby took the box and stood looking at it, momentarily at a loss. "Did your grandfather ever mention what was inside?"

"No. Once the box went into the closet, everybody forgot it existed." She looked at the box. "I only remembered it because I dreamed about my grandfather a couple of nights ago. I was a little girl, and he was up here showing me things from the closet. This box was in the dream, name tag and all. Grandad's been dead for twenty years, so I don't guess there's anybody alive who knows what's inside that thing."

Selby blew out his cheeks. He wasn't sure he wanted to know, either.

"This stuff has been here for half a century. I'm surprised nobody ever came for it before," Alice said.

"I'm even more surprised you kept it."

She shrugged. "I live way out in Woodlake. I use the apartment now and then when the weather's bad and I can't get home. There's no outside entrance, so we can't rent it. It's mostly storage. That closet is full of things from my grandfather's time that we've never gotten around to throwing out. Once a year, I pull everything out, chase off the mice, think about throwing it all away, and then put it all back."

"I didn't even know this apartment existed. In my time, that door at the bottom of the stairs was always kept locked. I thought it was a storage closet. My father probably brought his girlfriends here. My mother and I were not privy to this part of his life."

Selby looked at Alice's expression, and he blushed. "I'm sorry. I'm sure that's too much information." He shook the box. It felt empty. "I'd better let you get back to your customers."

In the shop below, the two women looking for budget romance had been replaced by a weedy young man with a beard and horn-rimmed glasses, also looking for budget romance. He turned to gaze at Alice with a book in his hand and a yearning expression in his eyes.

"Thank you for your time—and for this," Selby said, holding up the box.

"Don't be a stranger."

Selby smiled and nodded. By dinnertime, he suspected, Just Alice would have forgotten all about the visit from the eccentric old man with a courtly writing style. He tucked the box under his arm and walked out of the shop.

At the bus stop, Selby eased down onto the bench, wincing at the stiffness in his knee.

I've got to quit all this roughhousing, he thought.

A young man of about fifteen sat down next to him. The youngster's jeans were in shreds, but his sneakers and white hoodie were immaculate. His hair was styled in short, precise dreadlocks. They exchanged nods, and Selby went back to contemplating the box.

The knot wasn't complicated, but it had been tied a long

time ago and had stiffened into a single impenetrable lump. A considerable quantity of transparent packing tape had also been used to seal the lid down, and this had become a yellow skin bonded permanently to the cardboard. Selby picked at the fastenings for a few minutes but dropped the box hastily when a knife intruded into his field of vision.

"Whoa! Be cool. I thought you might have better luck with this."

Selby laughed weakly, looking over at the teenager next to him. He accepted the knife.

"Thank you."

"We're not all out to stab you and take your money, you know."

Selby nodded. "I apologize. I have terrible peripheral vision, so I'm easily startled by things coming into view from the sides. Nothing personal."

"No worries."

Selby sawed through the string and the tape. He handed the knife back to the stranger with thanks and lifted the lid.

Ashes. Pale flakes. Selby shook the box but almost dropped it when what he thought were a half dozen or so human teeth came to the top of the layer of debris. He realized his mistake when some of the "teeth" split to extrude wings and then flung themselves out of the box with an erratic, bumbling flight.

With a teenager's quick reflexes, the boy caught one as it flew past his face.

"Just a bug," he said, disappointed, examining his prize. It was a beetle, chalky white, half an inch long. "Prickly little feet." He tossed the beetle into the air, but it simply tumbled to the pavement, stunned. After a moment, it spread its wings and flew away. In a few minutes, all the insects had vanished.

"Nobody's opened this box in fifty years," Selby said.

"Huh. What's that in bug years?"

Selby set the lid to one side. Like Al Capone's underground

vaults, the prize did not live up to the drama of the opening. Once the beetles had departed, about a cup and a half of dry, flaky material was all that was left.

"Well, that sucks," the youngster said. "No jewels, no piles of cash, not even a secret formula. Maybe those're somebody's ashes?"

Selby had been stirring the powder with his finger. He jerked his hand back, then shook his head. "No, the texture is wrong. Human ashes look more like crunched-up kitty litter. This isn't even ashes. It's more like paper or thin cardboard that's been put through a food processor."

The boy nodded, impressed by Selby's arcane knowledge. "The plans for the North Korean atomic fusion super-submarine," he said.

"That's one possibility," Selby said, peering down at the drift of coarse gray powder. This was Maleva's box. The contents were all that remained of the cards. This box came from his dream, or the dream came from the box. Either way, it was impossible.

Ashes. My father's legacy, he thought. *Ashes and still more unanswered questions.*

When Selby's bus arrived, he changed his mind and didn't get on. Instead, he waited for the connection for downtown.

He needed to see Owen.

. . .

Fiona's Baby Diary:
Bongo had another one of his funny spells this morning. He was in the middle of telling me some story about him and Mitch loading hay and finding a snake in the barn, and he just faded away. He sat there for a minute, looking lost, and then he smiled at me, but it wasn't his normal smile, it was the smile he'd use for a stranger, somebody he was being polite to but didn't know. By the time I could react, he was over it, and everything was back to normal. Ruth told me this was something that

wouldn't go away, but I guess I was hoping. This is only the second time it's happened since we got married, so I probably shouldn't obsess on it.

CHAPTER SEVEN

Owen Mosley turned in his chair to face his visitor.

"You again? I'll have to start charging you an hourly rate."

Selby blinked. "Oh. I suppose you're right. How much do you think—?"

"Forget it. I was joking. Juliet says I need to cultivate a sense of humor before I retire, and she has to put up with me 24/7. I've been practicing, but I guess I'm not quite there yet."

Selby experienced a surge of sympathy. "I'm probably not the best audience," he said, his ears pink. "I tend to be somewhat literal sometimes."

Mosley nodded. "I've heard that about you. What can I do for you today?"

Selby took a deep breath, sorting himself out. "Ruth Coates."

"The woman from the accident. The one with her lips sewn up."

"Exactly." Selby showed Mosley the box from the bookstore closet. "Ruth Coates and my father, Sullivan Coates. I need to know more about both of them. My father left this behind when he disappeared. I picked it up this morning."

Mosley took the box and looked at the label on the lid. He opened the box, shook it, then replaced the lid and handed the box back to Selby. "A box of sawdust?"

"Pulverized paper, I think. There were beetles in the box. I think they reduced the contents to this."

"Probably their larvae," Mosley said.

Selby made a face. "Their larvae, then."

"Your father left—when?"

"When I was ten."

Mosley nodded. "Fifty-something years ago."

"Right."

"Durable little buggers. Continue."

"There have been other … incidents. Odd things coming to the surface. Maybe I have too much time to think about this stuff now. I don't know. I want to know what happened to my father. Why he left. Where he ended up afterward. Is Ruth Coates my sister?"

"I imagine she'd be your half-sister."

"My half-sister, then. If so, then she was part of my father's life after he left us. I want to talk to her."

Mosley nodded thoughtfully. "It's not as easy as it is in the movies. Aside from social media and the government, most people don't have a readily available public footprint. Will you need to verify or corroborate any of the information?"

"What do you mean?"

"Legal stuff. You're not going to put anything I give you in a book or bandy it about publicly, are you?"

"No. This is a personal thing. I'm mostly interested in anything I can learn about my father. Ruth is just a step."

"All right. There are some sources that I can get into as a representative of a major media company. People in this place go to them all the time for 'deep background' stuff. Subscription sites, voter rolls, DMV, court records, paid services. I wouldn't use them for an outside project if I thought there might be public disclosures, but if you're going to be discreet, I can justify breaking the rules for you. I'll need a couple of days."

"Thank you. Won't this be a distraction from your work?"

"What work? I'm marking time, Coates. Another year, and I'm out of here, too." He gestured, a wave that took in his entire subterranean empire. "Nobody cares about the past anymore. Once a story has been posted somewhere, printed, read out on a podcast, or whatever ... it's forgotten. Vapor. None of what we have here, all this history, none of it matters to the kids upstairs." Mosley looked up at Coates, his expression grave. "What's retirement like for you?"

Selby shrugged. "All right. A little directionless. I need to get this family stuff out of the way and zero in on a project."

Mosley nodded. "I haven't been without a regular job since I was in my teens. I worry about what will happen when the rug gets pulled out from under me. Juliet has made it clear that DIY home improvement projects will not be permitted. She even monitors my YouTube viewing to make sure I don't get any crazy ideas. Beekeeping. Pygmy goats. That sort of thing."

"You find new interests. Or you vegetate and die."

Mosley nodded again. "That was what I figured. I guess we'll find out soon enough. Meanwhile, I'm going to need a few days to do your searches. Today's what? Thursday? Check back with me on Tuesday or Wednesday. If I find anything before then that I think you'll want to see immediately, I'll zip it up and email it to you."

"That'll be perfect. I owe you one, Owen."

"Forget about it. Tracking down your mysterious father will be more interesting than sitting around down here counting down the days to the end of my career.

The patch of pavement in front of the Herald-Star that had been the scene of Selby's abrupt demise only days before was unmarked, undamaged. No blood, no skin. Not even a smear of cake frosting.

The bus was half full. Selby sat near the front, on the aisle, listening to the conversations going on around him. Roy always called it eavesdropping, but he preferred to think of it as an expression of his burning desire to get to know his fellow human beings a little better.

"She'll have to get some time off," a woman's voice was saying. "I know, but this is important."

She was talking on the phone. Selby felt a pang of guilt as he wondered where his cell phone was. Probably on his desk. He always sat at his desk to talk on the telephone. It was a portable phone; he was supposed to carry it around with him. He didn't treat the device properly.

"This job is for what? A year? She's got to think about the long term."

Bossy. There's always somebody who knows what's best for you, Selby thought.

"We got three pairs," a male voice across the aisle announced in an excited murmur.

"You're kidding! Those are so sick. You're going to make out like a bandit when you flip them."

Two men, young. Selby recognized all the words but had no idea what they meant.

"They have such a strange family." This one was a woman directly behind him, someone with an educated, rather pleasant voice. "So many marriages and divorces—"

"We *assume* there are divorces," a man's voice put in.

"True. We hope that there are some divorces in between all those wives."

"How many kids?"

"Who knows?"

Who knows, indeed? Selby thought as they pulled into the central terminal.

Selby climbed down from the Number Seven bus, his box of sawdust under his arm, and looked around for the bus that would take him the rest of the way home. The walkway that led under the road to the correct platform was closed off, with yellow caution tape tied between the railings. Plumbing problems, Selby assumed. That little pedestrian tunnel was notorious for getting flooded every time it rained. The detour involved climbing a flight of steps to the upper level instead, crossing over, and then descending on the other side. Selby could have taken the elevator, but he was determined not to behave like a person who was old and infirm until he was one. Which, he suspected, was likely to be any day now.

The overpass looked out onto the buses coming and going below but was otherwise uninteresting. As Selby labored up the steps, his knee making him wonder whether the time had come to reconsider the elevator, he noticed a woman coming up behind him. He shifted to the side, but she stopped and waved him on. Selby thanked her and continued to climb.

On the overpass, Selby paused to catch his breath. These buses were all electric now; Selby could remember a time when the diesel fumes made breathing inside the terminal a hazardous undertaking. Now, everything smelled of ozone and human exhalations.

The woman reached the top of the steps and hesitated. She was about Selby's height, stocky but by no means fat, wearing a tailored skirt and jacket, gray with white accents here and there. Executive clothes. Probably expensive. A pale gray hat, something like a fedora but more graceful in its lines, covered her hair, and a COVID mask covered her mouth and nose. Selby nodded hello and went back to looking at the buses. His own hadn't pulled in yet.

Selby staggered and almost fell when hard, strong hands grabbed the box from under his arm and jerked it away.

"Hey! What are you doing?"

The woman in gray and white yanked the lid off the box, flung the contents out over the platforms below to be scattered in the slight breeze generated by the activity of the buses and their passengers, and dropped the box and the lid onto the walkway at her feet. She faced Selby for a moment, her face unreadable through the mask, her eyes flinty, then turned and hustled away, her heels clattering on the non-slip metal of the steps.

Shocked, Selby stood motionless, staring after her, then he craned over the railing to see where the woman went; he knew he couldn't move fast enough to catch her in the crowd. He thought he caught a glimpse of her hat exiting the terminal on the far side, but he couldn't be sure.

Below, the bus that would take him home was pulling in. Bewildered, Selby collected the empty box and its lid and hobbled off to meet it.

After supper, Selby washed and dried the dishes and tidied up the kitchen, then warmed up a cinnamon roll for dessert. Licking off the icing, he stood at the counter and looked over at his desk. The blue box sat there, dented and reproachful.

The loss of the contents was not a big deal. Nobody was going to learn much from a pile of sawdust. At the same time, Selby was angry.

Angry at what? he asked himself, nibbling pastry. *At whom?*

At himself, of course. He shook his head. Everybody was walking all over him lately: the boys in the basement, the pale woman in the park, the vandal who came into his apartment, now the woman at the bus station. Selby couldn't imagine what he might have done differently, but he felt deeply dissatisfied with his responses to things, his inability to fight back.

He finished the cinnamon roll and washed his hands, draping the towel carefully over the oven handle to dry.

A thought struck him. Could the woman at the bus station have been a *man*? She would have fit Rita's description of the person who went into Selby's apartment. For that matter, perhaps the vandal was a woman dressed as a man.

What difference did it make?

Selby's life had become a sequence of random events over which he seemed to have no control.

Was it ever anything else? he wondered as he tidied up the kitchen and got ready for bed.

That night, DeQuinn Pitts stalked through Selby's dreams, naked and sweating, wrestling a younger, stronger, more exciting Selby Coates through a series of ever more unlikely scenarios.

At sunrise, Selby awoke frustrated and depressed. He lay in his bed heavy with the knowledge that the fit, desirable, thirty-year-old Selby Coates of his dream was as dead and gone as the sawdust in Maleva's blue box.

He heaved himself out of bed and staggered into the bathroom to pee.

Outside Selby's tenth-floor window, the October sky shaded from pink and yellow into an uneven pale gray while the sounds of early morning traffic rose from the street below, as pastel and remote as the firmament overhead.

Today is Friday. Tomorrow, I'm going away for the weekend. His shiver of apprehension and anticipation had nothing to do with his search for Sullivan Coates. Like his dreams of the night before, this was nothing but nerves and blood and hormones. He had an overdue appointment with biology.

Selby showered, dressed, drank coffee, and ate a banana muffin—the last of a box of four he had bought in the aftermath of his encounter with Doma in the park. It was old and stale, but who was he to throw stones? Even an old, stale muffin was better than no muffin at all.

Pancake stalked across the room on his way to the window, making the little ratcheting noise in his throat that meant a bird was on the windowsill. Selby twisted in his chair, half expecting crows, but saw that it was just a pigeon.

"What secrets are *you* hiding?"

The cat jumped up onto the bookcase, bringing himself up to the level of the windowsill. The pigeon cocked one eye at him, then flung itself off the sill and into the air. Just a pigeon.

Pancake sat down to wash his paws.

"Good job, Pancake. You showed him."

Selby licked muffin crumbs off his fingertips, unconsciously mirroring the cat's movements. He climbed out of his chair and went to finish getting dressed.

CHAPTER EIGHT

The neighborhood discount store a block south of the Circle Tavern had, for many years, been a Woolworth's, and long-time residents of the area still called it that, even though that name had come down from the long plaque over the door decades ago. Amid the smells of dust and mothballs, Selby bought boxer shorts and a new toothbrush.

He then rode the bus to a downtown barbershop up the street from the Herald-Star. Selby had been getting his hair cut by the same barber for more than a decade. He loved the familiar smells: the bay rum, the talcum powder, old Mr. Lewenholt's wintergreen chewing gum. The ancient rituals were soothing and predictable, and Mr. Lewenholt never felt compelled to make conversation once the required social niceties had been attended to. Selby sat in the chair, lost in the enormous black plastic cape, while the barber snipped and fiddled, coaxing his fidgeting customer's remaining yellow-gray fluff into an appearance of low-maintenance respectability.

Feeling adventurous, Selby ate lunch downtown at a diner he had frequented when he was still working at the Herald-Star. He stopped in at a used bookstore to pick up a paperback to read on the train—

Tomorrow!

—then he climbed onto the same bus that had propelled him to the edge of the afterlife only days ago. This time, he was hop ing it would just take him as far as his own neighborhood.

By the time Selby climbed down at the 29th Avenue stop and circled the roundabout to climb Tower Lane, his knee was bothering him, and he wanted a nap.

A nap. If that's not a sure sign that the end is nigh, I don't know what is, he thought as he trudged up the cracked sidewalk. According to his mother, he had been desperately nap-averse as a toddler.

A light rain had begun to fall while Selby was crossing greater metropolitan Buckley in the Number Seven bus. What anemic gray sunlight made it through the clouds failed to penetrate the overhanging trees on Tower Lane.

As Selby started up the hill, two men walked out of the driveway of the former Seventh Day Adventist Church and stood in the shadows in the middle of the alley, looking at him.

The young men from the Herald-Star basement. *I'm not in the mood for this*, Selby thought.

Selby put his head down and marched on. When he reached the men—they were indeed the same two men, wearing the same nerdy outfits they had worn the first time he met them, their mouths neatly stitched shut—they each raised their right hands, but he didn't wait. With a courage he didn't feel and a strength he didn't know he had, he shoved past them and kept walking.

The silence slammed into his back, a physical force, knocking him off his feet. When his bruised knee hit the pavement, Selby knelt there, gasping, until the first shock passed, then he crawled to the side of the road and struggled to his feet, bracing himself against a "Children at Play" sign that must have dated back to the days when the church was still there. The two silhouettes kicking a ball back and forth were grandparents by this time.

Selby turned and looked back at the two men. They were standing in the street in front of the Colonel's house, each holding up one hand, palm out. The silence was absolute, oppressive, surging like a tide. Wetness slithered across onto his chin, and he discovered that he had split his lip.

A second pulse hit him, but this time, Selby kept to his feet, holding on to the metal pole with both hands. His vision, never the most reliable, fractured, and a shooting pain ran up from his right ear all the way to the top of his head, like someone sliding a thin metal blade between his scalp and his skull.

Now would be a good time for the hero to show up and slug these guys, he thought, struggling to breathe.

Another sharp pain skewered his head, and the world suddenly went sideways.

Everything froze: the nerdy boys, the slow drips of rain coming through the trees, the beating of his heart.

Pieces clicked together inside Selby's skull as though an unplugged machine had been plugged back in, and Selby's awareness folded open, leaving a space, an empty room in the tumbledown mansion of his mind that he hadn't known about before.

He wondered what a stroke felt like.

Time rebooted, and Selby once again felt the weight of the silence gathering itself to hammer him down.

Cavalry. Now, definitely. That thought plunged into the empty room, stirring whispers.

Without warning, a jagged, high-pitched noise sliced into the silence like shards of glass shot into bread dough. The shorter of the two men did a silly dance, stumbling backward from a vicious little bundle of teeth and spite whirling around his ankles.

Bolívar. Selby laughed, his pain momentarily eclipsed by absurdity.

The man under attack tripped and fell, landing on his butt as his partner stood gaping, one hand still held up foolishly. The silence dissipated instantly.

"That's going to leave a bruise," Selby murmured, glad to be able to hear the sound of his own voice. He dithered for a moment, then staggered back down toward the action. Seeing his tormentors themselves tormented gave him courage. This might be an opportunity to learn something—or, at the very least, to recover some of his self-respect.

Bolívar let out a shriek as the taller man ran forward and kicked the dog away.

With a roar, the Colonel erupted from the front door of his house, shouting in Spanish, spitting with rage. Selby had no idea what he was saying, but it did not sound conciliatory. The Colonel shoved the tall man down, scooping Bolívar off the pavement and holding him against his chest.

The silent men scrabbled back across the cracked asphalt, dismayed, and when they got to their feet, they did not stay to deal with this new distraction but instead crashed into the undergrowth next to the Colonel's house and vanished from sight.

Selby walked down to where the old man stood glaring.

"Hello, Colonel," he sniffled, dabbing at his lip with the back of his hand, trying to reassemble the fragments of his dignity.

"Your friends tried to hurt my dog," the old autocrat growled. He stepped up close enough that Selby could have leaned forward and bitten him on his mottled bulb of a nose. Selby noted that he and the other man were of the same height. The Colonel reached into his pocket with his free hand and pulled out a tissue. "You are bleeding."

"They're not my friends." Selby accepted the tissue with some trepidation—it looked as though it might have seen active duty—and poked at his mouth gingerly. "Thank you."

To his surprise, the Colonel grinned, narrowing his eyes and baring a mismatched assortment of yellow teeth and off-white bridgework.

"I saw you confront them. The little *maricón* has *cojones.*"

The Colonel's breath reeked of wine and tobacco and poor dental hygiene. He had strange little hairs, like gray fishhooks, growing on the outside of his nose. With a grimace of distaste, Selby eased back a step.

"I don't like your dog, but I'm grateful for his assistance. I'm sorry they kicked him."

The Colonel nodded. "My Bolívar is not beautiful, but he is a good companion." He petted the dog and nodded toward the trampled bushes where the two strangers had pushed their way through. "I have seen women do that," he said. "That thing with the lips. Back when I served my country as its President—"

"You took power in a coup, Colonel, after assassinating your predecessor."

The Colonel spat on the pavement at Selby's feet but responded without heat. "As you like. You know *nothing* of my country and what I had to do and why I had to do it, but that is not what we are talking about right now, so I will be *mag-na-ni-mous*." He pronounced the last word carefully and elaborately.

The grim old man walked to the gap in the shrubbery and squinted into the shadows, petting the dog in his arms, who bared his teeth in Selby's direction the whole time. "The women in my country, they were protesting. They sewed their lips to make a point. These two, they are not like that." The Colonel looked back at Selby, his froglike face intent, almost gleeful. "These two are like you; something unholy has touched them."

"What? What are you talking about? What do you mean 'like me'? Touched by what?"

"I am not a fool. Do not pretend you don't know what I am talking about. You have the smell of the Whore of Babylon about you."

Selby frowned. This felt like a good time to walk away, but he wasn't sure what his knee was going to do, and he didn't want to risk embarrassing himself. "'The Whore of Babylon'?"

"Incense and unholy rituals," the Colonel elaborated. "Men who lust after little boys. Vast temples filled with gold and silk in cities where people are starving in the streets. You are a servant of the Mother of Harlots."

This whole conversation was getting weirder and weirder. *Whore of Babylon? Mother of Harlots?* "Wait a minute. You mean *Catholic?* I'm not Catholic. I'm not religious at all. I was raised Lutheran, for Heaven's sake."

The Colonel nodded. "So. Maybe you are not past redemption," he said. "The scarlet woman turns men into slaves and keeps them from God, all the while pretending to do God's bidding. Maybe you are not a slave to Rome, but you stink of false angels and devils."

Selby took a deep breath, staring at the former dictator, once nicknamed *El Carroñero*, "the carrion-eater," by the press of his own country. Why was he even talking to this awful man?

"Colonel, I have no idea what you're going on about. I don't even believe in angels and devils, let alone have dealings with them. I'm sorry you have such a problem with Catholics. Some of my best friends have been Catholic. I'm grateful to you and your dog for rescuing me from those men, but you're talking like a lunatic."

Bolívar, safe in his master's arms, delivered a nasal growl, and the Colonel smacked him lightly on the head. "*Callate, chiquito.* You can bite him another time." The old man turned his attention back to Selby. "Perhaps I am the criminal people have named me. But you associate with some strange people, my friend, dangerous people, so do not be too quick to judge me and mine." With a nod and a grotesque smile, the Colonel turned and vanished inside his house.

Selby blew out his cheeks. He looked up and down the dark, narrow street, but he was finally alone. No silent people, no creepy ex-dictators, no demonic lapdogs. High time he went home and stayed there.

. . .

Weather permitting, Barry Ratliffe and his border collie mix

Moby spent an hour every afternoon at the dog park half a mile from Ratliffe's house. The idea was to give man and dog an hour of exercise and fresh air during the interval between the confined rigors of the school day and the vegetative inertia of dinner and Netflix. Not that teaching eighth-grade science to a roomful of hormone-addled kids wasn't strenuous, but Ratliffe liked to clear his head of the overpowering funk of adolescent sweat and dominance games before he started dinner. His definition of exercise was flexible enough to include spending an hour dozing on a bench while Moby sprawled in the grass at his feet.

"Hello. This is Daisy."

Ratliffe grunted. "I'm not asleep. Just resting my eyes."

"You should say hello back."

Ratliffe groaned and opened his eyes.

"Oh. Hello."

A little girl stood in front of his bench, gazing at him with patient disapproval. She held up a doll, a stuffed monkey with a cylindrical body and limbs of plain black fabric, like plush sausages, surmounted by a molded plastic face frozen in an expression of maniacal, open-mouthed joy.

"She's not really mine. I just borrowed her for today," the little girl continued. "I'm taking her for a walk."

"Hello, Daisy," Ratliffe said. He glanced around. Where was this child's adult? "Are you here with your mom?"

The little girl was a wisp of a thing, with dark hair and an olive-sallow complexion. Her eyes were distinctive, luminous, a pale greenish hazel that stood out against her skin. She seemed familiar to Ratliffe, as though he had seen her, maybe more than once, but he couldn't quite remember where. He wondered if she might belong to one of the Afghan refugee families that had moved into the neighborhood a few years back.

"I don't have a mom," she said. "I never had one."

"Oh." That complicated things. Ratliffe was still foggy-headed and dull, half asleep, and he struggled to find a way forward through the conversation. "Do you have a dog?"

The little girl laughed. She wiggled her fingers at Moby, who ignored her.

"No. Dogs won't talk to me. I like birds better."

"You know, you shouldn't just go up to strangers in the park," Ratliffe said. "I'm sure someone has told you that before."

She smiled but didn't answer. Ratliffe stirred uneasily.

"I think Daisy would like to go play," he said. "She's probably bored listening to us talk. Maybe you should find your … babysitter? … and see what—"

"I think Barry is the one who's bored," the little girl said, her high, clear voice interrupting his nasal baritone ramble.

"What?"

"Barry is bored with his life right now," the little girl said, turning Daisy to face her and talking into the manic monkey face. "He used to have so much excitement, but now he just takes lots of naps."

That didn't just happen. "Are you here with your daddy?" Ratliffe asked, his apprehension increasing. "A grandparent? Can you point to them?"

"Six years ago," the little girl continued. She turned Daisy back around and hugged the doll to her chest so that Barry found himself addressed by two faces, one above the other, grave child and delirious toy. "I wasn't hardly even born yet, but you were big already. You went around in the ambulance to help people who got hurt. You met a lady who couldn't talk. Remember her?"

Ratliffe climbed to his feet, his lanky frame towering over the child. "Let's go find your people," he suggested.

"*Remember her,* Barry."

Ratliffe froze, unaccustomed to being addressed by small children in such a tone of command.

"Look, kid, we need to find your—"

Moby stuck her wet nose under Ratliffe's hand where it rested on his knee, and he awoke with a start, smacking his elbow into the back of the bench painfully. The dog settled onto her haunches, looking up at him.

"What the fuck was that?" Ratliffe rubbed his elbow, blinking and shaking his head.

Moby wagged her tail in response.

The schoolteacher stood up and looked around the park. A blonde fourth-grader, a couple of toddlers. Two little boys on the far side of the park blowing bubbles for their Yorkie to chase. No Afghan child with a toy monkey named Daisy and eyes like afternoon sunlight through the trees. He shook his head slowly, baffled. He picked up Moby's leash where it had fallen from his fingers as he dozed.

"Come on, Mobe. I think we've had enough exercise for one day."

. . .

Rita Okorie was coming out of the building as he was going in, and Selby almost flinched.

"Hello, Mr. Coates," Rita said. "You're limping. More than usual, I mean. And there's blood on your shirt. Are you all right?"

"I'm fine. Thank you for asking." He looked down at his shirt. *There goes another one.* "I had a little accident, that's all."

She nodded, accepting his non-explanation without question. Her husband moved in circles where bloody accidents were commonplace. "You should get some rest."

Selby smiled grimly. "You're probably right."

Rita moved to go but then stopped abruptly. "By the way, did you ever find out who was in your place?"

"No," he told her. "Fortunately, nothing was stolen. I'm going to be more careful about locking my door in the future."

"Always pays to be careful."

"That's true. How are Mari and Jonas?"

She brightened. "They're fine. I'm on my way now to pick them up at daycare."

"I won't keep you then."

Inside his apartment, Selby took off his shoes and placed them side by side on the mat next to the door. He topped up Pancake's food and water and hung his windbreaker in the closet, then he walked into the bathroom, flipped the light on, and turned on the shower.

While he waited for the hot water, he stared at himself in the mirror over the sink.

The man grimacing back at him looked *old*. There was a crust of dried blood around his right nostril and blood on the front of his shirt. His right eye was bloodshot. His expression was not so much one of anger as weary disappointment.

I look like roadkill.

He took off his glasses, and the image blurred and distorted. He turned from the mirror and undressed. His left knee was swollen and felt hot to the touch, but at least it was still functioning. He breathed, in and out, in and out, feeling naked and foolish and alone.

He climbed into the shower and scrubbed away the sweat and grime, inhaling the steam, letting the water beat down on his face, washing off everything but the frustration he felt. The cultists had beaten the crap out of him. If the Colonel and his little monster dog hadn't shown up when they did ...

When the hot water started to run out, he turned off the shower, climbed out, and toweled himself down carefully, leaning on the wall with one hand. He wrapped up in a bathrobe and went to sit in his comfortable chair, his phone in his hand. Pancake jumped into his lap and snuggled down into the folds of the robe.

Selby ordered delivery from the Salvadorean restaurant

down the block, then sat back and relaxed. His head still felt strange, a familiar structure that had changed in an instant, adding rooms, moving stairways, carving doors in previously blank walls. In the aftermath of the attack in front of the Colonel's house, he felt old and weak and inadequate. Alone.

No, he thought, *not alone. Lonely. Say the word. Lonely.*

The new thing in his brain, this latest mystery, only made it all worse.

He looked down at his phone for a long moment, then he found a number on his contact list and dialed it. His voice shaking, he explained who he was.

Of course, Mr. Coates. I can confirm your reservation for one night, arriving tomorrow, leaving Sunday. Your usual room. We look forward to seeing you again, Mr. Coates.

After he disconnected from that call, he called Reggie.

We haven't forgotten. Tomorrow and Sunday. We'll be happy to look after him. Have a loverly weekend. Enjoy yourself.

He eased the cat off his lap and went to get dressed to greet the delivery driver. Tonight, he would eat, relax, watch a movie, and then sleep the sleep of the dead.

As it happened, dinner segued almost directly into sleep, and Selby dozed fitfully in his chair, full of cheese *pupusas* and fried *yuca,* while the *Beast From 20,000 Fathoms* rampaged through the streets of New York with the sound turned off.

CHAPTER NINE

Selby, like his mother, had only ever possessed the capacity for one great love. Naomi's had been Sullivan Coates. For Selby, the object of his undying passion was a broad-shouldered cello player from the Pautasquot Valley Chamber Orchestra named Mario. Mario was a musician of only middling skill, but besides his Olympic shoulders, Mario also had thick, curly black hair and a gap between his front teeth that made Selby laugh every time he saw it. Mario was everything Selby had ever wanted, and for three years, as Selby's career began to pick up steam, the two men shared a bed in a dingy apartment overlooking a district of warehouses and small factories on the northern edge of Fallwood.

Life, in Selby's opinion, was good.

The twenty-first of June 1991 was one of those summer days when the boundary between sluggish river and soggy air blurred, and fifteen minutes outdoors required a shower and a change of clothes. Selby finished work for the day, rode the bus home, and arrived at the apartment sweating and headachy.

He had been away from home for nine hours.

In that short span, a lifetime of changes had taken place.

The apartment had been emptied of everything that would fit into Mario's car—not to mention Mario himself—and in exchange, Mario had left a note. Three short sentences scrawled in black Sharpie on the back of last month's water bill.

Thank you for everything, the note read. *I've gone to follow my bliss. Wish me well.*

At thirty-three, Selby's chance for love had come and gone. From that point onward, he would focus on his career and on creating a life for himself that was structured and self-contained, with no need for further entanglements.

By and large, he succeeded.

Two or three times a year, however, driven by a biological imperative he could neither ignore nor override, Selby took a weekend mini-vacation.

A few weeks ahead of time, he would call the Climbing Rose Inn in Port Sebastian and make a reservation with the owner, a quiet man, friendly but not unctuous, who always sounded genuinely pleased to hear from him.

One night. Of course, Mr. Coates. We're always happy to see you.

Selby, vibrating with anxiety, would board the empty Saturday morning commuter train and ride eastward along the shore of the river to the line's Port Sebastian terminus at the Pautasquot Valley International Airport. At the station, he would climb into a taxi and ask to be driven to the B&B.

The owner of the Climbing Rose Inn would greet him with impeccable courtesy, and the two men would have a meandering conversation that would have meant nothing to a casual eavesdropper but which always left Selby feeling wilted and desperate.

That evening at around sundown, Selby would answer a knock at the door of his room. He would find a man there, a stranger, smiling pleasantly. The visitor would be attractive, but not extravagantly so. Pleasant but also cool and professional. He would introduce himself, and Selby would invite Bob or Sean or Carlos to come inside and make himself at home. After a brief, pointless conversation about nothing in particular, Antoine or Mike or Levi would undress, and Selby would do the same. From that point, events would follow a predictable path to an even more predictable conclusion.

After a couple of hours, both men would dress with a minimum of fuss or conversation, and Arnie or Bill or Tito would take his leave. Selby would shower, put on the dressy clothes that he had packed for this one evening, and go out to dinner, someplace fancy, alone. That night, he would sleep without dreams, and the following afternoon, he would thank his host, pay his bill without looking at it, and ride the train back to Buckley.

Selby watched the strip malls and tract housing scroll by as the train whisked him westward on Sunday afternoon. Buckley and Port Sebastian had, over time, bled across the landscape like dye, mingling in the middle, staining former farmlands and villages with the stark tints of urban life. Cities, or maybe one big city, Selby sometimes thought, a dumbbell shape a hundred miles long, skinny in the middle but heavy with importance at either end.

Selby often felt old and useless these days, and a one-night stand in another city wasn't going to fix that. He had enjoyed his evening with Caleb—a chunky farm boy from Charlotte putting himself through graduate school by leasing out his sturdy virility to lonely old men—and did not regret having made the trip. At the same time, he couldn't ignore the fact that it was merely a stopgap, a substitute for something he would almost certainly never have.

For him, sex was biology but not life; it was a part of him that he had never successfully integrated into who he was. His father, on the other hand, had been the slave of a frantic libido. What was it Aunt Martha had said? "Everything in a skirt, and some things in pants," or words to that effect. It was hard to believe two men so closely related could be so different in something so fundamental.

Sullivan Coates had been a careless, affectionate parent, inappropriate in manner and speech by modern standards, overly permissive by any standards, but infinitely lovable.

While Sullivan's parenting style might have been classified as benign neglect, Naomi's was fiercely protective, if inconsistent. Only after Sullivan had vanished and Selby had outgrown his mother's embrace did Naomi start to manifest the theatrical snarkiness that would come to dominate their relationship throughout her son's adult life.

Sooner or later, Selby was going to have to talk to his mother. He didn't look forward to that. She was prone to tantrums, explosive rage triggered by seemingly trivial things: a smile in the wrong place, a comment phrased just so, a pause in a conversation held a beat too long. His father was the intersection of all the triggers.

Selby was apprehensive, but he had taken on this task, and Naomi Goodwin Coates was a lode of information he had not yet had the courage to mine.

Pancake was so excited by the return of his lord and master that he raised his scruffy yellow head briefly to look over his shoulder, his one green eye glinting with momentary interest as Selby came through the door with his overnight bag and a container of tikka masala. Selby wondered which had caught the cat's attention: the man or the food. Pancake yawned and went back to his nap.

"I missed you, too, big guy."

Selby made himself a cup of coffee—usually verboten this late in the day, but he needed the pick-me-up—and changed into his sweatpants and a t-shirt. He unpacked, putting everything away or into the laundry basket, as appropriate, then put his bag up on the closet shelf where it belonged.

Outside, the setting sun gleamed on Zeus' shoulders and butt and back-thrust calf, and Selby wondered who had been the model for that figure. A workman, he supposed, somebody who did heavy manual labor every day of his life. A man with no name who probably never got enough to eat and lived in a squalid warren with a dozen of his relatives, working ten-hour days to build that skyline and those muscles that Selby so enjoyed looking at from his safe little nest. An immigrant laborer, or somebody from one of the failed farms, drafted into baring his all for a few extra dollars. In the middle of the Great Depression, he would have done anything for those crumbs. Selby thought about Caleb with a pang of guilt, quickly squashed. *I've never had to sell my body to survive*, he thought. *As if that would have even been an option.*

A flight of pigeons drifted across his view, several stories below his perch, the sun glinting on their wings against the backdrop of the shadows down at street level. For a moment, the world was beautiful and breathless, and Selby laughed, the dark mood pushed aside.

Enough of that.

Since the cat had taken over the comfortable chair, Selby sat down at his desk and checked his email. There was a message from Owen Mosley glinting among the chaff.

"Regarding the accident in 2018," the message read: "The first responders would have been from Bay Counties Emergency Services. The ambulance crew was not identified by name, but see attached."

The attachment was a PDF of a recent article from the Herald-Star, a filler, a short human-interest piece, the kind of thing the editors churned out by the yard to fill holes or add variety on slow news days. "New STEM Class Recognized," read the headline. Selby frowned, doing a quick Wikipedia search for the acronym. Science, Technology, Engineering, and Mathematics, he read. He made a face. *Acronyms are devouring our language.* A middle school in the Buckley system had hired a new science teacher at the beginning of the previous school year, and apparently, the class had seen some good results—

good enough, at least, for the teacher to merit the expense of a brass trophy. The photo showed a skinny, middle-aged man with a balding dome of a forehead and deep-set eyes over a long nose and a crooked mouth. "Barry Ratliffe, hired 2020 in the Mentor Teachers program," the caption read.

The name of the program required another search, and Selby found that it was a local initiative whereby the school system could hire professionals from out in the community to come into the schools to teach certain subjects, hopefully transmitting some of their hard-earned workplace experience to their students—for less expense than a professional teacher who might demand a living wage and some healthcare, Selby thought, reading between the lines.

Ratliffe's former occupation had been that of a paramedic working for Bay Counties Emergency Services, a position he held from 2005 until 2020.

"Bay Counties" was a portmanteau term lumping together Candless, Melrose, Turner, Ogalacat, and Wolfe counties. Selby glanced back up at Mosley's note.

In 2018, this Barry Ratliffe would have worked for the company that responded to the accident on the Maryville Highway.

Selby mourned the good old days of telephone books—then immediately chastised himself for even thinking the phrase "the good old days," which always suggested that one's best years were long past and that a chair in the sunroom at an assisted living facility was waiting right around the corner.

Ratliffe's probably on Facebook, Selby thought. Selby had an account but used it only rarely. He logged in. A cursory survey told him that the quality of the discourse had not improved since his last visit, so he sidestepped the various traps set before his feet and searched for Barry Ratliffe.

There were, to his surprise, quite a few Barry Ratliffes, representing a number of variants of the name. Fortunately, only one listed his job as "Educator" and his location as Buckley.

Foolishly, this Barry Ratliffe had also provided his telephone number. Selby shook his head at the man's carelessness with his personal data while making a note of the number. Barry Ratliffe had posted five pictures: one of him fishing with two other men, one of him in paramedic gear, standing next to a short, tough-looking woman in the same uniform, two of a black and white border collie being cute, and one of Ratliffe in a suit and a lot more hair, standing next to a pretty, dark-haired woman in a somewhat plain bridal gown, his expression and body language amazed and delighted.

Selby picked up his phone and dialed Ratliffe's number. Pancake came over and rubbed against his ankles but stalked away when Selby reached down to pet him. "You think I smell like the Mother of Harlots too?"

"I beg your pardon?" The voice was lazy, a little nasal, clearly amused.

Selby went blank for a moment. Something about the telephone, talking to someone who wasn't there, rattled him every time. Out of the corner of his eye, he saw Pancake pounce on a pale object that looked like a garbanzo bean or a tiny ball of paper, and Selby made a mental note to run the sweeper over the floor when he got off the phone.

"Hello? Can I help you?"

"Oh, I'm sorry. Mr. Ratliffe?"

"Yes?"

"My name is Coates. Selby Coates."

This time, it was Ratliffe's turn to fall silent.

"Coates. That's interesting," he said after a moment.

Selby frowned. They had barely begun, and the script was already going astray. Pancake batted his prey against the wall under the window, then back out into the middle of the floor.

"Yes. I used to be a writer for the Herald-Star. You may have heard of me."

"Yes. I've heard of you. It's ... well, it's funny you should happen to call. Let me ask you, Mr. Coates: do you have any siblings?"

Pancake batted his toy up to Selby's shoe and then flopped down next to it, kicking at it with his hind feet.

"None that I know of, but I might. I don't know. As a matter of fact, that's why I called you."

Ratliffe chuckled. "Okay. That makes no sense, but I'll bite. What can I do for you?"

"I should preface this by telling you that my father's name is —or possibly was—Sullivan Coates."

"I'll be damned."

"So that rings a bell?"

Ratliffe laughed. "Yeah. Like the Hunchback of Notre Dame. For reasons I won't go into because you'll think I'm demented, I spent yesterday going through my notes of an accident in 2018 involving a woman named Ruth Sullivan Coates."

"Your notes?"

"Yeah. I keep notebooks—journals, if you like—documenting my world. Stuff that happens, people I meet, all that. I've done it since I was a teenager. Anyway, that incident was weird enough that I wrote it up pretty thoroughly in my notes at the time."

"I'd like to see those notes."

Ratliffe said nothing for a long moment, then, "I don't think I can do that. There's a lot of stuff in there that I'd as soon not pass around. I can give you a summary, though, or answer questions."

"I understand."

Pancake performed his best creep-and-leap maneuver, stalking the white object and then kicking it under the bed. He sat down abruptly, looking off in a completely different direction, then spent a minute washing his face before slinking under the bed after his toy.

"Sullivan Coates abandoned my mother and me in 1968,

and I'm wondering if he then went on to start another family here in the area. Ruth could be a product of that."

Ratliffe exhaled slowly into the phone. "I can tell you a few things. Her name, as you know, was Ruth Sullivan Coates. The address on her driver's license and registration was in Welles-ley, a couple of miles from downtown Buckley, but Deputy Smith found out that she hadn't lived there for more than three years, and the current occupants of the house had no idea who she was."

"Who's Deputy Smith?"

"Your basic stereotypical rural sheriff's deputy. Over-weight, underqualified, bit of a butthole, if you'll pardon the ex-pression. He ran for Sheriff in 2021 and won. I voted for the other guy."

"Where is he now? Do you think he'd talk to me?"

Ratliffe chuckled. "I would hope not. He died last year of a heart attack."

"Oh. I see."

"My partner on that job was a woman named Sherri Devere. Ex-military. We both served in Iraq, but at different times and in different roles. I was a field medic; she was combat." He made a noise. "Amateur bodybuilder. You should have seen the arms on that gal. She could bench press a Buick."

"Where is she now?"

"She got married not long after the Ruth Coates episode and moved to Idaho or Montana or one of those places. You know: God's Country. That was her thing. She believed that Ruth Coates belonged to some Satanic cult in Vale or somewhere. Up in the hills."

"You don't think so?"

Selby could almost hear the shrug. "Who knows? Not ev-erybody in a cult runs around in togas with tattoos on their fore-heads, and not everybody with crazy ideas about personal adornment is in a cult."

Pancake's little white chickpea shot out from under the bed, with the cat in hot pursuit. The object fetched up against the wall, and he lost interest. He sauntered over to where his food and water dishes were, and Selby soon heard the crunching of chicken-flavored kibble.

"Listen," Ratliffe said. "This is totally subjective and probably wrong, but I didn't get the impression that Ruth Coates was hanging around some ramshackle farmhouse with a bunch of losers praying over their ammunition while they waited for the Apocalypse. She didn't talk—obviously—but she gave me the impression that she was sharp. Educated. She acted like somebody used to being in charge."

"A doctor or a lawyer? Somebody like that?"

"Exactly."

Selby thought for a moment, then asked, "What about the staff at the clinic in Mary's Gap? Would any of them still be around?"

"Hm. That's a good question, but my first answer would be no. Those places see a really high turnover. I know for a fact that Dr. Shulman moved to Taiwan, and the nurse on duty that afternoon died during the Pandemic. There were a couple of techs, but I didn't catch their names, and they usually only hang around a place like that until something better comes along. If you're thinking about hitting up the clinic for information, I can tell you up front that's a non-starter. HIPAA and all that."

Selby made a noise of agreement and sat staring at Pancake, who had cornered his toy against one leg of the comfortable chair and was waiting for it to make a break for freedom. *What else? There must be more I can ask. This gets me no closer to Ruth than I was a week ago.*

Ratliffe cleared his throat. "Here's another bit of speculation on my part if you'd care to hear it."

"I'll take anything I can get."

"Yeah, but this is where I get into some questionable legality. Ah, never mind. You never heard it from me. Listen: when we were trying to ease Coates out of her car, I noticed some mail on her passenger seat. Three or four items. The address on them was a place down by the river, in the Intermodal District."

"Do you remember the exact address?"

"No, but I might have made a note of it in my journal. I'll check. Give me your email address, and if I find something, I'll send it along."

"I really appreciate this, Mr. Ratliffe."

Ratliffe laughed. "Don't mention it. I've been told I need to find some new interests."

They exchanged email addresses and goodbyes, and Selby put down the phone.

He bent to see what Pancake was playing with.

The object was not, as he had thought, a dried chickpea or a wadded-up cash register receipt. It was a chalky white beetle.

Selby climbed out of his chair, careful not to step on the thing, shooing Pancake away. He fished an empty spice bottle out of the recycling bin. To the cat's annoyance, Selby swept the beetle into the jar, careful not to touch it. He screwed on the lid and carried the jar to the window to examine his catch.

The creature's legs were curled tightly to its armored belly, and one of its antennae was broken off. Selby wasn't fooled. He knew, more than most, how fickle death could be. He was certain this was the same kind of beetle that had occupied Maleva's box until he opened it.

He put the jar down on the windowsill and checked the closet. The box was where he had left it; nothing had changed.

"How did you get into my house?" Selby wondered, returning to the window to pick up the jar.

The beetle could have embedded itself in Selby's clothing when he opened the box at the bus stop, but he would have found it by now. He always shook out his clothes before he put them into the laundry, checking his pockets and turning his trousers inside out, and he had washed everything he had been wearing at the time.

Who else had been inside the apartment?

"I've been accused of being over-fastidious, which means I don't carry large white insects around in or on my clothing without knowing it. Could you have flown up to the tenth floor and gotten through the screens? No, those screens kept the mosquitoes out all summer. They certainly wouldn't have passed you." He shook the jar gently, rattling the contents. "Another possibility would be someone else bringing you in here. Rita hasn't come past the doorway in weeks, and I've had no other visitors."

He held the container up to the light, peering in at the creature inside.

"Except one."

. . .

Fiona's Baby Diary:
Bongo and Mitch spent all weekend winterizing the house. We used the fireplace last night for the first time in months. I've asked Bongo to get us a fire screen that's heavy enough that Bingo can't knock it down. Last winter, the baby was a little nugget sleeping in a crib all the time, but now he's a deranged Roomba, scooting all over the floors, mostly backward, bouncing off everything. Bongo put felt corners on the coffee table so when Bingo starts walking he won't always be banging his head on it. I threw out a bunch of stuff from the fridge that was past its prime, and a whole flock of crows (somebody said you call them a "murder." I wonder if that's true) moved in. Bingo sat in the window seat for an hour, absolutely spellbound.

CHAPTER TEN

When Selby stepped off the elevator into the Herald-Star archives on Monday, he was startled by the growl and rasp of power tools.

He rounded the corner and saw that two workmen had dismantled the ceiling at the end of the hall, right outside the server room, and had dragged a rainbow of brightly colored cables into view. One man was standing on the ladder, buried down to the waist in the ceiling, while his partner stood at the foot of the ladder handing up tools. Boxy sections of sheet metal ductwork lay on the floor next to the wall.

"What's that all about?" Selby asked as he dragged the chair from the viewing room into Mosley's office and closed the door.

"Water damage or something up in the ceiling. We've got twenty-first-century technology housed in a building that used to communicate with the outside world via a switchboard in that room behind the lobby, operated for decades by a woman named Opal. It's always something."

Selby nodded. The Herald-Star Building was iconic, but it could also be a challenge to work in.

A ratcheting buzz penetrated the walls, and Selby waited for a moment of silence.

"Your message said you had some information for me."

"Yes, I do. Not as much as I would have hoped, but something." He looked down at his notes, then back up at Selby. "I have to say that your father is a strange man."

"You're saying 'is.' He's still alive, then?"

"Don't get ahead of me." Mosley pulled over his scratch pad and consulted the dense tapestry of notes and diagrams that covered it. Something clattered to the floor outside, and the workmen laughed. Mosley composed himself.

"The earliest record of a Sullivan Coates in this area—and by 'this area,' I mean the five Bay Counties plus Truax and Lake counties, a square a couple of hundred miles on a side—is from 1947. A man of that name bought a two-bedroom house in a new subdivision in Woodville, west of Roebuck. These were what is usually described as 'starter homes,' small houses for newlywed couples. In 1964, the house at that address became the property of Linda Wells Coates. Her husband had gone missing seven years previously, and she had him declared dead."

Mosley looked at Selby. "You with me so far?"

Selby shook his head. "Give me a second. I was born in 1958. Naomi and Sullivan met in January or February of that year. If this was the same guy …" Selby struggled to do the math in his head. Mosley took pity on him and showed him another page from his scratch pad.

"See this? Sullivan buys a house in 1947. He is presumably married to this Linda Wells person. Ten years later, in 1957, he disappears. His wife does all the usual things to find him but with no success. Seven years after that, Sullivan—let's call him Sullivan One—is declared dead. Meanwhile, Sullivan Two— your father—meets and marries your mother only a few months after Sullivan One abandons his wife, Linda. Where did you live as a child?"

"East Side, at least at first."

"If Sullivan One and Sullivan Two are the same man, he somehow managed to evade detection after he moved from Woodville to the East Side. That's clear across Buckley, in a different county, but it's still an accomplishment."

Another crash out in the hall made Mosley flinch. "I hate that. I wish they'd hurry the hell up and finish. This morning we had mice coming down through that damned hole in the ceiling."

He returned to his notes. "This brings us to Sullivan Two. He comes on the scene in 1958 and disappears in 1968. We know he existed because ... Well, here you are."

"Yes. We can take that one on faith."

"Indeed. Next up is a marriage license issued to Sullivan Coates and Elizabeth Harwell across the river in Ogden. Let's call this one Sullivan Three. The year is 1972. Ruth Sullivan Coates could be their child."

One of the workmen said something in Spanish, and both laughed. A metal-on-metal tapping ensued for the next five minutes. Mosley studied Selby as Selby studied Mosley's diagram.

The noise ceased with a mighty metallic crash, and Mosley shook his heavy head wearily. He flipped to another page of his pad.

"Anyway, you see the pattern. Every decade or so, a man named Sullivan Coates leaves his family and starts a new one. We have two more wives, one for the eighties and one for the nineties, right on schedule, but no more kids. In 2011, a woman named Alexa Coates files for divorce from one Sullivan Coates on the grounds of abandonment. I haven't found anything at all for the period from 2011 to the present, but if we assume that he's holding to his pattern, that gives us yet another wife, for a total of seven—that we know of. All the wives have either died —as is the case with Linda Wells and Elizabeth Harwell—or moved away, like your mother."

"Seven wives over seven decades. If we assume he was around twenty in 1947, then he'd have to be nearly a hundred by now."

"Records surrounding your father and his families are a mess. Documents are missing or damaged, digital records corrupted … you name it. The bits and pieces that survive are flukes. I've never seen anything quite like it. It's as if Sullivan Coates was some kind of walking information virus. Merely by existing, he obscures the fact of his existence."

"Seven wives. And he's still getting married every ten years?"

"He's a spry old bird," Mosley said.

Roy was seating a party of what she called "Botox Babes" when Selby walked into the Circle Tavern. As she returned behind the bar, she caught his eye and used the heels of her hands to drag back the skin at her temples, stretching her eyes.

"See that tall one?" Roy said as she pulled Selby a beer. "That bun she wears isn't hair; it's all the skin she's had yanked back and pinned up. I'm surprised she can still blink her eyes."

Roy had poured her lean physique into a high-collared plum-colored catsuit that showed sparkly highlights where the fabric stretched tight across shoulders, collarbones, and hips. A clutch of purple dragonflies mounted on invisibly thin wires bobbed and waggled over her hair. Her lips, eyelids, and fingernails all glimmered with a dusty purple sheen.

"Did you enjoy your weekend?" she asked as she tapped Selby's sandwich order into the pad.

"Yes, I did. Thank you for taking care of Pancake."

"Not at all. As pets go, Pancake's about as much trouble as a sofa cushion." She grinned at him. "Everything peachy in Port Seb?"

Selby laughed awkwardly, blushing. "Yes. I … yes."

Roy laughed and slipped away to take a drink order. Selby had told her the purpose of his quarterly visits to the city on the bay long ago but still preferred not to talk about what happened there.

"Speaking of Saturday," Roy said, as she began mixing a batch of Bloody Marys, "there was a woman in here asking about you."

"Me? A woman?" A chill blossomed in Selby's belly. "Who was she? What did she want?"

"She wouldn't give a name. She was shorter than me, chunky, butch haircut. Looked mean. No clue how to wear makeup. Nice threads, though. The outfit she had on wasn't something you'd look at twice, but I bet it cost more than I spend in a year on clothes. And that's saying something."

"Was she wearing a mask?"

"A mask? Oh, you mean like for the coronavirus? No, no mask. Hard mouth. Squeezed the words out like she was having to pay extra for them."

Selby puffed his cheeks and blew out a long, meditative breath.

"Certainly not Laylah, then. I'm not sure who she could be. Did she leave a message?"

"Nope. Wouldn't give me a name, either. Told me to let you know she'd been by. You figure she's something to do with your other fun new friends?"

"I have no idea. Maybe."

Selby thought about the woman at the bus terminal. Roy's description might fit her. "I guess she wanted me to know that she knew I came here a lot."

"You think she's threatening you, Coates?"

"No. I don't know. Maybe."

Roy put Selby's sandwich in front of him and hurried away to greet newcomers at the door.

Selby chewed his sandwich, frowning. The woman's visit to the Tavern served little purpose. Somebody had already been inside his apartment. Laylah was even in his dreams. Little remained of his life that hadn't already been exposed to Laylah and Doma and whatever they were up to.

So they know Selby Coates hangs out at the Circle Tavern. So what?

Roy poured iced tea and collected a basket of chips from the service window, giving Selby a wink in passing. Selby stared at her, watching the dragonflies as if hypnotized by their movements.

What if it isn't me they're threatening? he thought.

"What's up, Coates? You look like you've seen a ghost. And with you, that's not always just a figure of speech."

Selby shook his head, frowning, fidgeting with his food, scattering crumbs, hastening to sweep them up and deposit them on his plate. Roy looked down at him, waiting.

"That woman," he said after a minute, "what if she was here to call my attention to you?"

Roy tidied the stray crumbs off the bar. "What if she was? I live for attention."

"I don't want my problems affecting you and Reggie."

Roy put down the towel. Selby started to say something else, but she cut him off, tapping a glittery purple fingernail on the bar in front of him.

"Coates, look at me. I mean, *really* look at me. I'm a skinny, thirty-four-year-old Black dude from rural North Carolina who gets up every day and dresses like a bitch from an old James Bond movie. My poor dick spends all day jammed up in a jock-strap a size too small, and I get pimples from putting foundation on over shaving bumps, but I look *good,* right? Hell, yeah, I do. Reggie's an incredible woman, successful and strong, who can love a man who looks better than she does in women's clothes. Walking out the front door looking like me is a challenge that would *kill* a nice person. Do you honestly think we're all that easily intimidated?"

"No. Of course not. I just don't want to be responsible for bringing something awful into your life."

Roy laughed, her dragonflies dancing. "Coates, all you're

bringing us is something crazy to talk about over the breakfast table. Your missionary boys show up at my house; they're gonna need a lot more stitches when we're done with them."

. . .

Barry Ratliffe sat on his bench at the dog park and watched Moby do a round of butt-sniffing with a half-grown Lab and a snooty poodle. The late afternoon sky glowed a lurid yellow low in the west, but it was heavy and gray everywhere else. The weather suited his mood.

He was not good at being depressed. He didn't enjoy it the way some people did. His wife's younger sister wallowed in misery like a stripper in a tub of whipped cream, slathering it on herself, flinging great sodden masses of it at everyone she came into contact with. If she won a hundred million dollars in the lottery, she would weep for days over the taxes. Unhappiness nourished her.

For his own part, Ratliffe preferred to be busy, to be needed, to be productive. He enjoyed teaching. He had enjoyed being a paramedic even more, before his wife's illness had convinced him to switch to something with more predictable hours. He had even enjoyed serving in Iraq as an Army field medic. He certainly enjoyed being a husband; he enjoyed it enough that he wished he still was, every single day. He liked having clearly defined responsibilities. Things to do, even dangerous things. *Especially* dangerous things.

The Lab got a little uppity, and Moby gave him her "Back off, punk" stance, head turned to one side, shoulders hunched, all four feet braced. The puppy flounced around for a moment longer, then the message penetrated, and he ducked his head and backed away. The poodle ignored this entire exchange, only rejoining the party after Moby had asserted herself and the Lab had adopted a properly submissive posture.

Things had gotten too quiet, too easy. The challenges were

too abstract. They didn't engage his attention.

Go ahead and say the word, Ratliffe told himself, watching the dogs. *Bored. I'm fucking bored.* The creepy little girl with the monkey was right. He needed something more to occupy his mind. Something out of the ordinary.

The Herald-Star guy. Coates. I wonder what that's all about.

Ratliffe called Moby down before a situation with the poodle could escalate, and she ambled over to flop at his feet.

I completely forgot about the guy who picked up Ruth Coates at the clinic the day of the accident. I was there when she left. I couldn't see much of the guy driving the Subaru, just a baseball cap and a fleecy coat with the collar turned up, but I paid attention.

He climbed to his feet and stretched. Moby jumped up, tongue lolling.

"You had enough of these yahoos?" he asked her as he clipped on her leash. "Let's go heat up the rest of that pizza and do some detective work."

. . .

Selby's conversation with Roy left him unsettled for the rest of the day.

Talking about the things that had been happening lately made those events seem more *real*, harder to deny. A part of him still clung to the idea that it was all a paranoid delusion; with the right prescription twice a day, Laylah and her sister and the creepy boys would all vanish.

He looked at the spice jar on his desk, the one with the white beetle inside, and blew out his cheeks.

Not that simple, he thought. *Nothing's ever that simple.*

Selby addressed himself to the task of making red beans and rice for supper—not a complicated dish, but one that involved a lot of preparation. He chopped onions, peppers, and celery, sautéed garlic, rinsed a can of beans. Small tasks, one after another.

After dinner, he cleaned the kitchen and settled in with Pancake and a book.

He read for an hour, until he realized he had gotten through several chapters without the slightest idea what he had read.

He chased Pancake off his lap and made himself a cup of hot chocolate, then finally gave up and went to bed.

For most of the night, Selby's dreams were ordinary ones: being lost in a strange place with no money and no idea how to get home, struggling to fill out some sort of paperwork with eyes that refused to focus, walking into the laundry room stark naked to be laughed at by Chioke Okorie.

During the wee hours, the curtain rose on something different.

. . .

Mary Shelley sits picking at her needlepoint while a storm rages on the lake outside. Lord Byron poses and pontificates at the window. The room is somehow cavernous and cozy at the same time.

The Bride of Frankenstein, Selby thinks. *Elsa Lanchester in the introductory scene.* He has always loved that movie. Selby knows he's asleep this time, but the experience seems more real than his other dreams. The brocade of the sofa cushions is nubbly under his elbow, and he can smell the resinous wood burning in the enormous fireplace. The empty place in his head, the one that opened up when Doma's minions attacked him on Tower Lane, whispers to him.

"The story begins a long time ago," Mary says, putting her needlepoint down on her lap and gazing off into the distance.

The room has no ceiling; the enclosed space extends upwards into remote shadows. Everything is gray, from charcoal to nearly white, except for Mary's eyes, which are the yellow-green of fading willow leaves. The woman's clothing is entirely wrong for the scene: instead of the puffy sleeves and tight bodice of Mary Shelley's dress, the actress is wearing the long white robe of the Bride, who shouldn't appear before the third reel. Her hair, likewise, is not the opening scene's tight bun and demure spit curls; instead, a wiry, white-striped mass towers over her head, wobbling with every movement. Stitches run along the line of her jaw.

"Authority, however well-intentioned, can sometimes seem arbitrary. There are always those who push back, who refuse to accept limitations," Mary says.

From the window, Lord Byron makes a grand gesture. "As must we all if we wish to be frrrree!"

Mary rolls her eyes and purses her cupid's-bow lips. "Oh, do be quiet, Lord Byron." Ubiquitous but forgettable Southern actor Gavin Gordon, in the role of the tempestuous poet, subsides with sulky, cleft-chinned grace, draping himself alongside the window's deep embrasure.

Mary reaches out and almost, but not quite, touches Selby's sleeve, reclaiming his attention.

"Defiance comes with consequences. Sometimes proportional to the scale of that defiance, sometimes not."

Selby squirms in his seat. *This is ridiculous*, he thinks. He wonders what Laylah—he *knows* this is Laylah—is trying to accomplish with these elaborate little tableaux, tossing him these Delphic scraps one by one. "Please don't be so elliptical. If you have something to tell me, why can't you just spit it out? If you don't have anything useful, can't we dispense with all this play-acting?"

Mary/Laylah smiles but ignores the interruption. "All were punished for the crime of one." She closes her eyes for a moment as though in pain. The moment passes, and she sighs, lifting her needlepoint, picking at it, putting it back down.

Currents stir in Selby's conceptual empty room, his Empty

Room, reminding him that what he is experiencing is only a dream.

I'd forgotten how badly acted this scene was, he thinks.

"Punished," Selby prompted.

She smiles, revealing tiny teeth, like a child's, between the plump lips; her pale eyes gaze off into the past.

"One in particular paid a heavy price. Some would see that one restored, along with all those caught up in the mayhem. Others, less bold or more in thrall to authority, fear to incur further punishment."

"And both sides use innocents as their pawns. That's awfully arrogant, don't you think?"

The woman smiles down at her work. "'Innocents,' dear Selby? Can there ever truly be such a thing?"

Selby sits back, pulling away from her. "You're limited, in some way, aren't you, Laylah?" he asks. The willow-green eyes tighten, but her gentle smile never wavers. "You can't tell me anything straight out. Doma and her goons can chase me around the countryside, literally beating me over the head to get her point across, but you don't have that kind of leeway. You can't even speak directly. You're a shadow on the wall."

Mary/Laylah smiles, then she holds up her embroidery. Selby peers at the work in the uncertain lighting, not quite sure what he's looking at. She angles the frame to catch the light, and Selby sees that she has picked out a portrait on the white fabric, a face depicted in threads of every possible shade of gray. A smiling man, handsome, untrustworthy, adorable. The man of the photograph in Selby's apartment.

Laylah as Elsa Lanchester as Mary Shelley in the costume of the Bride of Frankenstein's Monster smiles. "Dear Selby," she says.

. . .

Selby woke up as if he'd been slapped. His pillow smelled

105

of spices and burning pine.

CHAPTER ELEVEN

On Tuesday, right after lunch, Selby hobbled down to the grocery store. His objective was to buy an ice pack for his knee, but he hated the thought of putting something cold against his skin, so he bought a Black Forest cake instead.

Back home in his comfortable chair, he put his foot up and devoured cherries and chocolate cake and whipped cream while he watched Vincent Price as *The Abominable Doctor Phibes* murder a succession of doctors in delightfully inventive ways, assisted by the beautiful and mysterious Vulnavia.

"Such a ham," Selby murmured approvingly. He spooned some more whipped cream onto Pancake's dish on the floor next to his chair.

Price's Doctor Phibes was able to communicate by plugging an assortment of audio devices into a socket on the side of his neck. *How does Doma speak to her hench-boys?* Selby wondered, watching Phibes and Vulnavia sort Brussels sprouts in Phibes' underground lab. *Could someone plan and execute a campaign of terror entirely through handwritten notes? Text-messaging? Instagram?* He supposed that telepathy was not impossible, but he had seen no evidence of it. Certainly, no one had tried to talk to him that way. *Except Laylah, but that's only when I'm asleep.*

Phibes' death at the end of the movie was obviously intended to be only temporary, a trick Selby could appreciate. He cleaned up the debris of the cake binge and set out veggies for a stir-fry later. *A healthy diet is essential*, he reminded himself.

The photo of Sullivan Coates and that nervous little boy still rested against the wall. Tomorrow, Selby had an appointment with a gentleman in Van Baar who was said to be a wizard with vintage and damaged photographs.

That picture. That's all I have left of him. Maybe that's all I ever had.

Wednesday morning dawned cloudless and bright, and by the time Selby had completed his morning routines and wrapped up his father's photograph, he felt quite chipper. Even his knee had returned to something approximating its original size and color.

"Black Forest cake," Selby told Pancake. "Good for whatever ails you."

Selby took the photograph across town to Mr. Garabedian, who tut-tutted at the mistreatment it had suffered but assured Selby that he could restore it.

"I can repair it maybe eighty percent? It won't look like it did before it was damaged," he warned, his single massive eyebrow flexing gravely. "There will always be a flaw on the side of the face."

"Whatever you can do," Selby said. "It's the only picture I have of my father, and that's the only print."

"You need a high-resolution digital scan," Garabedian told him. "After I'm done, I'll scan it for you. That way, you can replace the picture if, God forbid, something else should happen to it."

"Thank you. You'll call me when it's ready?"

"This time next week."

"That'll be fine. Thank you."

At the bus stop, Selby found himself sharing the bench with a young woman and her two little boys. The children were playing a complicated-looking game with special playing cards.

Selby had a deck of Old Maid cards as a child, but he could never find anyone to play with.

As soon as he had framed that thought, he bit down on it.

That's nonsense. I was alone so much because I was afraid of the other kids. I don't know why, but it's true. The problem wasn't with them; it was with me.

I'm as bad as my mother, nursing old grievances, inventing abuses that never took place.

Distracted by his internal monologue, he failed to identify a persistent four-note chime, repeated over and over.

"I think that's you," the young woman said as the sound finally ceased.

"What? Oh. I'll bet that's my phone."

The woman nodded, smiling. "I imagine it is."

Grampa's off his meds, Selby thought, wrestling the device out of his pocket.

Owen Mosley had called. Selby could not recall having spoken to Mosley by telephone in over a year. He selected redial, and a woman answered immediately.

"Hello?"

"This is Selby Coates. I believe someone called me from this number?"

"Oh, hello, Mr. Coates. That was me. This is Juliet Mosley. Owen's wife?"

The voice was pleasant, with a faint British accent. Selby remembered Juliet Mosley as a small, active woman with frizzy hair and an anxious, hurried way of talking, as though she expected to be interrupted by something happening offstage at any moment.

"Of course, Mrs. Mosley. We met at the Christmas Party a few years ago."

"Yes, I remember that party. We won theatre tickets in the gift drawing. The show was terrible, but it's the thought that counts, isn't it? I called you on Owen's phone because I thought you might recognize the number. Owen said you wouldn't answer a call from a number you didn't know."

Selby blinked, surprised that Mosley would know such a thing. Was he that transparent in his habits? "I'm not good with the telephone. What did you need to talk to me about?"

"My husband would like to see you."

"At the Herald-Star?"

"No, here at home."

This was wildly out of character. In all their years working in the same building, Selby and Owen Mosley had never once met outside of work.

Mosley's wife gave Selby the address and described the house. "Will you come?"

"Of course. Can you tell me what this is about?"

"Not really. Owen had some sort of accident at the office yesterday. He spent the night in the hospital, but he's home now, and he wants to see you."

"Is he all right?"

"He'll be fine, Mr. Coates, but he's anxious to talk to you."

"I can be there in twenty minutes, Mrs. Mosley."

"Thank you."

Owen and Juliet Mosley lived in a neighborhood of neat two- and three-bedroom cottages built at the end of the 1930s to house workers at the new Buckley Dam and Locks and the PP&L power station. During the decades since then, a few houses had been torn down and replaced with townhomes or mini-mansions, but most had been maintained or restored, and the neighborhood still held on to much of its original flavor.

Three-twenty-nine Poplar Terrace could be distinguished from its neighbors by the enormous honeysuckle that grew in an unruly mass on a trellis that framed the door. The front door and the window trim were all painted a deep royal blue against a background of pale gray siding.

Juliet Mosley greeted Selby graciously and ushered him into the small living room. Mosley met him in the middle of the brown and gray oval rug, and the two men shook hands. In his own home, the archivist looked taller, and instead of his usual white shirt, gray slacks, and lab coat, he was wearing fawn corduroys and a green-and-black flannel shirt. Lumberjack drag. He waved Selby to a loveseat covered with a crocheted afghan.

"Thanks for coming out," Mosley said, settling into a well-worn recliner.

"Your wife said you had been in the hospital," Selby said. "I hope everything's okay."

Mosley waved away Selby's concern. "I'm fine. I just needed a day to recover."

Juliet had shown Selby into the room but then excused herself, closing the door as she left. Mosley looked over at the door and then at Selby. Waiting.

"Recover from what, exactly?" Selby asked after an uncomfortable interval.

"Something strange happened yesterday."

"At the Herald-Star?"

"Yes." Mosley took a deep breath and sat back in the chair. "In the basement. In the hallway outside my office."

"Can you tell me about it?"

Mosley smiled his lumpy half-smile. "That's why I asked you here." He closed his eyes, then opened them and stared up at nothing.

"You saw the construction going on down in the basement," he said after a moment.

"Heard it, too."

"Exactly. The noise and confusion have been intolerable. Yesterday was the worst. I left the building and ran personal errands until noon. When I got back to my office, I found that the workmen had gone to lunch. I sat down to try to get as much done as possible while I had the chance."

Selby waited, watching Mosley's fingers pick at the ridges of his corduroy trousers.

"I finished a couple of things, then I followed up on an idea I'd had about your project." He seemed to run out of steam at this point. Juliet Mosley poked her head in to ask if anyone would like some tea. Selby took his lead from Mosley and politely declined.

"I needed to run down the hall to use the bathroom. As I was getting out of my chair, everything got very … quiet," Mosley said after his wife had left the room.

"Quiet," Selby echoed, his cheerful day cracking and peeling around the edges.

"In the archives. Quiet. Unnaturally quiet. I thought something had happened to me. I had just lost all my hearing. I stepped out into the hall."

Selby started to say something about his own experience in the Herald-Star basement but thought better of it. "Go on."

Mosley stared at him, reading his face. "You know something about this," he said.

"Finish your story, and I'll tell you mine," Selby said.

"Yes. You damn sure will."

Mosley sat back in his chair.

"Something was pouring out of the hole in the ceiling, where the workers were replacing all that ductwork."

"More mice?"

"Not this time. My first thought was that it was smoke, with a lot of big flakes of ash in it, but after a moment, I saw that the cloud was all flakes. There was no smoke."

He took a deep breath.

"The flakes weren't ashes, either. You know what they were?"

Selby shook his head.

"*Moths*, Coates. Thousands of moths. White moths. There were so many of them they filled up that end of the hallway. I was startled, but then I decided there must have been some vast rookery of moths up in the hollow spaces that got disturbed when the work started. They were just moths, after all. Nobody's ever been attacked by a moth."

Mosley paused.

"Owen, if you—"

"No, wait your turn. I need to get through this." He shifted his weight in the chair. His fingers moved from his thighs to the arms of the chair, but they continued their picking, tugging, scratching.

"The moths were all trying to gather in the middle of the hallway, so there got to be this dense mass in the center, five, six feet tall, surrounded by strays. They were moths, remember, just moths, so I stepped a little closer."

Selby could see that Mosley had reached a critical juncture in his narrative. He wanted desperately to offer his condolences and walk out the door, but he couldn't do that. This horror belonged to him; he had inflicted it on a man who thought he was his friend. The least he could do was hear the full scope of his crime.

"As I approached, the moths at the top part of the densest area began to … What's a good word? To *seethe*. Like the surface of a pot of soup. The moths in the middle rolled back, and the mass … folded open."

Mosley paused for breath, his face gray and his mouth tight.

"There was a woman inside that clump of insects, Coates. A *woman*. Her face. Pale skin, beautiful eyes. Her mouth was covered by the moths, at least at first. Her hands emerged on her chest, folded like this." Mosley interlaced his fingers over his chest.

"We looked at each other, this woman and me, for what seemed like forever, and then the moths moved away from her mouth."

Selby knew what was coming next.

"Owen …"

"It was *horrible*. Disgusting. Her mouth was sewn up, big black stitches, some kind of skinny yarn, I guess, or string. She stood there, looking at me like I was … I don't know what. Something on her living room floor that the cleaning lady had missed.

"I don't know what I did then. I think I tried to shout or something, but I was utterly deaf, so I don't know. She looked at me, this woman made of moths with her mouth all sewn up, and I wet my pants. I'm sixty-four years old, and I wet myself right there in the hall."

Mosley stopped again, looking away. Selby would have given anything to take this away from him.

"The HVAC workers came back and found me on the floor, soaked in my own piss, mumbling and thrashing. They hauled me upstairs, and DeQuinn called for an ambulance. I finally pulled myself together in the emergency room. They decided to keep me overnight so the neurologist could look at me in the morning. Juliet brought me some pajamas and things." He let his head roll back against the headrest of the chair. "The neurologist was convinced I had experienced an epileptic seizure. I had no idea I was epileptic."

He sat staring at Selby.

"That's my story," he said, his voice grim, controlled. "Now you."

Mosley was clearly not in any condition to hear the entire saga. Selby gave him an edited summary of his first encounter with the two young men. As he spoke, the other man's face grew gray. His entire body became rigid.

"You fucking bastard. *You never told me*. You never said a *fucking thing*! You *knew* this insanity was down there! Down there with me! In my space! And you couldn't warn me?"

"I'm so sorry. I thought what had happened was something to do with me alone. I never dreamed it might affect you."

"'Affect me'? I'm lucky I didn't have a fucking heart attack!"

Selby wanted to curl up and cover his face, or cry, or something, but there wasn't space in the moment for him to indulge himself. That would come later. "I'm so sorry," he said again.

"*Campea perlata*," Mosley said, his voice suddenly calm, deliberate, like throwing a switch. "The Pale Beauty Moth. Fairly common in this part of the world. Common, but not generally known to congregate in huge numbers. You can find them knocking their brains out against your porch light on any given summer evening, one or two at a time. There's nothing on Wikipedia about them gathering in the thousands to take on human form."

The diversion into trivia was a lifeline, and Selby clutched at it eagerly. "How did you identify them?"

"Juliet found two dead moths in my clothes when we got home. I looked them up on the internet, and then I flushed them down the toilet." He stared at Selby, unblinking, his face set, grim.

Selby looked down at his hands and then met Mosley's stare.

"Owen, I don't know what to say."

"The fact that you're taking this insanity at face value tells me all I need to know. I heard about your strange behavior with the fire alarm the other day. I wish you could have told me the whole story."

"I didn't realize—"

"Forget it, Coates," Mosley said, slumping back in his chair, his outrage spent. "I know you didn't do this on purpose. Just listen. I'm going to retire next year. I've got some money set aside to take Juliet to England to see her family. She has twin grandnephews about to start college, boys she's never even met. I'm going to get out of that basement, breathe some real air, get used to honest daylight." He leaned forward again, planting his elbows on his knees. "I'm not like you, Coates. You'll go nuts if a picture is hanging crooked or if somebody doesn't put the cap back on a ballpoint pen, but you don't bat an eyelash at the idea of a woman made out of living insects. In a year, I'll be gone. I want you to stay out of the archives until then. I'm asking you as a colleague and maybe even a friend. Don't bring any more of your madness to my doorstep. One year. Give me another year of sanity, and then you can burn the place to the ground if you want to."

Selby looked at him, at his earnest wedge of a face. Mosley was drawn and gray, years older than a few days before. *I did that to him*, Selby thought.

"Of course. I'll do whatever you say. Whatever I can."

Mosley nodded, looking away. "I don't blame you, Coates. Not really. It's something attached to you, something in your life, like your father, like the Ruth Coates story. You're not the disease; you're just the carrier. But whatever it is, I don't want it."

Juliet Mosley stepped into the room. "Mr. Coates, will you be joining us for lunch?"

Selby glanced at Mosley and then at his wife. "I'd love to, Mrs. Mosley, but I have some errands to run, so I have to get going. Thank you, though."

"Maybe next time, then."

Selby climbed to his feet and stepped forward. He and Mosley shook hands.

"Thank you for coming over," Mosley said.

When Selby got home, he immediately climbed into the shower, but all the hot water in the world couldn't flush away his guilt.

Even as events had grown more extreme, Selby had been confident that only he was affected. His friends, the people around him—he was sure they were outside the circle of risk.

The Colonel had been exposed to Doma's acolytes, and Rita and Roy had encountered other people connected with her, but they had not been attacked, not molested in any way. On the contrary, their arrival on the scene appeared to drive the sinister visitors away.

I was wrong, Selby thought. He dried himself off and wrapped up in his bathrobe. Pancake waited next to the comfortable chair, and when Selby sat down, he jumped up into his master's lap. Selby scratched him behind the ears. The cat stretched, merging with the folds of the bathrobe.

They don't care about collateral damage.

Selby couldn't remember the bus ride home from the Mosley house. The image of Owen's face, the betrayal in his voice—these things had left him blind and deaf.

I've been like a child on an adventure.

No. If he were being honest, Selby told himself, he had been more like a monkey in an explosives factory, playing with matches. How could he have been so stupid? So careless? He couldn't just walk away, not now. He had to know. Why was he still alive? Who was his father, that he could be a part of all this insanity?

Who am I?

The door to the Empty Room—he had begun to think of it that way, in capital letters, something special, not just a symptom of an as-yet-undetermined malady—stood open, and strange currents stirred the silent whispering.

And what about this? This new thing in my head? Even as he asked himself the question, he knew he had worded it wrong. This was not a new thing: it was something intrinsic to him, to his nature, something that had simply not been accessible until now.

Like the apartment upstairs from the bookstore, the Empty Room had always been there, only up until now the door had always been shut.

Laylah. Selby spoke the name into the turbulent silence of the Empty Room. *Laylah. I don't know what this is or what it means, but I think you can hear me. Believe me when I say that I'd rather occupy a jar on Roy's mantelpiece than bring danger to her doorstep. You keep Doma away from Owen, and Roy, and the Colonel's nasty little dog, and everyone else, or I'll put an end to this whole stupid game. I died once: I'm not afraid to do it again. These people are my family, for better or for worse, and I won't put up with this.*

The whispers came and went, endless purposeless motion, but there was no other answer.

Pancake yawned and jumped down to wash his face. Selby climbed out of the chair to get dressed, then he padded into the kitchen to put water on for pasta.

The scent of garlic and chopped parsley slowly replaced that of exotic perfumes and burning beeswax.

. . .

Fiona's Baby Diary:
Bongo has nightmares from time to time. I wonder if they're connected to his spells of forgetfulness? The doctor says he may be suffering from a very mild form of epilepsy. In his dreams, he starts talking in his sleep, arguing with somebody in a language I've never heard before. Sometimes he cries, and I wake him up. He never remembers the dream afterward. I asked him if he speaks any languages other than English, and he said he didn't think so. I would think most people would KNOW whether they spoke more than one language, but not my husband.

CHAPTER TWELVE

If Selby Coates had to sit down and make a list of the things that terrified him most, close to the top of that list would be Naomi Coates.

Selby would be the first to admit that his mother had been a paragon throughout his childhood: fiercely protective, dedicated to her son's health and safety, engaged with his interests. Sometimes, these goals clashed with the reality of Selby's father's careless philandering, leading Naomi to rely heavily on prescription tranquilizers for many years, but Selby couldn't fault her good intentions.

It was only after Sullivan left and Selby sidled uneasily into adolescence that Naomi's hoarded bitterness worked its way to the surface. Her son's departure at nineteen was a relief to them both.

Dinner was out of the way, and the kitchen was clean; there was nothing else he needed to do. Selby sat down at his desk and composed a cautious email to his mother.

Mom,
I trust you're doing well. I called last week, but you were out. I'd like to come down for a couple of days. Some things have happened here, and I need information. I have to ask you a few questions about Sullivan Coates.
I know Dad is normally off-limits, but I need to know what you know. I don't exaggerate when I say that it could be a mat-

ter of life and death.
   Selby

He read through the message, looking for triggers, then read it twice more. If nothing else, the message would stimulate her curiosity.

He clicked send.

. . .

Across town, Barry Ratliffe scratched his chest through his threadbare Fort Walton Beach sweatshirt and sneezed.

Under the harsh light of the overhead fixture, the former paramedic sat at his kitchen table, pawing over a growing pile of spiral-bound notebooks, all in varying stages of disrepair. In the shadows underneath the table, Moby dreamed of sheep, emitting an occasional snort and, once every so often, a long, trailing whine, warning the stray lambs to get their shit together.

"The more I don't find the fucking thing, the more I know it's here," Ratliffe muttered. He knew what he was looking for: an appointment card from the desk at the doc-in-a-box at Mary's Gap. An ordinary business card. It was here somewhere.

The notebook that included his ruminations and recollections from April 2018 lay to one side, while a dozen others were scattered haphazardly across the table. Ratliffe's journals were handwritten on a random assortment of cheap notebooks packed in banker's boxes and stored in the closet of the spare bedroom. Nagged by the certainty that he had more information on the Maryville Road accident than he had given Selby Coates, he had pulled down the relevant box to look. Bit by bit, he filled in gaps in his memory until he remembered the appointment card.

A lot of trouble for a total stranger, Ratliffe thought, looking at the mess he was making. *But then, all my career choices have involved going to a lot of trouble for total strangers.*

Selby Coates was an odd one. Talking to him was like talking to Ratliffe's wife's Aunt Judith, all creaky politeness and unexpected confusions. *Seems like a nice guy, though. Not somebody you'd ever sit down and drink a beer with, maybe, but trustworthy.*

He flipped through another notebook and set it aside, chuckling. *I'm judging people according to the qualities I look for in dogs*, he thought. He nudged Moby with his bony bare foot, and she grunted.

He had never arrived at a workable system for organizing his journals. A given notebook might cover a year, or it might cover a few days. During the months on either side of Laura's death, he had gone for weeks at a time without writing a word, only to erupt in pages and pages of desperate questions for which there could be no answers.

Apart from the notebooks themselves, there were also movie tickets, greeting cards, a shopping list, and a receipt from a computer store. *Here* was a creased photocopy of his birth certificate. *Here* was a branded bookmark from Northside Books. *Here* was a snapshot of Ratliffe leaving the animal shelter with Moby nine months after his wife's funeral. He smiled.

"She'd have loved you, Mobe."

Ratliffe tucked the photo into a notebook and added that one to the pile.

Selby Coates didn't seem like the sort of man who would be associated with a cult. At least, not based on the telephone conversation Ratliffe had had with him. For all the schoolteacher knew, Coates could be sacrificing black roosters under the full moon in some vacant lot in Fallwood. You never really knew, but his instincts told him that was unlikely.

The man who collected Ruth Coates from the doc-in-a-box didn't look like a cultist, either. But then, a COVID mask and a fifty-thousand-dollar SUV could cover a multitude of sins.

"I'm going about this wrong," Ratliffe said, slapping down

another notebook. He got up and pulled the last few notebooks out of the box, pushed the pile aside, and then flipped the box over on the table and thumped the bottom.

When he took the box away, he found a litter of additional odds and ends, including two dead spiders and something with about a million legs that was all too alive.

Not fucking here. Ratliffe sighed, scratching his chest. *I was so sure.*

He picked up a handful of notebooks and squared them to put them back in the box, but midway through the movement, he sneezed: once, twice, then a third time.

"Jesus. Batten down the hatches. Women and children first," he muttered, blinking away tears. He grabbed a paper towel from the counter and blew his nose. Moby grunted and rolled to her feet, shook herself, and ambled out of the room.

"Sorry, Mobe. It startled me, too. Where does all this fucking dust come from, anyway?"

Blinking, Ratliffe looked down into the box. "Hello." He put the notebooks back down on the table and flipped up one of the cardboard flaps that made up the bottom of the box. Another multi-legged critter dashed up the side of the box and away.

A rectangle the size and shape of a business card had slid under the flap, leaving only a corner showing. Ratliffe picked up the card and flipped it over. He grinned.

"Bingo," he said.

. . .

When Selby Coates was thirteen years old, he and his mother rode the train to Port Sebastian to look for a Christmas gift for his Aunt Martha.

Selby was a late bloomer, smaller than the other kids in his classes, clumsy at sports, socially inept, oscillating between a blushing shyness and outbursts of astonishing rage—astonishing not only to the targets but also to Selby himself. Puberty was a stealthy adversary, sneaking up on the boy without warning, churning his ideas of who he was, shoving him headlong into adulthood before he had fully come to grips with childhood.

Selby was both irritable and irritating on the shopping excursion, and he and his mother bickered all the way to the mall in Port Sebastian. Selby thought it was ridiculous to buy Aunt Martha a gift since all the money they had was hers in the first place, but Naomi insisted it was important, struggling to explain.

"There are things you don't do for yourself, even though you can," she told her son. "She's taken on a lot of responsibility with us, and it's important to remind her that she's still a person in her own right, not just a meal ticket for impoverished relatives. It's our way of telling her we appreciate what she's doing for us without burdening her with our gratitude."

None of this made any sense to Selby, and even if it had, he would have dismissed it out of hand. What did his mother know about anything? This was the woman who had chased Selby's father away. Her advice was worthless.

After two hours of browsing, while Selby's corrosive self-absorption slowly ate its way down to the bones of his mother's composure, Naomi finally purchased a tennis bracelet and had it engraved with her sister's name. Martha had recently taken up tennis, and Naomi hoped the gift would be something she would not have thought about buying for herself. Mother and son ate a grim lunch and caught the afternoon train back to Buckley.

When Christmas finally rolled around, Martha was delighted with the present and thanked her sister and her nephew enthusiastically and sincerely. Selby offered a surly "You're welcome" and then helpfully pointed out that Martha was awfully old to be taking up a sport as a beginner.

Martha and Naomi soon forgot the incident, buried as it was by so many other adolescent mishaps, but fifty years later, Selby still tortured himself with that memory.

. . .

Selby had stayed at the Coconut Key Inn in Fort Myers on previous visits, so he knew what to expect. The rooms were dim, not overlarge, and completely generic in their furnishings and decor, but they were scrupulously clean, which was always Selby's first priority. Martha had booked him into a double room, perhaps clinging to the hope, faded but never extinguished, that Selby would one day turn up with a Significant Other in tow. He shook his head and unpacked his bag on one of the beds, arranging his belongings neatly across the beige and brown coverlet.

Tonight, Selby would relax, recovering from the plane ride and the pointless hours spent waiting in the airport between the desk and security, between security and the gate, between the gate and loading, and between loading and finally getting the damned thing into the air.

Tomorrow, Selby and Naomi would go shopping.

"I thought you'd be more upset with my asking about Sullivan," Selby said as he and his mother picked over a tray of jewelry.

"I stopped being angry with Sullivan about the time you moved away to go to college," Naomi said. "Thing was, my anger had crowded out everything else, so even after the whole mess had died down, I couldn't change the way I behaved. I kept on acting like I was on fire when the fire had burned out long ago."

Selby picked up a cloisonné pendant and held it up to the light. His mother squinted at it, then shook her head. They moved on.

"You were certainly convincing."

"You've always believed whatever you wanted to believe," Naomi said. She led the way into a shop filled with small artworks, mostly framed woodcuts of women drinking coffee, putting on clothes, laughing. She punctuated her comments with taps of her cane on the floor. "Nobody could ever tell you a fucking thing. I'm sure you've grokked that by now."

Selby chuckled. He had forgotten how his mother liked to sprinkle her speech with obscure neologisms. He glanced over at her surreptitiously. Her age was apparent in her face, and she walked with an elegant rosewood cane, but she was erect of posture, firm of step. She was old, but she wore it well.

"And maybe I played into that," Naomi went on after a pause. "Being an angry bitch is so much less … embarrassing than being a wife who's too stupid to stop loving the man who dumped her and her kid without so much as saying goodbye. You and me, between us, we had created a narrative that served neither of us but that we were both comfortable with." She held up a woodcut of a woman sitting on the front steps eating an ice cream cone and nodded.

They were wandering through a vast space, a former sugar refinery that had been converted to a combination flea market and fine art emporium. Selby paid for the woodcut, and they waited for the clerk to bring it back wrapped in brown paper. He took the package, and they continued walking.

"I'm surprised you've never asked about your father before," Naomi said as they wandered through the stalls and booths.

"I suppose I had put him out of my mind," Selby said. "The longer I didn't think about him, the easier it was to keep not thinking about him. Besides, you always seemed so angry about it. About him. I was afraid my questions might trigger a … a reaction."

"Still? I thought I'd cleaned up my act."

"Last time I visited, you were a holy terror," Selby said.

"Last time you visited, you were a supercilious prick, and I had just had gallbladder surgery."

Selby's ears turned pink. "Oh."

Naomi chuckled. "There was never a snowball's chance in hell we were ever going to be a family like the ones on TV," she said. "Your dad was … what he was; you were weird and withdrawn all the time, and I was going slowly insane trying to live with both of you."

"Martha implies that you and Dad experienced something like love at first sight," he said.

Naomi scoffed. "I'd say she was sugar-coating the facts, but I know damn well she didn't say it like that, so we'll let that pass. It wasn't love; it was lust, pure and simple. I thought he was the sexiest man I had ever laid eyes on. Louise—my friend who was dating him when we met—was holding out for protestations of eternal devotion or something, but I wanted to see what he looked like naked. I wanted to know what his skin tasted like."

"I'm not sure I need to hear this," Selby said.

"You've always been such a fucking prude, Selby. I can't imagine where you got it. Anyway, you're the one who wants to talk about Sullivan."

Selby blew out his cheeks. They stood gazing at a series of enormous paintings of antelopes.

"Copied from National Geographic," Naomi said, pointing with her walking stick. "That one over there is from 1991, June or July, I think."

Selby laughed. He had also forgotten his mother's bizarre ability to recall obscure nuggets of data when nobody was expecting it. Something he had inherited from her.

"You're right. I need to know more about him, and I guess that means hearing things a child never wants to hear."

"I'll try to edit out the juicier details."

They paused in front of a shop selling Quinceañera dresses to marvel at the variety of colors and the amount of tulle a fifteen-year-old girl might be expected to dance in. At one end of the shop, four wedding gowns, elaborate confections of lace and brocade, stood headless and armless, waiting for a bride to step in and inhabit one of them. Naomi shook her head at the display.

"A girl's dreams." She smiled. "There was something about Sullivan that broke down all your barriers. Five minutes in his presence, and you wanted to be near him for the rest of your life."

"You make him sound like a drug."

"That's exactly what he was. Addictive, seductive."

"Martha says you still love him."

"Martha needs to shut her fucking pie hole."

This was the Naomi Coates that Selby was accustomed to. He wondered which version he was more comfortable with.

They walked past a shop selling cell phone covers and another selling leather goods, then turned into a place selling rather unusual handmade dolls.

"You've changed," Naomi said.

"Me?"

"Who else is in this conversation, you twit? Yes, you. You're not so critical. You're listening to what I'm saying."

"I have no idea what to say to that."

Naomi laughed. "That's new, too. The old Selby would never have been at a loss for a witty riposte."

Really? he thought. *Maybe being dead has had some lingering aftereffects.*

"You've changed, too," he countered. "Mellowed."

Naomi held up a doll, Raggedy Ann reimagined as a Goth witch.

"Bambie Thug. I like this."

Selby chuckled, shaking his head. "Mellowed a little, anyway."

"There was a woman," Naomi said, putting down the Goth doll and picking up a more delicate white-haired doll. "She came around several times. She claimed to be Sullivan's cousin or some such shit, but he always seemed a little unsure as to whether he actually knew her or not. It was weird, but there was zero sexual energy there, so I didn't worry too much about it. She was … spooky. Quiet, kind of dreamy, but with an under-current of something absolutely terrifying. She was never anything but polite around us, but you knew she could stand there and watch somebody disemboweling children without turning a hair. She'd show up, spend the day, maybe have dinner or cock-tails, then disappear for another year or two."

"What was her name?"

Naomi started to speak, then frowned. She turned to stare at Selby. "You know, I can't remember. Isn't that odd? I'm eighty-nine years old. I wonder if some of the pages are starting to fall out of my book."

"Maybe it'll come to you later."

"Maybe. Sometimes, I have trouble remembering what Sullivan looked like."

Selby thought about the photo of his father that hung, re-cently repaired, next to his window.

"I worry about that, too," he said. "Letting him fade into nothing."

Naomi shrugged. "Maybe that's what he wants."

Outside, they waited for their taxi on a bench under a poin-ciana tree, a riot of scarlet spreading above their heads like a burning umbrella.

"When I met Sullivan, I felt like we had known each other for a thousand years but had only just now ended up in the same place at the same time. I've never felt anything like that with anyone else, not before, not since."

"Aunt Martha says he was charismatic."

Naomi made a face. "I suppose he was. I'd like to think I wasn't stupid enough to fall for a handsome face and a winning line of patter, though. Maybe I *was* that stupid. In retrospect, it was incredibly silly, the whole romance. It was like a bad ro-mantic comedy. All the clichés. A year into our marriage, I started realizing how thin the whole relationship was, how frag-ile."

"And there I was."

"Don't get me wrong," Naomi said, "he loved you. He was thrilled when you came along. I mean that. Ecstatic."

"I've always wondered whether he left because fatherhood was too much for him."

Naomi shook her head. "No. Don't think that for a moment. He said he had never had a child before, and I believed him. He adored you. We were so very, very happy." She smiled, looking back over the years. "The problem was that his love was so fucking indiscriminate. He loved *everybody*. There wasn't nearly enough of him to cover all the territory his love tried to claim."

The cab arrived, and Selby helped his mother into the back seat and then climbed in next to her. She gave the driver the address, and they rolled away into traffic.

"You used the phrase 'matter of life and death'," Naomi said. "The questions you wanted to ask. Explain that."

Selby made a face, and his mother laughed. "My god, you still do that? You used to make that face when you were five. Martha always told you your face would stick that way forever if you didn't stop."

"But I didn't stop."

"Nope. You would always wait until she turned her back, and then you'd make the face at her. You were such a little shit sometimes. You definitely got that from me. So. Life and death."

Selby took a deep breath, then another. "I've been attacked twice—no, three times—by someone who doesn't want me try-ing to find my father."

"'Attacked'? What the fuck do you mean, 'attacked'?"

"Physically. Hit with … things. Nothing more than some bruises, but alarming nonetheless. One of my friends was terrorized."

"Jesus fucking Christ, Selby! What have you gotten your-self into?"

"That's what I'm hoping to find out."

Naomi caught the driver's eye in the rearview mirror and scowled at him until he looked away.

"When we get home, we'll talk more about this."

CHAPTER THIRTEEN

Martha was delighted with the woodcut.

"I love it, Selby. I forgive you all your trespasses."

"Even the tennis bracelet?"

"What tennis bracelet?"

"When I was thirteen, Mom bought you a tennis bracelet for a Christmas gift. I made some reprehensible crack about you being too old to take up tennis. I've been angry at my thirteen-year-old self ever since."

Martha looked at her sister, then back at Selby. "Oh, Selby. You fucking idiot. I was almost forty, and I was showing the early signs of MS. You were absolutely right."

"It was still an awful thing to say."

Martha smiled, the makeup at the corners of her mouth and eyes creasing and crackling. "Just goes to show you which side of the family you take after. You're your momma's little boy, all right."

"Jesus," Naomi said. "Is there any liquor in this house?"

After dinner, Martha went to her room to watch TV while Naomi and Selby stretched out on lounge chairs at the Village's communal pool with glasses of wine.

"Nice out here," Selby said. He didn't normally drink wine, but at Blue Spring Village, it seemed the thing to do in the evening, having a glass of wine by the pool.

Naomi shrugged. "It's okay. I like it like this, at night, with the lights on down in the pool, everything quiet, no leather-skinned geriatric Baywatch babes wallowing in coconut oil, no geezers in Speedos leering at everything that moves, munching Viagra like M&Ms."

Selby nodded into the dimness.

"So, life and death," Naomi said. "Attacks. What have you gotten yourself into?"

"I don't altogether know. It's something to do with Dad. People who want me to track him down, and other people who want me to leave him alone."

"Sullivan."

Selby looked at his mother, her face lit from beneath by the pool lights. "I can't help but feel as though the more I know, the better equipped I'll be to deal with things," he said.

"Hell of a thing to spring on your old mother after all this time."

"I know. I wouldn't have involved you—"

"You shit. I'm your mother! Don't you think I might have some interest in what's going on in your life?"

"Sorry."

Naomi lay back and laughed. "No, I'm sorry. Do you remember the time you almost cut your finger off trying to whittle a statue of some Greek god or other? You used one of Martha's German kitchen knives."

"The yelling. There was so much yelling."

"I was worried about you. I thought you were going to bleed to death."

"I still have a little scar on my hand." He held up two fingers and wiggled them.

Naomi chuckled. "Probably some emotional ones, too. I couldn't stop shouting at you. You had almost taken my Selby away from me, and I wasn't dealing with that very well."

"I guess motherhood was never as easy as it looked on *Leave It To Beaver*."

"Ain't it the truth." Naomi sipped her wine, looking back over the years. "You know, people always like to tell stories about how wonderful and transcendent pregnancy is. I can tell you from personal experience that they're full of shit. Pregnancy is months of being jammed into a skin that's too small with an evil leprechaun kicking your bladder up into your lungs all night long. When I went into labor, Sullivan was away on a book-buying trip. You were early, and he was almost certainly not buying books, but let's leave that for another time. Marty van Bever took me to the hospital, where I made a general nuisance of myself, screaming for blood, cursing you, your father, the doctor, God, and probably President Eisenhower, with all the eloquence at my disposal."

"Oh, dear."

"You might well say that. Anyway, they doped me up to within an inch of both our lives. By the time they wheeled me into the delivery room, I was higher than Jesus' kite."

Naomi paused, shifting her position, adjusting the chair. "Fucking hip. Every position is comfortable for three minutes, and then it's torture. As I'm sure you've noticed, bad joints abound on my side of the family. Don't ever get old, Selby."

"I think that horse has already left the barn."

She chuckled. "It hasn't gotten all that far yet. There may still be time to rope it in. Anyway, as I lay there giving birth for what felt like weeks but was actually two hours, I noticed that the room was full of whispering and muttering."

Selby blinked. "The hospital staff?"

"Different from that. You know that sound in a theater just before the play, after everybody has settled down and put their art-appreciation faces on, but before the lights go down? It was like that. A whole fucking Greek chorus standing around commenting on my efforts to expel a Volkswagen from my body."

"Could you hear what they were saying?"

"That's what was so weird. It was all just babble, noise, until this one voice jumped out. It was a woman's voice; I could hear her clear as I'm hearing you."

"You could understand her?"

Naomi nodded, her face strangely youthful in the exotic lighting. "Yep."

"What did she say?"

"She said, 'Maybe this one.'" Selby's mother lay back. "After that, all I could hear was you hollering and the doctor congratulating me, and I figured it was nothing but a hallucination. It may well have been."

She looked over into her son's face, her eyes shadowed and strange. "But sometimes I wonder."

. . .

Juliet Mosley did everything but throw herself in front of her husband's car, but Owen was determined. He was on a one-week medical leave, and he had left microfilm in the reader and his computer logged in to the servers. He needed to go and shut down his office and make sure everything was as it should be during his absence. Only when it became evident that he was going to fret himself into a relapse if the situation wasn't addressed did his wife relent.

"No monkey business, Owen. You go do what you think you have to do, and then you come right home. Do you hear me?"

"I hear you." Owen Mosley smiled at his wife. "An hour, no more. I'll get the film back into its vault and shut down my computer and the readers in the viewing room, and then I'll head right home. Do you want me to stop and pick up anything on my way back?"

"No. Just go, do your thing, come home. We'll order out for lunch as soon as you get back."

Owen chuckled. Having Thai food delivered was an expensive luxury they indulged only on special occasions. This was

Juliet's way of making him pay for his willfulness.

"I think that's a grand idea, Jules."

The Herald-Star archives were as he had left them. No strange insects fluttered under the lights, and no scent of mystery hung in the sterile hallways. Mosley took the microfilm reel off the scanner and returned it to the climate-controlled cabinet where it belonged. The computer in the viewing room was cycling through a screensaver consisting of rectangles in various colors appearing and disappearing randomly across the screen. He wiggled the mouse to dismiss the screensaver, then powered down the machine.

In his office, SpongeBob SquarePants cavorted across the undersea landscape of Bikini Bottom. He clicked the mouse, and the screensaver vanished to reveal a digital capture from an issue of the Herald-Star stored on microfilm.

In all the confusion, he had forgotten about this, the last bit of information he had scavenged for Selby Coates's search.

The item was a feel-good photo piece from 1936, one of several that the Herald-Star would scatter through the paper every day in an effort to offset the bad news that covered the front page.

A milkman in his white uniform and cap hands a bottle of milk to a smiling housewife while another woman looks on, also smiling, and a small boy peers into the back of the milk truck. All very Norman Rockwell. In a brief caption, the reader learns that the scene is taking place in one of the "wonderful new housing estates in Van Baar, built to house workers on the PP&L dam and locks project." The milkman is identified as "S. Coates."

Mosley stared at the screen for a minute, debating whether to delete the capture and move on. With an impatient gesture, he finally saved the item and attached it to an email. For the subject line, he wrote "Coates." He took a breath and sent the message, then shut down his computer and turned out the lights.

Please, Coates, Mosley thought as he stepped onto the elevator. *Let this be the end of it.*

. . .

The man in the aisle seat had the thick dark hair and breezy, amiable face of Richard Long in *House on Haunted Hill.* Selby covertly watched the man stumble up the aisle of the claustrophobic Embraer 190 aircraft, admiring his athletic build and imagining him dodging an assortment of rather sophomoric murder plots either by or against Vincent Price and the sultry Carol Ohmart.

Selby blushed when the object of his attention glanced first at the seat numbers, then at Selby, and dropped into the seat next to him. He smelled of freshly cut grass. A *lot* of it.

The stranger immediately struck up a conversation. This, unfortunately, consisted entirely of a profanity-laden tirade about the size of the plane, the fee for his checked luggage, and the ethnicity and attractiveness of the female flight attendants.

"It's only a two-hour flight," Selby pointed out.

The stranger grunted. "Doesn't matter. That's no reason to have a bunch of dogs on the job."

There was nowhere to go with this. Selby made a noise that meant nothing and settled into his seat, closing his eyes. With the reefs of social interaction out of the way, the next couple of hours would represent an island of forced inactivity in the turbulent sea of his existence. He hoped to use the opportunity to explore the odd things that had been going on inside his head of late.

When Selby was eight years old, he developed an inner ear infection that brought with it a 104-degree fever. Even almost sixty years later, Selby could still remember the strange synesthesia he had experienced as he drifted in and out of delirium. He could *smell* the fever: it was a rope of soft clay that someone had squeezed in their hands so that the material oozed up between their fingers. The fever made a sound, too, a sneaky, poisonous noise that he interpreted as dark water with ambiguous green and pink shapes suspended in its depths, barely visible, swimming lazily. Even after the fever broke, later that night, Selby had struggled to sort sight and smell and taste and hearing back into their proper cubbyholes.

The Empty Room was like that. Selby thought of it as an open space confined within walls, but it was also a smell (garden soil, mothballs, burning sycamore leaves) and a sound (voices whispering just on the other side of intelligibility). The door was a door, but it was also everything that enclosed the room: opening the door meant removing the walls. The room's only occupants were presences that surged and drifted and flirted among themselves, following lines of attraction and repulsion that also wandered and evolved from moment to moment.

The disappointing man in Seat 14-C made play with an elbow, but Selby gathered without opening his eyes that this was part of a territorial expansion and not a social overture. Selby slowed his breathing—How much Polo can one man wear at a time?—and shut out the offending presence.

Though what they were saying could not be distinguished, the voices in the Empty Room still had individuality. There were aggressive voices, frightened voices, weary voices, even enthusiastic voices. Whose voices *were* these? *The voices in my head*, Selby thought. *Grampa's gone off his meds.*

As he often did at the Circle Tavern, Selby eavesdropped, but no matter how he concentrated, he could not find words among the whispers. He did notice that voices came and went, entering or leaving the Empty Room.

The Room doesn't represent confinement, Selby realized, but a resource. *A meeting place? Do I have a Discord server inside my skull?* He attempted to thrust his own awareness into the space, but he sensed that the idea he was employing was wrong.

He was trying to push a large container inside a smaller container that was itself already inside the large container, while that small container also encompassed the large container's entire universe …

The combination of 14-C's cologne and the conceptual intricacies of the Empty Room gave Selby a headache, and he considered asking the flight attendant for an aspirin. That would involve admitting that he was awake, which might mean being forced to interact with his neighbor. He decided to tough it out.

Though he could not enter the Empty Room himself, he could make his thoughts happen there. He generated a simple *Hello*—or rather, the concept of *Hello*—and inserted it into the chorus of whispers.

The response was underwhelming. The currents flowed around his thought, only interacting with it to the extent of avoiding it entirely.

He framed another thought and tossed it through the open door: *Who are you?*

This time, he triggered a response. The voice that spoke to him was so clear and so forceful that he flinched against the constraints of his seat belt.

This is not for you, Selby, dear.

Laylah. Here was Laylah, speaking to him from the Empty Room.

Why not? It's my head. I can go where I want in here.

His headache intensified.

Don't play with tools you can't possibly understand. Focus on your task.

The passenger in seat 14-C abruptly lurched to his feet and stomped off to the bathroom, and Selby inhaled a lungful of Polo-free air.

Some of Naomi Coates's stubborn disregard for the expectations of others had rubbed off on her son over the last couple of days. He squared his figurative shoulders and faced the invisible entity that was trying to order him around inside the confines of his own mind. He had always hated being told *can't* and *don't* without solid explanations.

Can you stop me? Explain what I'm dealing with, politely and in detail, or get used to having me drop by from time to time. You started this. You're going to have to live with the process you set in motion—or end it.

Selby waited for a replay, both anxious and defiant—mostly anxious—but Laylah's presence vanished in a cloud of brimstone and vexation without another word.

Curiouser and curiouser, Selby thought.

His traveling companion returned to his seat, and Selby, his ears hot, wondered what the man's skin tasted like.

As Selby let himself into his apartment, Pancake stood up and stretched, then flopped down next to the food dish in an attitude of haggard desperation.

"There's food in your dish already, you faker."

Selby unpacked his things and took a shower, flushing away the last traces of 14-C's cologne, and then wrapped up in his big white bathrobe and padded into the kitchen.

Coffee, first.

According to the news, Port Sebastian was experiencing the first winter storm of the season, but Buckley, seventy miles inland, was merely gray and depressing. Zeus looked like he wished he had stayed in Greece. Selby thought about his fellow passenger on the Breeze Airways flight.

Maybe it's hard for someone so pretty to develop a personality, he thought. He smiled into his coffee, his ears going pink. "I sound like my mother's son."

Selby's email was, as usual, mostly junk, but he spotted Owen's address glinting among the dross. He opened the message, looked at the photograph for a long minute, then closed the message. He saved the attachment to his hard drive and then to his cloud storage. *Later*, he thought.

He sat back in the desk chair, looking at the computer screen without actually seeing it.

Naomi's right, he thought. *I've changed.*

The Empty Room was part of it, but the visit to his mother, talking to her without either of them being self-absorbed and bratty ... Selby felt positively giddy.

He felt for his pulse, counted the beats.

Nope. Everything normal. This is me.

Seeing his mother at eighty-nine years of age reminded him that he was only sixty-six. *Not old. Not ancient, anyway. Just upper middle age. Still room to grow. If Mom can do it, so can I.*

There was time for a late lunch at the Tavern. Selby drank the rest of his coffee and went to get dressed.

CHAPTER FOURTEEN

"Damn, Coates! You're getting pretty adventuresome these days," Roy said as he walked into the Circle Tavern and slid onto his stool. "Almost two o'clock in the afternoon, and on a Saturday, yet!"

"I just got back from Florida. Pancake says to thank you for taking care of him."

"Always a pleasure. The usual?"

Selby hesitated, toying with the idea of doing something outrageous, like having a veggie burger or even a fish taco, but decided not to press his luck.

"The usual."

Roy was wearing a cream-colored catsuit ornamented with large nested rectangles in green, orange, and chocolate brown. Her nails were the orange of her outfit, but her lips were a soft tan color that was only slightly lighter than her skin, while her eyeshadow was a shade darker.

"How was your trip?" she said after she had tapped in his order and slid his beer across the bar.

Selby made a face, then looked down with a chuckle, remembering his mother's comments about that particular facial expression. "It was interesting. My mother and I bonded."

"Better late than never, I always say."

"Exactly. I also learned that my father was a walking invitation to sexual indiscretion."

"Your mom told you that? Spicy."

"I've known for years that he was a philanderer, but I never really thought about what that meant. He had no money to speak of, so there had to be something that was encouraging all these women out of their petticoats."

Roy laughed. "A charmer. Runs in the family."

Selby didn't catch on to that immediately, but when he did, he splashed beer in his lap and blushed.

"I'm my mother's child, I suspect," he said, looking down into his beer. "I got the brains, instead."

Roy handed him a bar towel, and he wiped up the spilled beer, dabbing at his pants.

"Who says brains aren't charming?"

Selby laughed, uncomfortable with this sort of banter, and Roy changed the subject.

"We've got new crows at our house," she announced. Selby's sandwich appeared in the window, and she put it in front of him.

"Rescues?"

"Nope." A young couple at one of the tables flagged her, and Roy held up one finger. "Hold that thought."

Only half a dozen late-lunch stragglers remained in the place, Selby saw. The couple ordering dessert, the three young architects from across the Circle, and Selby himself. The architects were unusually subdued; as far as Selby could determine from scraps of conversation that drifted his way, one of the three had lost a large bet on a boxing match, and their mid-afternoon visit to the bar was along the lines of a wake.

Roy placed the dessert orders and turned her attention back to Selby.

"Crows," he said.

"Crows. Four of 'em. They showed up first thing Thursday morning. There was some fuss for about half a day, but by din-nertime, the new guys and our babies were all best buddies."

"They're still there?"

"Oh, yeah. They go poking around, but they don't get far from the hacienda. They've attacked the mail carrier, the UPS driver, and the snotty kid from next door. Reggie went out and explained to them who's who, and we haven't had any further difficulties. Except with the kid. I think Reggie sicced them on him intentionally."

"I'm glad they're fitting in well."

Roy gave him a suspicious look. "Do you know something about these birds?"

Selby's ears pinked, and he shook his head. "Of course not. You're the one who talks to crows."

Roy sighed and shook her head. "You're lying like a rug, but we'll let it go for now. The crows aren't a sign of trouble, are they?"

Selby looked at her and decided to come clean. "They're insurance. I think Laylah sent them. I told her that if anything happened to you or Reggie, I'd see to it that I ended up in a jar on your mantelpiece, and Laylah could go shop elsewhere for lackeys."

Roy stared. "Never say anything like that again, Coates. If anything happens to me or Reggie, I expect you to look after the birds. You dig?"

"Yes, ma'am."

She shook her head. "Lordy. What a world we live in."

"Have you given them names yet?"

"The crows? No. We'll have to see how they shape up. If they piss me off, they'll end up being Number This and Number That. If they become a part of the family, I'll give 'em names out of Shakespeare or something. Maybe I'll name one after you."

Selby bought groceries on the way back to his apartment. After he had put everything away, he sat down at the desk and pulled up the message from Owen.

When the picture opened up, Selby chuckled. "A milkman. How apt."

He looked at the dates.

How is this possible? he thought. If Sullivan Coates was already an adult in 1936, then he'd have been in his forties when Selby was born, and pushing fifty when he left. Selby was quite certain his father hadn't been fifty years old. Besides, that means that now he'd be … what?

Selby pulled up a calculator and did some figuring, shaking his head at the results. Alexa Coates filed for divorce from Sullivan in 2011, at which time he would have been ninety-seven years old. Shades of Rupert Murdoch.

"Assuming he was about twenty-two when the paper took this picture, he'd be 110 now. That seems unlikely," Selby murmured, trying out different combinations of numbers. "On the other hand … Suppose 'S. Coates' was Sullivan's father? Would that work? Might. That makes a lot more sense."

A grandfather. I never had a grandfather, Selby thought. Naomi's father had died when she and Martha were still in their teens, and Sullivan had hatched from the egg fully-grown. Selby blew out his cheeks and shook his head slowly, staring at the handsome man and his adoring customers.

The existence of another generation was more believable than an eternally youthful Sullivan Coates, but it felt contrived, somehow. *And it sure as the Dickens* looks *like him*.

Selby filed the new item away with everything else he had accumulated so far.

Outside, Zeus was standing tall, basking in the spotlights that illuminated him from sunset to sunrise. Selby stood at the window watching the last of the pigeons settling onto their roosts among the girders and blocks of the god's pedestal, listening to the faint sounds of traffic coming through the glass.

Laylah had done what he asked. Selby did not doubt for a moment that the new crows in Roy's backyard were there to protect his friends. This meant a couple of things that were worth thinking about. One was that he could talk to Laylah through the Empty Room. The other was that Laylah needed him badly enough that his threats carried weight.

She could walk in a person's dreams, command the birds, even thwart death. Even so, Selby Coates had told her what to do, and she did it.

That would need a lot of thinking about.

The week that followed Selby's trip to Blue Spring Village was remarkable for being unremarkable. No attacks by deranged cultists, no strange encounters with exiled Latin American dictators, no cinematic dreams filled with Laylah delivering meaningless snippets of lore. Naomi called to tell him that she had enjoyed his visit, and Aunt Martha sent her nephew a semi-pornographic greeting card with a few lines scribbled on it · thanking him for the woodcut.

The only thing that stood out was Roy's report on the new crows. By Friday, they had learned to accept the FedEx driver, the pizza delivery boy, and most children under nine years of age. Still on the "prohibited" list were two political pollsters, someone collecting signatures for a petition, and a man claiming to be an inspector for Buckley Municipal Services looking for a leak in a water line somewhere in the neighborhood.

"The supposed water guy ..." Roy said, pushing Selby's beer across the bar. "Reggie said there was definitely something sketchy about him."

November had brought rain, and the Tavern was surprisingly busy, full of wet, noisy people drinking hot drinks and eating chili served in coffee mugs from a vat on a hotplate behind the bar.

"How so? What made her suspicious?"

Roy interrupted the conversation to pass orders over to Joboss, a relentlessly good-natured twenty-something space cadet who was always available to come in at a moment's notice when needed. Joboss waited on customers with a blithe indifference to who ordered what, smoothing over any pushback with a rueful chuckle and a "Really? Where's my head at, right?" while ignoring the problem entirely. Customers soon found that outrage was wasted on him and made do with what he served them, and everyone got along.

"That guy," Roy said, getting back to her story. "Reggie was working in her office when she heard this godawful commotion out in front of the house." Roy's wife, Régine Bernard, was a CPA and worked in an office downtown two days a week and from home the other three days. "She grabbed her phone and went out to investigate, and found this farmer type in jeans and a down vest standing on the curb while the new crows marched back and forth in front of the stoop, hollering what she assumed was something nasty in the language of their people."

"Who was he?"

"He said he was with BMS and that he was checking around the neighborhood looking for a water leak. Reggie said, 'Where's your truck?' and he said, 'Oh, it's around the corner.' Reggie says the street was pretty much empty at the time, so she told him, 'Why don't you park it right here in front of the house? That should be more convenient for you.' He hemmed and hawed until Reggie took his picture with her phone, which pissed him off royally, she said. He started to come up into the yard at that point, but the crows made a fuss, and he backed off while she took a couple more photos. Reggie had BMS on her contacts list—she has everybody on her contacts list, from Domino's Pizza to Lady Gaga's hairdresser—so she called 'em up and asked about a leak. At that point, Mr Puffy Vest turned around and marched away."

"No leak?"

"BMS told Reggie they would always send out an email, text, or robocall any time somebody might need to go door to door, and workers would always be in uniform. There was no leak."

Roy delivered Selby's sandwich, and he squared everything up on the mat and looked at her.

"I don't like that."

Roy shrugged. "That's how life is, Coates. Next time you talk to the Wicked Witch of the West, tell her thanks for me. Those crows are a treasure."

Roy hustled off to deal with a conflict that Joboss's stoner charm was insufficient to resolve, and Selby ate his sandwich thoughtfully.

There were other scammers and crooks on the street besides Doma's henchpeople, but this incident was disturbing. Selby had no idea what the stranger might have intended to do once he gained access to the property, but he assumed it would not be in Roy and Reggie's best interests.

Now that Selby was back home, his problems should resume their focus on him and leave his friends alone. But if things didn't work out that way, what could he do about it? He thought back over his exchange with Laylah on the plane.

I may have options, he thought, watching Roy spoon chili into bowls and pour oil on troubled waters. *I just don't know what they are.*

Selby chewed a bite of his sandwich.

Yet.

River City Grocery was the anchor of what might have been called a strip mall, except that it had been there since the 1950s, built at a time before modern strip malls had so completely taken over the landscape. A tiny bakery that was only open from eight in the morning until noon squeezed in between River City and a florist whose staid and predictable arrangements had graced the funerals of Fallwood's bourgeoisie for three generations. A laundromat clung to the end of the row. Underneath that, its location made possible by the abrupt slope of the ground at that point, an after-hours dive bar crouched in the fragrant, steamy shadows like a demented uncle hiding in the bushes at the family picnic.

At lunchtime, any bread left over from the morning's production at the bakery went to a food bank, while the grocery store next door sold the more perishable items at a discount. This arrangement encouraged Selby's addiction to sweets. Having discovered a four-pack of his favorite devil's food cupcakes, Selby cruised the aisles looking for something to legitimize his visit. He hated going through the checkout with nothing but cake in his basket.

"Ha! Mr. Coates, my old friend."

Selby was startled to find the Colonel in the breakfast cereal aisle, Froot Loops in one hand and Lucky Charms in the other. In the bright overhead lighting, the old autocrat looked like some forgotten specimen from a taxidermist's attic.

"Colonel. Fancy meeting you here."

The Colonel produced a phlegmy chuckle. "My Bolívar enjoys some milk and cereal for breakfast every day. He prefers Cap'n Crunch, but they appear to be out of that one."

Selby struggled to find a reply to that, but in the end, the best he could do was a weak smile and a feeble "Really."

"I spoil him, but he is all I have. I seem to have outlived all my friends and colleagues." He grinned, making Selby take an involuntary step back. "And, of course, most of my enemies. Nobody left but me and my little friend."

"The price of longevity, I suppose," Selby said. "Not to mention systematic political assassination."

"Indeed." The Colonel put the Lucky Charms back on the shelf and turned to face Selby, holding the box of Froot Loops in front of his belly like a shield. "Mr. Coates, I would like you to come to my house, maybe today, maybe tomorrow, as you like. I have been thinking about the incident in the street with those unfortunate young men, and I have some documents I think you should see."

Dear god in heaven. Is he inviting me up to see his etchings?

"I … I'm not sure I—"

"Rest easy, Mr. Coates. I am not inviting you into my house for sinister purposes." He chuckled in a way that would have put one of Selby's horror movie villains to shame. "Learn about a man named Grigorio Cudhill. He was a minor functionary in the Ministry of Internal Security during my time in power. Then come to my house whenever you are ready."

With this strange invitation, the old man bowed slightly and walked away.

Selby blew out his cheeks. *That evil little dog eats Cap'n Crunch?* He glanced down at the cupcakes in his basket and went looking for some broccoli or kale or something to balance the load.

Sitting at his desk in his sweatpants and t-shirt that evening after supper, Selby forked day-old devil's food cake into his mouth and scrolled through the high points of the Wikipedia entries on both Grigorio Cudhill and his one-time boss, Selby's neighbor, the Colonel.

The Colonel's home country was known primarily for the long and bitter period of political and social instability that it experienced during the middle decades of the twentieth century, a crisis driven by the Cold War politics of the US and the Soviet Union. A succession of military dictatorships took and held power during that time, none lasting more than a couple of years.

On January 6, 1982, in an event later tagged the "Epiphany Revolution," forces loyal to Colonel Carlos Cabrera López, erstwhile Minister of Internal Security, seized control of the capital and promptly shot everyone connected to the previous series of ad hoc administrations.

Eighteen months later, the Colonel was, in his turn, chased out of office, escaping to Houston with twenty kilos of high-quality cocaine and a suitcase full of cash in a yacht chartered by a shell company controlled by the US Department of State. From Houston, he was moved to Fort Bennings, losing the cocaine somewhere along the way, then to Alexandria, Virginia, and finally to Buckley, where the tide of assassination attempts finally dried up, and the monster was allowed to settle down to an obscure retirement.

Grigorio Cudhill had been Deputy Minister of Justice under the Colonel's regime. After the Colonel's sudden departure, Cudhill helped put together an election that brought democracy of a sort to the country, and then he quietly evaporated.

"Fascinating, but what does this have to do with me?" Selby wondered aloud. He spooned a bit of cream cheese icing onto a plate on the floor for Pancake, careful to avoid including any of the cake. He had heard that chocolate was not good for cats.

A photograph of Cudhill accompanied a Wikipedia post about the massacres. The photographer had taken the picture at an official function, everyone in suits, plus a couple of older men in boxy uniforms stiff with medals and decorations. The photo depicted a heavy-set man, almost fat, with a round face and no chin to speak of. Short dark hair, hooded eyes, a forehead like a melon. Cudhill was standing in the posture of a big man trying to stay out of the spotlight: his head turned slightly, his face angled down, his shoulders slumped, his hands behind his back.

Why did the Colonel think his former hatchet man was relevant to the weird things that were happening to Selby Coates? Selby looked down at Pancake, who looked back with the blank stare only a cat with cake icing on his face could pull off.

"You realize what this means, don't you? I'm going to have to go and let the Colonel show me his etchings."

. . .

Fiona's Baby Diary:
I'm so mad I could just SPIT! I asked Mitch whether he knew anything about Bongo's family since he never talks about them and I'm always a little afraid to ask in case there are skeletons in the closet or something. Mitch said, as far as he knows, I married an orphan. I asked about Bongo's sister, Ruth's boss, and Mitch got all flustered. Later, Ruth called and ORDERED me not to ask her husband questions about Bongo's past! It's not like I'm a reporter for the tabloids or something! I'm his wife and the mother of his baby! Some people.

CHAPTER FIFTEEN

Régine Bernard stood in her backyard, brandishing a broom and a threatening expression.

Feeding the crows had become far more complicated since the new birds joined the family. Each crow had a dish of its own, and over time, Reggie had trained the rescues to stick to their own food and leave their neighbors' dinner alone. The newcomers, however, still cheerfully pushed away the disabled birds and helped themselves to whatever was available, and Reggie had to shove them back when they got grabby. *Patience*, she told herself. *They'll learn*. She waved the broom at a crow who was sidling over to examine his neighbor's bowl. *That, or I'll fricassee the little bastards*. The early morning feeding was always the worst.

Reggie was a small woman, almost delicate, with a child's eyes and mouth. Because of her appearance, strangers—and sometimes birds—underestimated her. Few made that mistake more than once.

The largest of the newcomers attacked one of the blind crows, and Reggie scooped him off his feet with the broom and flipped him neatly away from the feeding area. Outraged, the offender flapped up onto the privacy fence and shrieked at her.

"Yeah, whatever. I've been called worse," Reggie said. The new birds still didn't have names, not officially, but Roy had been calling that big one Othello, and that was probably going to stick. Woman and crow eyed each other warily.

"You want to eat my food, pretty boy? You do it according to my rules."

After a time, the birds lost interest in what remained of the melon, meat scraps, and oatmeal soaked in leftover cooking oil. They hopped around, preening and posing, occasionally peering thoughtfully at any food left on the dishes or at each other. Othello came down from his sulk and picked over the remains. Reggie watched for a few minutes to ensure that everybody was behaving, and then she turned to go back into the house.

She put the broom away and stood in the kitchen, sniffing the air.

Perfume, men's cologne. Expensive. Stinky.

Roy didn't wear cologne, and Reggie only wore perfume when she and Roy were going out someplace fancy.

She stepped out of her shoes and padded silently down the hall to the living room.

A stranger was standing in the middle of the living room floor.

"Ms. Bernard, right? I'm sorry to walk right in like this, but you need to—"

Whatever his excuse might have been, the intruder standing smack in the middle of her living room, big as life, didn't get a chance to articulate it. In one smooth movement, Reggie snatched the brass Buddha from the mantelpiece and swung it underhand, stepping into the swing. During her years at North Carolina A&T State, Régine Bernard had been celebrated as a softball pitcher who took no prisoners. The Enlightened One slammed into the stranger's crotch at considerable velocity, and the man went down like a rock.

"You're the guy who was pretending to be with Municipal Services," Reggie said. As the stranger moaned, clutching at himself, Reggie dashed into the kitchen and came back with a nasty-looking handgun in one hand and a cell phone in the other. She stood just out of reach of the man on the floor, holding the gun where he would see it when he opened his eyes. "You broke into my house," she said as she dialed the phone.

"The door … was … unlocked." He sounded as though he were strangling, but he could speak.

"And you saw that as an invitation to walk right in?"

"Need to … tell you …"

"A woman alone in her house, minding her own business, some joker walks right in without so much as ringing the doorbell … That's a castle doctrine scenario if ever I saw one. Hello? Yes, I have an intruder in my home. I'm alone here. I hit him with a little statue. No, in the nuts. Yes, that's what I said. He's alive, but he doesn't look happy. Yes, I'm okay, just pissed off. No, I don't think he's armed. He won't give me any more trouble as long as you get a move on." She gave the address and disconnected.

The man on the floor pulled himself up to a sitting position, and Reggie showed him the gun.

"Nothing moves but your lips. Do you hear me? If you feel like doing something stupid—and bear in mind that I'm the one who gets to define 'stupid'—remember those words: 'castle doctrine.' I was born in Haiti, Mister Burglar-slash-vandal-slash-rapist, and I will not hesitate to shoot your fucking balls off if that's what it takes to defend my home."

The man froze. "I'm not any of those things."

"Bull-fucking-shit. You're in my house without my permission. Unless you're the Secret Service or something, you're a criminal."

He groaned, and Reggie stepped back.

"You have something to tell me? Start by explaining what you're doing in my house."

"You have to tell Selby Coates—"

"Selby Coates? I'm not an answering service. If you want to tell Selby something, call him on the phone."

"Listen to me, goddammit—!"

"Oops. Too slow. Hear that?" Reggie nodded toward the front of the house. A police siren chirped twice somewhere nearby. "Police substation is only nine blocks from here. I think your speaking time is about up."

"No, listen—"

"You listen, *saloparde*. This is a civilized society. We have ways to communicate. There is the telephone, there's voicemail, there's email, there's texting. You can even write a letter. None of those choices involves breaking into somebody's house. If you're here to threaten one of my friends, then consider yourself lucky you didn't get to deliver the message because I really would have shot your balls off."

Two police cars pulled up in front of the house, lights flashing, pursued by a flock of kids on bicycles. Reggie walked over and opened the front door, then returned to stand in front of the man sitting on the rug. As the police bustled up the front walk, she unscrewed a cap on the butt of the gun and poured a quantity of red liquid into an empty candy dish on the coffee table, and tossed the gun onto a chair.

"Cabernet. The plastic makes the wine undrinkable after only a day or so."

The police appeared in the doorway, and Reggie turned to greet them with a smile.

. . .

The former dictator welcomed the former journalist in an entry hall lit only by a fanlight over the front door. A coat rack loomed in the shadows like a sinister butler, shrouded with cobwebs and dust, waiting to take a hat or an umbrella. Bolívar lurked at his master's heels but limited his reaction to Selby's presence to a snaggle-toothed snarl.

"Welcome, Mr. Coates," the Colonel said. "My house is your house."

Following the old man into the front room, Selby felt as though he might be entering the tomb of an obscure Pharaoh, locked away beyond the reach of daylight for a thousand years. Prints and photographs covered the dark floral-patterned wallpaper, many of them so faded or so small that Selby's vision was inadequate to determine their subjects. Beaded fringes dripped from lampshades, echoing the tasseled valence over the narrow window, and bric-a-brac covered every horizontal surface. Shelves groaned under stacks of books, magazines, and age-yellowed newspapers, and a battered guitar hung on the wall above the cold, dusty fireplace, its strings hanging limp. A smell of dust, dry rot, and dog piss permeated everything.

"It is a museum," the Colonel said, correctly interpreting Selby's expression.

"How did you get it all here?" Selby asked.

The old man chuckled. "It took time. I arrived in this country with little more than a pair of suitcases and the clothes on my back. Fortunately, I had money, and I still had friends back home, and they slowly passed my belongings along, smuggling things out, a box here, an envelope there. Once, a truck appeared at my door carrying a load of my furniture and my books. I sat on the front steps and wept like a woman in my gratitude."

Aside from some pictures and a collection of mementos that fit easily into a shoebox on the shelf in his closet, Selby had never accumulated a lot of things, but he couldn't help but be affected by the intensity of loneliness and homesickness that the room represented.

"It must have been hard, leaving everything behind."

The old man nodded. "I almost chose to remain and die, but in the end, I was weak. Your government was concerned that my successors would neglect to execute me, leaving me free to talk about my time in office. This involved events they did not want made public, so they convinced me to come here and disappear. So here I am, once a wolf, feared and respected, now a pitiful stray, toothless and half blind, hiding in his kennel." He shrugged and indicated a clear spot on the sofa. "Such is power. It comes and it goes. Please sit."

Selby sat, and the Colonel settled into a high-backed chair that creaked under his weight. Bolivar jumped up and coiled himself in his master's lap. The dog had given up snarling, but his upper lip was still caught on one eyetooth.

Keep making those faces, and you'll get stuck like that, Selby thought.

"I have seen and done many strange and terrible things in my life," the Colonel said. He reached out to pick up a tumbler half full of red wine that sat on a little table at his elbow. He took a sip and put the glass back.

"In my country, the modern world is nothing more than a thin skin covering thousands of years of blood and joy and terror. We pretend it is not so, but every scratch reveals the truth that lies beneath." The old man seemed to lose the thread, and he sat gazing off into space, his lips pursed into a bundle like the mouth of a drawstring bag. After a moment, he shook himself and picked up a stack of what appeared to be small placards from the side table. He set the cards in his lap, easing Bolívar to the side. After a brief search, the Colonel chose one of the items and passed it over to Selby, who saw that it was a photograph laminated onto thin pasteboard.

Selby held the picture up to catch the light from a floor lamp next to the sofa. In the creased and smudged black-and-white image, a group of men clustered on an elevated platform, one at a podium, the others arranged to either side. Selby puzzled out the handwritten caption and realized that the man at the podium was the Colonel as a young man, sturdy and dark, almost handsome.

"March of 1982. A rally soon after I took power," the Colonel said. "The others are men I brought into my circle to replace the lackeys and bootlickers that had filled the government during the time of the caudillos, the warlords. You see the fat man, the second man from the left?"

"Yes."

"That is Grigorio Cudhill. He was the only bureaucrat I kept from the previous government."

The Colonel passed over another photo. This was a reception or similar gathering, men in evening clothes smiling at each other. Cudhill was in this picture, too, off to one side.

"You see him?"

"This man here?"

The Colonel nodded. "That is Cudhill at the inauguration of Alejandro Montenegro, a year after my... departure. He engineered Montenegro's rise to power while the new caudillos were slaughtering each other, then served in Montenegro's 'democratic' government." He handed Selby the stack of images. "Some of those pictures are photographs. The man I call Cudhill is in all of them. Some of the pictures are—what do you call it? Engravings, yes, for newspapers in the old days. The oldest is from 1890—you would not believe the bribes I had to pay to get it. The newest is from four years ago."

The old man leaned forward, eliciting a squawk of protest from Bolívar. The dim light swam in the deposed dictator's cloudy eyes.

"Cudhill is in every one of these pictures."

Selby frowned. "Back to 1890? That hardly seems likely."

The Colonel scoffed. "You say this to me? You? You speak of what is likely and what is not? I know this man. I watched him weaving his webs for the eighteen months that I was President and for years more before that, when he and I were nothing but foot soldiers in someone else's army. You may believe me or not, but I know this man is in every one of these pictures!"

A spray of saliva caught the lamplight on the last word. The old man collected himself and sat back, stroking Bolívar's head.

"You are involved with something strange," the Colonel said after an uncomfortable moment. "You and I both know this to be true. Over all my many years, my many experiences, I have come to the conclusion that there are things in this world that are more than we can understand. I don't mean gods and devils and the ghosts of dead grandmothers floating along the upstairs hallway. I mean Cudhill and men like him. Your young men with their mouths sewn shut. People who take their places among humanity but partake of something more. They are all part of a larger thing. I called it 'unholy' before, but that was just my way of talking. This thing is not holy or unholy; it is something to the side of all that."

Selby leafed through the images.

In every picture, even the nineteenth-century caricature of a group of uniformed men drinking wine and dandling women on their knees, even there, that same jack o'lantern face hovered. Always to the side or in the background, but always there.

Selby looked at the images, thinking about the photo of the smiling milkman from a hundred years ago, the man who looked so very much like his father. *Two, three generations? Grandfather, father, son? That's the only possible explanation. The only rational explanation.*

"I'm sorry, Colonel," Selby said, handing the images back, "but I can't believe in immortals hiding among us. How would somebody like that not be noticed?"

The Colonel nodded. "I ask myself that question. I find that records are missing, fires break out in museums, someone steals documents. All that remains are scattered pieces of the story. I was able to make the connections I made because I was in a position of power, power that reached beyond my own borders."

Here, again, the situation was perilously close to what Owen had said about his search for information regarding Selby's father. *A walking information virus.* Selby looked at the ugly old man with his ugly old dog and wondered what his dreams looked like. The Colonel met his gaze without blinking.

"Thank you for sharing this," Selby said, finally, gesturing at the stack of pictures in the Colonel's hands. "You're right that things are going on in my life right now that I don't under-stand." Selby climbed to his feet, wincing at a twinge in his knee.

"Be careful, friend Coates," the Colonel rumbled. "You have not lived as I have. You do not have the habit of looking over your shoulder. Perhaps you should learn."

On that cheerful note, Selby said goodbye. The Colonel did not show him out, but Bolívar offered a farewell growl.

Selby hurried home without really seeing the familiar streets, preoccupied instead by the Colonel's strange notions.

Strange notions? Selby scoffed as he let himself into his building. The old autocrat hardly had a monopoly on strange notions. The Colonel was right: Selby was in no position to judge what was or was not possible.

When he stepped off the elevator on the tenth floor, Selby found Chioke Okorie banging on the door to the apartment he shared with his wife and children, just down the hall from Selby's. The other tenants of that floor were either out or hun-kered down, waiting for the storm to pass without their inter-vention. When Selby came near, he could see that Chioke's knuckles were bleeding and his shirt was torn.

"Chioke? Are you all right?"

A child was crying inside the apartment, and Selby could hear Rita, although he could not hear what she was saying.

Chioke shouted through the door, slamming into it with his shoulder. Selby could not recognize the language the man was speaking, but his intentions were clear, and at the rate he was going, he would soon tear the door out of its frame. Selby patted his pocket, looking for his phone, but it was, of course, inside his apartment, on his desk. He turned to fetch it, to call the po-lice, but it struck him that there might not be time.

"Chioke! Stop that!"

The other man turned, his face puffy with rage, and shouted something at Selby in the same language, then he added, in English, "Mind your own business, old faggot."

Selby had been around long enough to have dealt with that sort of attitude before, so he shrugged off the name-calling, but the violence that shivered in the air all around Chioke was frightening.

"This *is* my business, Chioke. This is my home," Selby said quietly, his voice trembling only slightly.

Chioke turned to face him fully, then stepped forward and grabbed the front of Selby's jacket.

"You want a fight, old pervert?" Chioke snarled into Selby's face. "I'll be happy to give you one."

Between one heartbeat and the next, the door to the Empty Room swung wide. Chioke blanched and stepped back, still clutching at Selby's windbreaker.

"Stop it, Chioke," Selby said, his voice barely more than a whisper. His chest was icy, but his ears were hot. His entire face felt swollen and feverish.

The whispers whirled. Selby *saw* Chioke's fear and rage and frustration seething around his head and shoulders like shards of hot glass. Chioke released Selby's jacket and snapped something in the language Selby couldn't understand. The agitated presence surrounding him gained energy, and Chioke narrowed his eyes and gritted his teeth.

Almost without realizing it, Selby reached into the Empty Room. The space breathed out, a long, slow whisper, then *inhaled*—

Chioke Okorie paled and staggered back as his violence was sucked away from him and swallowed up in the infinite space that occupied a tiny corner of Selby's head.

"*What the fuck?*"

"You need to go downstairs," Selby said gently, his heart pounding so hard it hurt. "Wait in the lobby."

Chioke stared, all the fight gone, leaving him barely able to stand up. After a moment, he rubbed his face with his hand and stumbled to the elevator.

When he was gone, Selby knocked on the apartment door. "Rita? It's Selby. Your neighbor. Are you all right?" His voice wavered. He sounded like a very old man. He *felt* like a very old man.

"Who is it?"

"Selby Coates," he said, speaking more carefully. "From next door."

The door opened a crack, and Rita Okorie peeked out.

"You have blood on your face, Mr. Coates."

Selby wiped at his lip and discovered that his nose was bleeding sluggishly.

"A nosebleed. I'll be fine. Are you all right?"

Rita opened the door fully, and Selby saw that her daughter Mari was clinging to her leg, eyes wide, snot running down onto her upper lip.

"Where is my husband?"

Selby blinked. "He's downstairs. I ... we agreed that he should go downstairs and cool off for a while."

Rita heaved a deep breath. "He means no harm. It's just that his business has not been going well. He discovered one of his partners has been stealing from him." She poked her head out into the hall and looked toward the elevators. "You are sure he's all right?"

Selby felt a vast weariness settle over him. "He was a moment ago. He was trying to break the door down."

Rita nodded. "I know. I locked the door because he was shouting. Maybe I should not have done that, but all the noise was frightening Mari." She reached down and stroked the little girl's head. "Jonas is sleeping over at a friend's house. They are going to see a movie." She looked away. "I hope Chioke doesn't get into trouble. You know how men are when they are upset."

Selby couldn't decide whether he wanted to hug her or yell at her, so he just sighed. "He'll be fine. He was much calmer when he went downstairs."

The woman nodded again, and Selby reached out to pat Mari's hair. The girl ducked back out of reach.

"If you need anything, I'm right next door," he said.

"Thank you, Mr. Coates."

After Rita had pulled Mari back inside and closed the door, Selby limped back to the elevator and rode down to the vestibule, snuffling blood.

Chioke Okorie stood outside, on the sidewalk next to the street, smoking a cigarette and fidgeting. As Selby watched through the plate glass of the front door, a late-model Tesla pulled up. Chioke stomped out his cigarette and climbed into the back seat. Selby watched the car make a U-turn in front of the building and drive away.

Back in his apartment, Selby took off his shoes and squared them on the mat next to the door. Turning, he noticed that Pancake's water dish needed to be topped up. He picked up the dish, emptied the water that was in it, and then spent the next ten minutes scouring the bowl, lathering it up with detergent, and scrubbing it with the green pad, inside and out, over and over. He rinsed the bowl, refilled it, and put it back in its place, then dumped the food that was in the food dish down the garbage disposal and gave that bowl the same treatment.

Pancake, curled up on the comfortable chair, didn't raise his head, but he watched the entire process with an alert, cautious eye.

When he finished with the cat dishes, Selby discovered that he had soaked the cuffs of his windbreaker, and a smear of blood ran along the zipper. With a snarl of frustration, he yanked off the jacket and hung it up in the bathroom, then stumbled back across the apartment to sit heavily on the edge of the bed.

He breathed, but his breaths were not the long, slow, calming breaths he needed, but jagged things that hurt his throat as they came and went.

What was that? What did I do?

Chioke Okorie was a man of a type that Selby had encountered many times in the past. A weak man who desperately wanted to appear strong. A man like Chioke was servile to those he saw as more powerful than himself while abusing those who were weaker. "Kissing up, punching down," Roy called such behavior. Selby didn't know enough about Chioke's background to understand how he got to be this way, but that wasn't really important.

What was important was that Selby had done something to the man, something *awful*. No matter how destructive Chioke's rage and fear might have been, they were *his* rage and fear; they belonged to him. Maybe they *were* him, what defined him. For better or for worse, they were his birthright, and Selby had stripped them away without hesitation.

Chioke was going to hurt someone. He might have hurt Rita or Mari. Or me.

It was true that Selby had assumed Chioke intended violence—but he couldn't really *know*. He made an assumption based on his interpretation of events, and he acted out of fear, out of cowardice.

I was afraid he would attack me, and I didn't know how to defend myself. I didn't wait to find out what he was going to do; I struck out with a weapon I didn't realize I possessed.

He reached into a man's heart and took away something that was a part of him.

What have I become?

CHAPTER SIXTEEN

For a day and a half, Selby did not leave his apartment, living on canned soup and leftover cupcakes, watching fifteen minutes of one movie, then half an hour of another, unable to connect with anything he was seeing.

He tried to access the Empty Room but discovered that the door was closed, and he couldn't open it. At first, Selby assumed this was because of what he had done, his attack on Chioke Okorie, but after a time, he understood that it was because he wasn't really trying. He had been seeing the Room as an asset, a tool—maybe even an adventure—but now he was forced to reassess that notion. The Empty Room was a resource, yes, but it was also a weapon, and he didn't know how to address the idea of Selby Coates with a weapon. His confusion kept the door closed.

He saw that Barry Ratliffe had emailed him on Friday, then again on Sunday.

Friday: *I've got info for you about Ruth Coates and the 2018 accident. I've tracked down the car that came and picked her up at the clinic. Call me, man!*

Sunday: *I'm guessing you're one of those guys who never checks his voicemail or reads his text messages. Hell, you've probably got a flip phone or something from ten years ago and can barely order a pizza. I've got a line on Ruth Coates. If you're interested, let's talk.*

Selby sat drumming his fingers on the desk. He wanted to

know what Ratliffe had found, but he was having second thoughts about involving the other man in his search. The incident with Chioke Okorie had rattled him badly, and he didn't want anybody else getting too close to what was happening.

Chioke came home on Sunday night. Selby heard him out in the hall talking with Rita. The conversation was just a conversation, no cursing or shouting. Chioke sounded contrite but otherwise perfectly normal. They moved inside their apartment, and Selby heard nothing more from them.

I did what I did, and everything seems to be okay, Selby thought. Maybe I even prevented further violence. Which still doesn't justify my carelessness, but I've got to get over myself and move on. I don't have the attention span to keep up all this sturm und drang *for so long.*

Selby looked over at Pancake, who was on the bookcase, growling at the pigeons. Pancake was right: it was time to get back to work. He picked up his ten-year-old flip phone and called Barry Ratliffe.

The schoolteacher had information, he told Selby. He was still waiting for a couple of details, which should be available Wednesday or Thursday.

"I have more free time on the weekends," Ratliffe told him. "Why don't we meet somewhere on Saturday? Or better yet, I'll come get you. We can visit the location that I found."

"Location for what? Of what?"

"Don't want to spoil the surprise, right? How about Saturday, first thing? Say, nine o'clock?"

Selby was grateful for the delay, as it would give him time to resolve his issues and indecision before addressing whatever Ratliffe had to tell him. He felt that—as usual—someone else was usurping his control of the situation.

"I don't want to involve you any more than necessary," he said.

Ratliffe chuckled. "It's a trade-off. I've got information you need, and you've got a puzzle I want to help you solve. You in or out?"

Selby blew out his cheeks. "Fine. Saturday at nine." He gave Ratliffe his address and directions.

"Got it. That's the Highlander, right? The building they used to call the Highdiver because of all the people who jumped out of the windows?"

"Only three."

"Say again?"

"Only three people jumped out of the windows, and that was over a period of many years," Selby said. "The record is not that much worse than any tall building. The building just got an unwarranted amount of press."

Selby didn't mention that one of the windows that had provided the gateway to the afterlife was his: Marilyn McCullough, aged 71, fell out backward in 1972, striking the building twice on the way down and then landing in the tiny lawn to the left of the front entrance. Selby had used that information to talk down the price of the apartment when he bought it.

Defenestration. Selby loved that word.

Ratliffe laughed. "How about I meet you out front? Ground level."

"That'll be fine. I'll see you on Saturday."

The door to the Empty Room unlocked on Tuesday while Selby was washing his breakfast dishes. The abrupt release of tension in his mind startled him so badly that he shattered a water glass and had to spend ten minutes picking the pieces out of the sink.

One piece, then another, then another. Carefully, methodically, Selby collected the fragments and dropped them into a bowl. The big pieces were no problem; they were large and easy to grasp. The small pieces were more challenging, harder to see.

He pricked his finger on one and grimaced.

I wanted the Empty Room to go away, and it did, and I was miserable. Now it's back, and I'm rattled by that, too. Just can't please some people.

Picking up the pieces and putting them in the bowl. One by one. When he thought he had them all, he ran water into the sink, flushing away any tiny bits that he might have missed. He dumped the fragments into a baggie and put the bag into the trash. When he had rinsed the bowl and set it into the drainer, he stood leaning on the edge of the sink.

After everything that had happened—to him, to the people near him—he still didn't know what the point was. What his role was. He was so ordinary. How did somebody as unexceptional as Selby Coates end up in the middle of all this craziness? *This one will do*, the whispers said at his birth. Do *what*?

Selby tidied up the kitchen, ran the sweeper over the floor, picked up a book he had left next to the comfortable chair, and placed it on the desk with the edges of the book and the desk carefully aligned.

I need to think. I need to stop letting events drag me along like a banged-up suitcase packed full of useless crap. I've got to start acting like an intelligent human being.

He looked out at Zeus, his brass backside glossy and resolute under a dreary gray drizzle.

"I have got to get out from under this cloud," Selby said aloud. "Am I a man or a mouse?" Pancake jumped up onto the bookcase and arched his back, demanding attention.

"You're right. This is no place for a mouse."

He scratched the cat behind the ears and went to get his rain coat.

Selby sat on the "quaint" bench in the rain and gazed out over the meadows and woods of Redmon Park. Water dripped from the hood of his raincoat, a fragile curtain screening him from the world outside. The landscape had moved from autumn to winter, and leafless trees etched fractal diagrams against a soft gray sky. Only two crows were abroad, dismantling something in the grass beyond the foot of the hill, a dead chipmunk or a chunk of bread they had brought from elsewhere. Selby found the scene relaxing, although he was disturbed to find that he couldn't think of an appropriate movie reference.

Breathe. One breath, in and out. Another, in and out. Breathe.

Selby relaxed, listening to the rain pattering against his hood, the crows murmuring and clacking at one another, the remote hiss of traffic outside the park.

One by one, he shut each input down: the rain, the crows, the traffic, even the chill that rose from the ground beneath his bench. He turned his attention inward.

Whispers. The voices in the Empty Room represented more than speech. He had been thinking about this a lot since the incident with Chioke. The Empty Room was full, crowded with fragments of identity and personality. Minds broken into small pieces and shuffled together, no longer coherent enough to do much more than hiss and mutter, coalescing for a moment, then drifting apart. The Empty Room had opened at the moment of his birth; the whispers had spoken to his mother as he was drawing his first breath.

Selby understood that the room wasn't a *room,* not really; it was the idea of something separated from something else by a conceptual barrier. With an effort, he could breach that barrier and peek inside.

Hello.

The whispers swirled, drawing back in something akin to distaste or perhaps derision.

What is this place?

Amusement.

Topos hyperuranios, a voice breathed.

Mshunia Kushta, another offered.

Gnosis.

Hekhalot.

The world outside the cave.

A current of voiceless laughter drifted past his awareness. The voices were playing with him. Teasing him with incomprehensible answers.

A prison. This voice scattered the others, stifling amusement. *You won't learn anything here.*

Selby recoiled from the flatness of this voice, a whisper that had never laughed, never raged, never wept. A voice that only existed in this non-place. The unheard voice of a milk-glass goddess, static and cold.

Where, then, Doma? If not here, where?

The air itself was a soup of meanings out of which ideas could evolve, inhabited by pockets of intellect that drifted and poked and manipulated those ideas, creating and dissolving. They were here, these entities, and yet they were elsewhere, too, in many places, all at the same time. They were of a nature that was so alien to his own that he could never hope to perceive more than a minute fraction of the whole, let alone understand what it was he saw. Were there answers here to the questions he was struggling with?

You will play your part. You will not be allowed to interfere.

Selby could have wept with frustration, and his frustration, in turn, made him irritable.

Play what part? Interfere with what? Could you possibly be any more cryptic? You're worse than Laylah.

Selby's eyes snapped open when a crash of thunder startled him out of a doze. He found that water had seeped under the skirts of his raincoat and soaked the back of his pants. The Empty Room remained open. Remained empty. The rain continued, unconcerned.

Selby showered and dressed and saw to Pancake's various needs, then organized ingredients for pasta Alfredo. He was putting water on for the fettuccine when he heard a shy tapping at the door.

That can only be Rita.

He took a few deep breaths, his guilt galloping back to the fore. He opened the door.

"Hello, Rita. Please come in."

"I can't stay, Mr. Coates." She smiled. "Chioke is trying to put Mari and Jonas to bed, and that never ends well." Rita held up a dish. "We want to thank you for your kindness the other night. I made you a date cake. It is Chioke's favorite."

Selby blushed. "You didn't have to do that."

"No, but I wanted to."

Selby took the plate. The cake was a dense brown disk glossy with syrup and topped with coconut. It looked and smelled delicious.

"Thank you," he said. "How is Chioke?"

Rita glanced back toward her apartment. "He is much better. He stayed with friends until Sunday, and he was still very quiet after he came home, but today he is more himself. He is more easy, I think. Maybe he has talked to his partners, and they are working out their business problems. He was much calmed by his conversation with you."

Conversation? Selby thought, but he just nodded. "I'm sure everything will be fine."

The sound of children shrieking and giggling drifted down the hall, and Rita sighed. "I must go. He will get them all excited, and no one will sleep tonight."

"I understand. Thank you for the cake. It looks delicious."

After dinner, Selby selected a movie, something mindless but entertaining. He cut himself a generous wedge of date cake and disposed himself in his comfortable chair.

So Chioke had been subdued but not damaged by what

Selby did to him. Rita was no more capable of lying than Selby was, so if she said everything was back to normal, it probably was. Would there be permanent effects? Selby had no way of knowing, but at least he could let go of the worst of his guilt. Not all of it, but enough that he didn't feel the need to keep flagellating himself over the incident.

No more incidents, he thought.

He could not pretend that the Empty Room didn't exist, but he could be a lot more careful with how he interacted with it.

No more letting fear trigger my actions.

Selby ate cake while he watched smug, pointy-nosed Nyah, the *Devil Girl from Mars*, stalk the English countryside looking for men to take home to help repopulate her dying world. Oddly enough, no one seemed eager to become a mind-controlled zombie stud, and the Devil Girl had to get uppity.

No more dangerous stunts.

Despite Nyah's robot and ray gun, plain old human stubbornness and duplicity won out in the end. As Selby licked date syrup off his fork, the Devil Girl's flying saucer went up in a remarkably unconvincing explosion.

No more mistakes.

. . .

Fiona's Baby Diary:
Dire doings around here these days. Mitch and Ruth are staying in Buckley for a couple of weeks, all very mysterious. Bongo's been going over and taking care of the animals and checking on things while they're away. This is unusual for them, but I guess when you live on a farm in the middle of nowhere, you do your vacations in the city. I went to the farm with Bongo yesterday and brought the baby. He was absolutely fascinated by the chickens, which scare me, but wasn't all that interested in the cows, which I adore. Go figure!

CHAPTER SEVENTEEN

Selby traveled in private automobiles so rarely that he always found himself behaving like a fidgety child, touching the dashboard, adjusting the vents, and fiddling with his seat belt. Barry Ratliffe's somewhat elderly Rav 4 mini-SUV was remarkably neat inside, although Selby would have dusted the dashboard more thoroughly and not allowed chewing gum wrappers to accumulate in the cupholder.

"When I got off duty that day," Ratliffe said as he worked his way around to 15th Avenue, heading west, "I went back to the clinic. I was curious how the whole Ruth Coates thing had played out. As it happened, she was still there, sitting out front on a covered bench with a hospital mask on. This was pre-COVID, mind you, so the mask was a little weird but not crazy, seeing as we were at a medical facility. I went in to chat with the assistant at the desk, and a car pulled up, a brand-new Subaru, and Ruth got in."

"What did the driver look like?"

"No idea. Just a guy. Fleecy coat, John Deere cap. He was about as generic for Mary's Gap as you could get. I'd say two-thirds of the population of that area look just like him."

Ratliffe tapped his horn a couple of times to warn off a red Ford Ranger with no taillights and a black passenger side door that was veering into his lane.

"Fuckwad. Anyway, the Subaru pulled around to leave, and I grabbed an appointment card off the desk and jotted down the license plate number. I stuck the card in my notes."

"And you still have it?"

"I do, indeed."

"Were you able to find out whose car it was from the tag number?"

"Yep. The green Subaru that came and collected Ruth Sullivan Coates from the doc-in-a-box in Mary's Gap was—and still is—registered to a company called Unified Global Logistics Consulting. UGLC has its headquarters, as you might imagine from the name, in the Intermodal Transport District, and that's where we're headed now."

Selby squinted out into the traffic. The headlights reflecting on wet pavements made it appear that cars and trucks were driving on top of each other. His inability to sort those visual impressions reliably was one of the reasons he did not drive.

"So we don't actually have a lead on Ruth, but only on the man who picked her up. Maybe not even him, but rather the company he worked for six years ago."

"Oh, ye of little faith," Ratliffe said. "Unified Global, etc., has a website. On that website, the company lists its officers. One of those officers is R. S. Coates, Director of International Development."

Selby's expression cleared, and his ears warmed. "You're a genius."

"I'm a guy who deals with kids all day. You've got to have some basic internet skills, or they think you don't know your ass from your elbow."

"I should have thought of that myself. I've been getting lazy."

"Maybe you've been distracted."

Selby looked over at Ratliffe, unsure as to how much the other man knew about Selby's adventures. He hadn't told him about the cultists' peculiar abilities or about Laylah and Doma. He had certainly said nothing about his own death and resurrection. He had, however, repeated the story Roy had told him about the return of the fake utility man, an episode that was keeping him up at night. Reggie had dealt with the problem quickly and efficiently, but what about next time?

"I worry about people getting caught up in my problems," Selby said. "Sometimes that becomes a preoccupation."

"I spend all day in a classroom full of eighth-graders, so I've seen the true face of terror. I also served in Iraq, which wasn't nearly as bad but still pretty tough going. I'm not all that easy to intimidate."

I have seen and done some strange and terrible things, the Colonel had said.

"I can't be responsible for somebody other than myself," Selby said, reluctantly exposing the core of the issue. "I don't want to be the reason someone else suffers. I can't keep people safe or keep my problems from hurting them."

"Maybe nobody's asking you to. We're all grownups here. You're not my daddy, and I don't expect you to look after me."

In the distance, cranes and winches reared up like titanic praying mantises, freed from the ice that had trapped them for millions of years, stalking the riverfront from the bottom of the locks all the way to the walls and fences of posh Bluff Park, searching for prey, for shelter, for mates. Maybe just looking around for some high-tension power lines to knock over.

Barry Ratliffe was not easy to intimidate—or so he said—but he intimidated Selby Coates. Ratliffe was a head taller than Selby, with a way of moving that made Selby think of springs and wires. He was affable and pleasant, and Selby didn't know how to talk to him.

I'm out of the habit of people, Selby thought. *When did that happen?*

Ratliffe turned onto a side street before the car came within reach of the riverfront monsters.

"It's along here," he said, slowing. They were passing into

an area of fairly modern glass-and-brick office buildings, with carefully landscaped parking lots and tasteful signage surrounded by dwarf evergreens. "This is all pretty upscale. Your sister does well for herself."

"Half-sister."

"Right, half-sister."

They drove another hundred yards, and Ratliffe pointed. "There it is."

The offices of Unified Global Logistics Consulting occupied one of the smaller buildings in the area, a compact three-story L-shaped structure built around two sides of a courtyard of evergreens and Japanese maples. Ratliffe parked the car, and the two men sat looking at the building.

"Well? What's the plan, boss?"

Selby blew out his cheeks. "I go in. I ask for Ruth Coates. If necessary, I tell them I'm her brother. See what happens from there."

Ratliffe nodded. "I guess that's a plan. It's Saturday morning. Are you sure she's in there?"

"Yes. I don't know why I think that, but I do."

Ratliffe accepted that assertion with a shrug. "Okay. The rain's stopped. Do you want me to come in with you, or would you rather I lurked outside in the shrubbery?"

"Lurking might be best. You're more intimidating than I am. No security guard is ever going to look at me and pull the red handle, but you look like somebody who might have dealt with middle schoolers and have combat skills."

There were not one but two security guards on duty in the small lobby, both male, both stocky, and neither much taller than Selby. One was young, around thirty, with a shaven head and tattoos creeping out from under his collar and cuffs. The other was ten years older and had thinning blond hair. The older man had a sour expression, the sort of person who would never eat any food he hadn't already become accustomed to by age five. Neither guard was as pretty as DeQuinn Pitts, but neither looked like he might turn rabid at any moment. Selby limped up to the desk.

"My name is Selby Coates. I'd like to see Ruth Coates."

"Do you have an appointment, Mr. Coates?"

The tattooed man had a voice like chocolate syrup, warm and rich. Selby's ears heated up, and he stood blinking for a moment before finally saying, "No, but I'm her brother. Well, half-brother. We share a father. If you'll let her know I'm here, I'm sure she'll see me."

Pull yourself together, Selby.

"Ms. Coates doesn't usually see anyone without an appointment, but I'll call upstairs."

"Thank you."

Selby stood with his hands clasped behind his back, rocking back and forth onto his heels, looking around.

The guards' desk was in the middle of the lobby; beyond it was a pair of elevators. Hallways ran to left and right. Low sofas rested beneath enormous abstract paintings that suggested oceans, islands, and high, white clouds. Everything was cool, impersonal, generic.

"Mr. Coates? Ms. Coates will be right down."

When the elevator disgorged Ruth Coates, Selby wasn't surprised to see the woman from the bus station. She also fit Roy's description of the woman who visited the Circle Tavern asking about Selby. She didn't appear to be wearing makeup, and her haircut looked as though it might have been self-inflicted, but her dove-gray pantsuit was immaculate, beautifully tailored, and her pearl earrings and choker looked to be of good quality. Ruth Coates made Selby think of a farmer's wife who had won big on the lottery.

"Ruth Coates? I'm Selby Coates. We've met after a fashion, but we've never actually been introduced."

"I know who you are. Why are you here?"

Selby breathed, in and out, in and out, trying not to fidget or allow his voice to wobble. The Empty Room was hushed, attentive.

"You have gone to considerable effort to intrude into my life. I thought we should at least meet face to face."

"We have nothing to say to one another, Mr. Coates."

"That's odd. I was told you were looking for me. I assume that was why you were stalking me at the bus terminal, why you showed up asking for me at the Circle Tavern, why you sent someone to break into my home—"

"He didn't break in. The door was unlocked."

Selby stared at her, brought up short, his eyes round as silver dollars behind his glasses. A radiating pattern of fine wrinkles surrounded Ruth's lips. Regular dots, puncture scars, were embedded in those wrinkles, marching all the way around her mouth.

She glanced over at the security guards and led Selby to a sofa on the far side of the room. Indicating that Selby should sit, she perched on an awkward-looking chair across from him.

"You've been making a nuisance of yourself," she said.

"Are you offering that as an explanation for your behavior? If so, I'm afraid you're going to have to flesh it out a bit."

Ruth's thin lips grew even thinner. "Why did you come here?" she said, squeezing the words through a hard, narrow slot.

"Are you my sister?"

"No, I am not."

Selby grimaced. "Half-sister, then, if you want to be pedantic."

"I'm not even your half-sister, Mr. Coates. We are not related in any way."

Selby blew out his cheeks. "Your name," he said. "Sullivan Coates was my father. And my mother's name is Naomi. Naomi and Ruth?"

"Sullivan Coates was also my mother's husband for a time," Ruth said. "Mother married Sullivan Coates when I was ten months old. She changed my name to match his, to spite my biological father. Whatever point you're trying to make about my given name and your mother's is just a coincidence. You and I don't share blood, Mr. Coates."

Selby sat back, staring at her, round-eyed. He had assumed that Ruth Coates's interest in him had something to do with a shared relationship, but if she was telling the truth, then this was not the case.

Ruth Coates had a face made for anger. Her lips could pinch down to a horizontal line in a moment, and the grooves on either side of her nose deepened with her emotions. Three vertical lines were carved between her eyebrows, a permanent frown. It was a highly expressive face, even if it could only express one mood. For all that, she seemed to resist any display of emotion. It was as if she were struggling to look impassive. Blank. Expressionless. Who did that remind him of?

"Oh!" Selby said after an awkward moment. "Doma. How stupid of me not to have seen that. The lip thing should have told me immediately. You aren't interested in me or my activities because you and I are related. You're working for Doma. Like me, you're a pawn of the Weird Sisters."

"I am not a pawn!" Ruth spat. The guards looked over, and the one with the velvet voice stood up.

"Ms. Coates?"

"It's nothing, Jason. As you were."

Selby blinked. Did people really say "as you were"? Apparently, Ruth Coates did. The guards settled back down to whatever it was they had been doing.

"I work for Doma because I believe in her," Ruth said. "Without her, I'd be a farmer's wife with manure on my shoes, drowning in boredom. She has given me this job, this life. I owe her *everything*."

"I believe in her, too, but I don't scramble to do her bidding. In fact, I try to avoid her as much as possible."

"Because you're a fool."

"Says the woman who used to run around with her lips sewn up." Selby calmed himself, counting his breaths. *In and out. In and out.*

Ruth stood, straightening her jacket and shooting her cuffs. "We have nothing to say to one another, and I have work to do."

Selby stared up at her, his hands gripping each other in his lap, whispers rushing to and fro in his ears. He started to speak, cleared his throat, started again.

"You're wrong, Ruth. You are a pawn, and we have a great deal to say to one another." Selby was shocked by the way that statement came out. He didn't usually talk to people like that.

But I'm not usually so angry.

"Leave now, Mr. Coates, or I will have the guards remove you."

Selby's conscience had been wrestling with his need to learn more about this annoying woman and her connection to the events in his life, but her threat resolved that struggle.

He reached into the Empty Room.

The whispers were agitated, uneasy. Selby was reminded of the behavior of the crows at Redmon Park during his confrontation with Doma. He looked at Ruth, at her anger and her hostility, and he let the Empty Room breathe through him.

"I'd like to see what you do," he said mildly, his eyes innocent and round. "I'm sure it's fascinating."

Something moved in the Empty Room, like whales swimming past a boat under the surface of the water, but Selby encountered no resistance, no backlash. The turbulent air of the Room rushed out, swirled around the woman in front of him, and was gone.

Ruth Coates took in a deep breath, held it for a moment, then released it through her nose. Her eyes betrayed a shadowy per-plexity, but she turned and headed for the elevators. "Fine. Come with me."

Selby climbed to his feet, the pain he felt in his knee from the episode with Doma in the park easing the guilt he felt for us-ing the Empty Room to manipulate another person. *I'll feel guilty later*, he told himself. *For now, this woman is the only lead I have, so I've got to use the tools that are available to me.*

As he followed Ruth Coates onto the elevator, he shook his head. *I'm reduced to sophistry. This had better be worth it.*

Ruth's third-floor office was not large, but, like the lobby below, it was furnished in exquisite—and utterly lifeless—taste. One wall was all windows, looking out over the courtyard, where presumably Barry Ratliffe was doing his lurking. A glass-topped desk sat in front of the windows, facing away from them, refusing the view. In front of the desk sat two blocky, low-backed chairs, furniture of the kind designed more for vis-ual appeal than for comfort.

Ruth moved behind the desk and slid into an expensive-looking desk chair. *Her* throne, Selby noted, was designed for both visual appeal *and* comfort.

Selby looked around the office and gestured at an enormous map of the world that completely covered one wall. Magnetic markers in various colors were attached to the map. He waved toward the map.

"Your activities?"

Ruth took a breath through her nose. "The company's activ-ities. When I find potential new clients, I make the initial assess-ment of their needs and of the companies we work with who might be able to meet those needs. Our clients are all over the world, naturally. We help them get products and services from one place to another."

Selby nodded, impressed in spite of himself. "That must be

a demanding job. Do you have to travel to all those places?"

Ruth shrugged. "Not so much these days. Online interactions are usually enough, and I can do more from here than from a hotel room in Singapore or Saigon or wherever."

Ruth's voice and manner were flat, deadened, stripped of the suppressed rage she had shown previously. Selby wondered what the Empty Room had taken from her.

"You seem far too connected, far too consequential, to be the kind of person who blindly follows an exotic religion."

Some of the woman's fire flared up briefly, but the necessary emotional oxygen was lacking, so it quickly died back down.

"I don't do anything blindly. I told you. The Silence has helped me get to where I am today. Doma guided me to fulfilling my true potential. If I'm connected and consequential, it's because of my service to Her."

Selby winced. Intense religious feeling was something he didn't understand, and what he didn't understand made him uneasy. Unanswered questions were holes through which chaos leaked into his universe.

"How does Sullivan Coates fit into all this?"

Ruth flapped one stubby hand. "He has nothing to do with this company."

"But if you're not his daughter, and he has nothing to do with your work, why are you interested in him at all? Why come into my home and vandalize a photograph of a man who means nothing to you?"

Ruth's hard eyes narrowed. "You need to leave him alone. He is under Doma's protection."

"He's my father."

"A man you haven't laid eyes upon in fifty years? How often do you even think about him?"

She had a point. Had Doma and Laylah not called his attention to Sullivan, Selby would have been perfectly content to leave him in the obscurity into which he had vanished all those years ago. "You're right," he said after a moment. "He would have to be an old man by now. I suppose I've assumed he was dead."

"They often do."

That was a remark worthy of Laylah. Selby was tired of strange women saying things that made no sense. He started to ask what she meant, but stopped himself. That was just another rabbit hole, and he needed to stay focused.

"He's my father. It's true that I haven't laid eyes on him in decades, but he's clearly central to whatever it is you're up to, and that's affecting my life. If you and yours hadn't gotten so pushy and weird, I would never have given Sullivan Coates another thought. Now I can see that until I get to the bottom of the Sullivan Coates mystery, I'm never going to get you people out of my life."

"Your *borrowed* life," Ruth said, her voice regaining some of its edge.

Selby blinked. He looked at her, owl-eyed, his ears hot. She seemed to know an awful lot. "If you like. My borrowed life. Although I don't see what that has to do with anything."

Selby could see that Ruth's apathy was fading, and her baseline anger was bubbling back into the foreground.

"Where is Sullivan Coates?" he asked quickly.

"Living his life," Ruth replied.

"Where?"

"None of your business." She leaned forward, her elbows on the desk. "The Silence has watched over the man you know as Sullivan Coates for lifetimes. The Goddess intends to right a cosmic injustice. You are interfering."

This was more than Selby knew how to process. While he sat blinking at her, Ruth Coates stood up and pressed a button on a console on her desk.

"Jason, would one of you please come up to my office? Mr.

Coates is ready to leave."

Selby nodded slowly and climbed to his feet. "It has been interesting to finally meet you, Ms. Coates," he said. "Will you stay out of my life from here on out?"

"I will do what I must to carry out the wishes of my Goddess."

That was a stock non-answer right out of a bad movie, and Selby Coates was an expert on bad movies.

"Then I'll do whatever it takes to keep you and yours from screwing around with me and the people I care about," he said.

There was a knock at the door, and the dyspeptic blond security guard stuck his head in.

"Ma'am?"

"Joe, Mr. Coates is leaving now. Please show him the way out."

"Yes, ma'am."

For a mad moment, Selby considered offering to shake hands with Ruth, but the set of her mouth was not encouraging. With a smile, he turned to the security guard.

"Thank you, Joe. It's been so long since I've been in a place like this. I get lost."

Joe glanced at Ruth, then waved Selby ahead of him. "We'll look after you, sir."

Selby glanced back as Joe closed the door. Ruth stood motionless behind the desk, silhouetted against the light from the windows. He could see nothing of her expression.

Upon reflection, he thought that was probably for the best.

When Selby and Joe stepped off the elevator, they found Ratliffe standing at the guard kiosk chatting comfortably with silver-tongued Jason.

"There you are," he said as Selby walked up. "Jason here went to the school where I teach. He was there before my time, but it sounds like nothing much has changed since then."

Joe slipped behind the desk, and Ratliffe turned to Selby. "Business all transacted?"

Selby nodded. Ratliffe shook Jason's hand and led Selby back out to the car.

The rain had ceased, leaving the landscape shiny and cold. Selby took hold of the passenger door handle but then stood without moving, looking back toward the building. Ratliffe waited on the other side of the car.

A silver Audi pulled in a few spaces over from where they were parked, and two men got out. The driver was tall, fit-looking, wearing a charcoal-gray suit and a silver-gray tie that matched the color of the car and of his hair. The other man was shorter, no taller than Selby, shapeless in rough jeans and work boots, with a puffy blue jacket and a green John Deere cap. The shorter man glanced over at Ratliffe and Selby but showed no interest, and they walked inside, talking quietly.

"Anything else you need to do here?" Ratliffe asked.

"Sorry? No, we're finished. I zoned out for a second."

Selby had made eye contact with the shorter of the two men for an instant, and something surged inside the Empty Room, but the moment passed without further disturbances.

"It's coming up on eleven-thirty," Ratliffe announced as they pulled into the casual Saturday morning traffic. "Do you want to get something to eat?"

Selby blinked. "I usually eat lunch about this time."

"I mean, together. You and me across a table from each other, eating a meal while we tell each other what we learned in that place we just left."

"Oh." Selby knew his social skills—always somewhat rudimentary—had deteriorated during the past year, but he was surprised at how stupid he sounded. "Yes, that would be nice. Are you familiar with the Circle Tavern in Fallwood? Near my apartment?"

"Across from the Tower? Used to be a super-sketchy biker

bar?"

"Yes. It's under new management now. I go there a lot."

"Sounds good to me."

As they headed back toward Selby's home turf, Ratliffe tapped the dashboard to get Selby's attention.

"So, are you going to tell me anything about what went on in there? I have news to trade if that helps."

"I'm still sorting out the whole Ruth Coates connection," Selby said. "Are you sure you want to get any deeper into this?"

Ratliffe scoffed. "Let me tell you why I was so surprised to hear from you," he said. He recounted his dream at the dog park, the little girl and her sock monkey.

Selby stopped fiddling with things on the dashboard.

"The monkey. What did it look like?"

"What?"

"The *monkey*. The sock monkey. Describe it. Please."

Ratliffe negotiated a turn, then shrugged. "Black, kind of faded. Not a normal sock monkey face."

"A molded plastic face that was stitched onto the head. Kind of psychotic?"

Ratliffe said nothing for a minute, then glanced over at his passenger. "Holy shit. How did you know that?"

"Did the little girl say the monkey's name?"

"Oh, yeah. She made a point of it. It was—"

"Daisy."

Another long silence, then, "Yeah. It was Daisy."

"What did the little girl look like?"

"Dark hair, tan skin. I thought she might belong to an Afghan family that moved into the neighborhood a few years ago."

"Her eyes. They were unusual, weren't they? I'm sure you noticed. Describe them."

Ratliffe took a deep breath, then released it noisily, glancing over at his passenger.

"Kind of green and yellow and brown all mixed up together. The reason I thought about her maybe belonging to one of the Afghan families was because of that magazine cover from decades ago, with the Afghan girl."

Selby nodded. They had already crossed that bridge. Barry Ratliffe was involved.

"Let's get to the Tavern, and I'll tell you a story."

CHAPTER EIGHTEEN

"Man! Has this place changed!" Ratliffe said, looking around as the two men slid onto stools at the bar. Roy brought Ratliffe a menu and Selby a beer, and Ratliffe hiked an eyebrow. "I guess you're a regular."

Selby blushed. "I do come here a lot."

"But you don't," Roy observed, reaching across the bar to shake Ratliffe's hand. "Royal Freeborn. I'm the owner. Call me Roy."

"Barry Ratliffe. Pleased to meet you. I came in here a couple of times back when it was still Bomber Boys."

Roy scoffed. "If you were expecting that bunch of lard-butt, drunk-ass biker dudes, you're gonna be disappointed."

"Not at all. Last time I was in this place, I ended up in the emergency room. Change is good."

Roy winked at Selby while addressing Ratliffe. "You could still end up in the emergency room. You haven't tried our food yet. What are you drinking?"

"Do you have sweet iced tea?"

"Honey, I'm from North Carolina."

"Sweet iced tea, please."

Roy poured a glass of iced tea from a pitcher dripping with condensation and took Ratliffe's sandwich order.

"I like Roy. Pronouns?" Ratliffe asked as Roy slipped away to seat a fresh batch of customers.

"What?"

"What does Roy prefer in the way of pronouns?"

"Oh. Um, 'she' and 'her' and so on. Feminine." He glanced over at Roy where she stood talking to a trio of Botox Babes who were struggling to place a drinks order through paralyzed facial muscles. He tried to imagine what Ratliffe saw. "I guess I never thought about it." Roy was in her "basic" costume, a black catsuit with pleather insets at the shoulders and down the outsides of the legs. A belt of square silver links rode low on her narrow hips, and she wore a silver comb in her hair. Her lipstick and eye shadow were dove gray. "She's just Roy."

"I try to keep up," Ratliffe said. "My wife used to tell me I was a dinosaur, all loaded up with old ideas and regressive social practices. Since she died, I've been working to change that."

Selby nodded and took another sip of his beer. "It's hard to keep up sometimes." *Evolve or die.*

Ratliffe tasted the tea and nodded approval.

"So," he said. "Selby Coates. You knew stuff about my dream."

"Yes."

Ratliffe rolled his eyes. "One-word answers ain't gonna cut it, pal. I never told a soul about that dream. How did you know about the monkey and the little girl's eyes?"

"I dragged Daisy around everywhere until I was three and slept with her on my bed until I was eight," Selby said, blushing into his beer. "I knew about the girl's eyes because … because that's an entity that calls herself, itself—whatever—Laylah." He took a deep breath. "Laylah brought me back to life after I was struck and killed by a bus a while ago, and she has been popping up in my dreams from time to time since." He took a sip of his beer. "I think that's the only way she can communicate with living people."

Roy had returned behind the bar in time to hear part of this, and she stood watching as Ratliffe took it all in.

"Okay. Maybe I was better off with the one-word answers," the schoolteacher said.

Roy laughed and went on about her business.

"I wouldn't expect you to believe it," Selby said. "I don't believe a lot of it, and it's happening to me."

Ratliffe frowned slightly, nodding. "My first instinct is to blow the whole thing off as a hot pile of bullshit. On the other hand, my life is not terribly interesting these days, and it sounds to me like yours is."

Roy reached over with the pitcher and topped up Ratliffe's tea. "Stick with Coates. The interesting stuff follows him around like a stray dog. A bitey one, with fleas."

Ratliffe looked at her, then at Selby, who blushed.

"Roy knows all or most of the story," Selby said.

"And you buy it?" Ratliffe asked her.

Roy put down the pitcher and wiped up a few dribbles of condensation that had landed on the bar.

"Yeah. I buy it. Coates is a smart guy and all that, but he can't lie worth shit. If he says something's true, then it is."

"He could believe it himself, even though it's completely nutso."

"Sure. How long have you known him?"

"Since this morning."

Roy grinned. "Give it time. You'll see."

Roy took their food orders and tapped them into the pad, then went to wait on other customers.

Selby found the whole conversation going back and forth past him as though he wasn't even there intensely irritating, but he said nothing. He waited, sipping his beer and trying to make out the labels on the premium liquor bottles lined up on a shelf next to the service window.

"I used to read your stuff in the Herald-Star," Ratliffe said after a time. "Back when there was still a daily print edition. It was well-researched and well-written. Sometimes it reminded me of my tenth-grade Grammar and Comp teacher, Mrs. Abercrombie. She'd have loved you."

Selby's ears pinked. "I've been told my writing is 'courtly.'"

"Yeah, I think that's a good word. Old-fashioned. I always felt like I could accept whatever you wrote at face value. You didn't go in for hyperbole or unsubstantiated information."

Selby grimaced. "Hyperbole is for carnival barkers, not for responsible journalism." As soon as the words left his mouth, he knew he sounded exactly like an elderly high school English teacher.

"I agree. I'm not saying all that to piss you off or to criticize your work. I want you and me both to understand why I'm prepared to listen to whatever you've got to tell me—and maybe even believe some of it."

An hour later, Selby stood in the bathroom splashing water in his face and struggling not to upchuck spicy baked tofu and avocado.

He had known Barry Ratliffe for a single morning, and he had poured out his entire saga, from the bus accident to this morning's meeting with Ruth Coates. The acolytes, Owen Mosley and the moths, Doma, the dreams, the Colonel … everything. What had he been thinking? There were aspects of those events that he hadn't even shared with Roy. The only person who wouldn't think Selby was out of his mind was someone who was even crazier.

Breathe, Selby. In and out. In and out.

He looked at the man in the mirror and made a face at him. Without his glasses, his face dripping, he looked like a wrinkled child caught in the rain.

He dried his face, put his glasses back on, disciplined his breathing, straightened his collar, and walked out of the bathroom.

Selby had hoped that Ratliffe might have disappeared while he was indisposed, but instead, he found Roy and the school-teacher in relaxed conversation. They looked up as he emerged.

"Lookin' a little green, there, Coates," Roy said. "You okay?" She filled a glass with water and slid it over the bar. Her tone was light, but her concern was real.

"I'm fine. Just …" *Grampa's off his meds*. He looked at Ratliffe, then away. "Talking about all this. Hearing myself lay-ing it all out like that, telling everything to a complete stranger. I sound like a demented old man."

"I'm hardly a complete stranger," Ratliffe pointed out. "We've talked on the phone twice, and we've been hanging out together since nine o'clock this morning. We're practically bros. Look, I'm not laughing at you, okay?"

"Why not?"

Ratliffe finished his sandwich and handed the plate to Roy.

"Let's say I'm currently predisposed to believe impossible things. That dream in the park, meeting Ruth Coates out in the boondocks back in the day, rethinking my life the way I have been lately. I'm willing to give you the benefit of the doubt." Roy topped off his tea, and he thanked her. "By the way, our pal Jason, the security guard at Unified Global, let slip that Ruth's husband was spending the morning in court after having been arrested for misdemeanor burglary of a residence about a week ago. Mitchell Coffey is the husband's name."

"Why didn't you mention this before?"

"I've been busy processing your info dump, Coates. Bur-glary seemed like pretty small potatoes by comparison."

Selby acknowledged this with a nod. "Sorry. It seems likely that the man who picked her up at the clinic is the same as the man Reggie knocked down with the Buddha."

"What do you bet that's the guy we saw at UGLC? Stumpy guy in casual clothes who arrived with Mr. Sharkskin?"

"I didn't think of that. I suppose the other man could have

been a lawyer."

"In that suit? Definitely a lawyer. That, or a narco kingpin. I'm going with lawyer."

Ratliffe finished his tea and crunched an ice cube. Selby flinched at the sound, touching his teeth with his tongue as if to confirm their safety.

"So what's next?" Ratliffe said around a mouthful of ice.

"I don't know, frankly. I need to sort out all the stuff we've learned."

Roy waved the tea pitcher in their direction, but Ratliffe shook his head. Outside, the rain had resumed, heavy and slow. Cars *shoosh*ed by on the wet pavements, headlights glittering in the shrouded afternoon light.

Ratliffe stretched, then twisted to look out the window.

"It's ugly out there. Can I give you a lift home?"

By reflex, Selby started to say no, then reconsidered. "Thank you. I'd appreciate that."

Selby paid for lunch, waving away Ratliffe's effort to pay for his own, and the two men said goodbye to Roy and hustled out to the parking lot.

In front of the Highlander, Selby checked his pockets to make sure he had everything he had left home with.

"Call me when you've got a next step mapped out," Ratliffe said.

"You're sure?"

"I'm a big boy. I've seen some things. I might even be useful. I definitely need to get out more."

Selby nodded. "Thank you. I'd better get inside. It's feeding time."

Ratliffe laughed. "Yeah, Moby's probably chewing up the sofa by now. What kind of dog do you have?"

"I don't have a dog. I have a cat."

"Oh. Somehow, I had you pegged as a dog person. Something small and a little mean. Maybe a Chihuahua."

Selby thought of Bolívar and shuddered. "No. Definitely not a Chihuahua."

In the evening, home and dry in his tenth-floor aerie, Selby assembled the ingredients for a quick stir-fry, occasionally dropping a sliver of water chestnut or a matchstick of carrot onto Pancake's dish. The day spent with Ratliffe had left him feeling disordered and jumpy, and he wondered why.

I feel like that gangster in Beast from Haunted Cave, *shopping for a henchman.*

He gave Pancake a morsel of marinated tofu. The cat sniffed at it, then pantomimed burying it. Selby picked up the offending treat and dropped it into the garbage disposal.

Except we're not buried in snow, and there are no giant spider monsters lurking offstage.

Selby crunched a piece of carrot, frowning.

At least, not yet, anyway.

How long had it been since Selby made a new friend? Mary-Louise at the grocery store, that was last summer. And Selby wasn't altogether sure he could call her a friend, exactly. More like a close acquaintance. Friendly, not friends. She was the cashier at the supermarket, and he was the old guy who chats up strangers in the checkout line.

Selby finished cutting vegetables and turned on the heat under the pan, squirting in a dollop of sesame oil and then some olive oil. He stood back, tidying up the piles of vegetables on the cutting board as he waited for the oil to get hot. Lining up the pieces of carrot. Stacking the garlic slices. Dabbing up a dribble of liquid from the water chestnuts with a paper towel.

Selby had no reason to disbelieve Ruth Coates's story of her family history. He suspected that his attitude was colored by his dislike for the woman, but he could see no reason why she would lie about something like that. This meant that Selby himself was the only offspring of Sullivan Coates, at least the only one he knew of. Given what he knew of Sullivan's enthusiastic sexuality, he thought there ought to be Coates children littering the countryside, but that did not seem to be the case. Apart from one large family scattered through the towns and villages north of the river and a smaller cluster in Port Sebastian, both of which Selby knew were unrelated to him, there were no other Coateses in the Bay Counties, at least none identified in publicly accessible records.

The ginger and garlic sizzled as it hit the hot oil. A few moments later, the veggies joined them. Selby put down a couple more pieces of water chestnut for Pancake to crunch on.

It seemed obvious that Ruth Coates knew more than she was telling—where Sullivan Coates was at the moment, for instance —but Selby couldn't see any way to get that information from her.

He stirred the pan, inhaling the smells of sesame and seasonings. He mixed up some soy sauce and honey and a pinch of cornstarch and poured them into the pan. He pulled the rice off the back burner and fluffed it with a fork.

I'm tired, Selby thought. *Too tired to think tonight. I'll eat dinner, clean up, read a book, and get a good night's sleep. Maybe that'll get my synapses firing again.*

Pancake tried to gulp down a too-large piece of water chestnut and threw up a slurry of cat food and crunchy vegetables on the floor next to his dish. Lost in thought, Selby didn't even notice.

. . .

Selby Coates is asleep, dreaming that he is back at the Unified Global Logistics Consulting building. He and Jason, the security guard, are in the courtyard in the pouring rain. Jason is wearing nothing but his brown UGLC cap and a lot of tattoos. He's walking Selby through the courtyard of the office building, pointing out each of the shrubs and small trees and identifying them in his rich, dark voice.

"*Acer palmatum*. Smooth Japanese Maple."

The tattoos shift with the guard's every movement as he raises his arm to point, bends down to indicate the shape of a leaf, stretches up to pluck a winged seed pod. His feet are blunt, square across the toes. He has a pattern of feathers tattooed down the top of each foot.

"*Acer shirasawanum*, Fullmoon Maple."

Under the tattoos, Jason is built like a wrestler, sturdy and compact, but the exact contours are confused by the riot of artwork.

"*Juniperus californica*. California Juniper."

Without all the ink, Selby thinks, the man might have modeled for the statue of Zeus atop the Pautasquot Power & Light building.

"Really, Selby. Don't you think this is a bit immature?"

Selby steps from among the little trees and finds himself in an open, grassy space. Jason has vanished, and the day has suddenly declined to dusk. Fifty yards away squats a metallic structure with a ramp leading down from a door well above ground level. In front of this object stands a humanoid statue, all cylinders and blank surfaces. The face of the statue is featureless apart from eyes set into a recessed band. In the distance, Selby can make out what he suspects is the Washington Monument.

Appearing next to him in what Selby believes is called a "swing dress"—tiny at the waist, inflated with petticoats to the knee, made of some plain black fabric—smoking a cigarette and scowling at him with tragic willow-green eyes, is Patricia Neal, circa 1950 or thereabouts. She is very thin, taller than he is, angular and tense in her movements.

"Oh," Selby says, looking back toward the metallic structure and its guard. "The spaceship. And that's not a statue; that's Gort, the super-robot. This is *The Day the Earth Stood Still*." He grins, and for a moment, he's a boy again, amazed and delighted by what the tiny black-and-white screen is showing him. "Klaatu barada nikto."

"I have to work with the materials that are available to me in your peculiar little mind," Laylah tells him, in the character of nervous widow Helen Benson. Her voice is an amalgam of Laylah's husky murmur and Neal's cracked contralto. "It's a challenge sometimes."

"You haven't been around much lately."

"I'm not sure there's any point, really, since you refuse to listen to anything I tell you."

This is a tone he has not heard from her before. A brittle intensity has replaced her usual smooth, almost maternal, delivery. He wonders how much of this is Laylah and how much is spillover from Neal's Helen Benson character. He wonders if he should be concerned by the change; she did, after all, once bring him back from the dead. He has no idea how far her abilities might extend in the reverse direction.

"If you told me something useful, I might be more inclined to pay attention. Thank you, by the way, for the crows."

She gestures impatiently with her cigarette. "I'm assuming you won't be needing them anymore. You've involved yet another person in your fumblings. Our Sister can't silence everybody in town."

Selby nods. "My father is alive," he says, changing the subject.

"Yes. At least you've come that far."

"You knew that."

"Yes." She blows out smoke, waving it away with a jerk of her arm. "I can't tell you anything you don't already know without risking … consequences. Now that you have learned of Sullivan Coates's continued existence, there is no need for me to hide the fact."

Selby steers their steps toward the robot towering at the foot of the ramp.

"Ruth Coates is not my sister—not Sullivan's daughter," he says.

"No."

Selby sighs. He would much rather be strolling with Jason. At least then he'd be learning the names of the shrubs and trees.

"I've used the Empty Room."

"Yes. You must not do that. The *topos hyperuranion* is not a hammer with which to flatten the obstacles in your path. I can't say more than that."

"I think we've had this conversation."

"Disregard me at your peril, dear Selby."

Selby stops to stare at her, his eyes round behind his glasses. "Did you really just say that? I thought only villains in comic books said that."

The woman exhales a slow cloud of sandalwood and cloves, tainted with something akin to hot asphalt. She gazes back at him through Patricia Neal's tragic face, then drops the cigarette and stomps it out with her shoe.

How is she walking in this grass with those heels? Selby asks himself.

"I might have hoped for a more cooperative tool." With that, she stalks up the ramp into the spacecraft and is gone.

Selby looks up at the robot and sees that the creature is built not of metal but of milky glass.

CHAPTER NINETEEN

Everyone, it seemed, wanted Selby to stay away from the Empty Room.

He cleaned up his breakfast things and stood at the window drying his hands on a towel, gazing out at Zeus and the pigeons, thinking about last night's dream. The rain had ceased during the wee hours, and patches of blue came and went overhead. Pale sunlight, like a thin yellow fluid, bathed Zeus, making him gleam and sparkle.

Ruth Coates had told Selby a number of important things—not least the fact that Sullivan Coates was still alive and kicking. Given UGLC's international reach and Doma's power, Selby thought it odd that Sullivan never seemed to wander far from the Bay Counties. Why not pack him up and ship him to some tropical island somewhere? Selby certainly didn't have the resources to go haring off to the Caribbean or the South Pacific in search of a delinquent elderly parent.

The implication of this was that Sullivan had to stay in the area for some reason. Why?

Find him, talk to him face to face, Selby thought. *This frantic cogitating is a waste of time.* The questions would haunt Selby until the day he died (again) unless he found Sullivan Coates and demanded answers from the man himself.

Selby gave Zeus a nod and went back to his Sunday morning housework.

Later, Selby sat listening to the whoosh of the washer and the grumbling and thumping of the dryer, a paperback copy of Howard Phillips Lovecraft's *At the Mountains of Madness* forgotten in his lap. Washing a load of towels, another of socks and t-shirts and underwear. Thinking about the strange thing that seemed to be occupying space in his head.

Although he thought of it as "the Empty Room," it wasn't a room, and it wasn't empty. Calling it a room was convenient and avoided the need for him to try to establish what exactly it really was. But empty? Selby had looked up the word Laylah/Patricia Neal had used: *hyperuranion*. It was from Plato, a place where the ideas of everything in the world were kept, like a filing cabinet full of blueprints. The molds the gods might use to make a chair, or a pencil, or a tomato, or a pensioner with bad knees.

All that was interesting, but not very useful. The whispers weren't ideas; they were voices. Maybe they were the idea of voices? The idea of people? Why were Laylah and Doma so anxious to keep him out of there?

Selby was finding it easier to access the Empty Room, as if it were a poem or an address he had memorized, coming to mind more and more easily the more often it was repeated. It was something he could do almost casually now. More and more, the Empty Room felt like a part of him: native, natural, inborn.

Tuning out the laundry sounds and smells, he looked inside.

Despite his increasing familiarity, the whispers didn't acknowledge Selby's existence, but when he intruded, he could sense a disruption in the currents, a clumping and dispersal of the skittering, fragmentary presences that haunted the place. They knew he was there; they just preferred not to pay any attention. Larger entities, with more heft and significance, stirred but ignored him utterly. Below everything else, vast intellects hung at terrible, crushing depths, godlike and remote, suspended in a medium that was not air or water but meaning itself, the idea of ideas, the primordial soup from which the DNA of thought might assemble itself.

An elderly woman entered the laundry room in a cloud of floral perfume and quiet muttering, startling Selby out of his ruminations. She was dwarfed by the basket she wrestled through the door.

"Hello, Mrs. Swainson. Can I help you with that?"

Selby climbed to his feet and took the basket from the woman's tiny claws. Mrs. Swainson lived on the third floor and had been in the building since before the first Highdiver took flight from the west-facing window of apartment 9-D in 1971. Her husband died of a heart attack a week after Bill Clinton was sworn in as President. The widow still wore black and still blamed the Democrats for her loss.

"Thank you," she said, flustered. She always used the washer and dryer down at the very end of the row, with the table next to it, convenient for folding the clothes. Selby took her basket there and stepped back.

"How have you been?" he asked.

"As well as can be expected," she said. "I guess I'll live to be a hundred. Just goes to show you."

Selby had no idea what she meant by that, but he suspected that her century was not all that far away. "You're still very active," he said politely. "A lot of people younger than you don't get around as well. Myself included."

She squinted up at him for a long moment, then nodded. "I do all right." She turned and began transferring her clothes from the basket to the washer, keeping her body between Selby and what she was doing.

Selby smiled and returned to his chair. *Doesn't want me to see the lacy underthings, no doubt.* Mrs. Swainson's great secret, a black lace bustier and a chiffon nightie.

Selby regretted that thought as he watched Mrs. Swainson covertly. Did she walk her dreams in a younger body, as Selby did, her wispy hair thick and black again, her pickled little face smooth and velvet-soft? He hoped there had been fancy lingerie in her past, at least one night of giggling and murmuring and the occasional gasp of surprise. Everyone deserved to have that in their lives, however briefly.

Mrs. Swainson finished loading the washer and started the cycle. She stood leaning on the edge of the folding table for a few moments, breathing, then nodded to Selby and left the room.

A buzzer sounded, and Selby moved his second load from the washer to the dryer, then returned to his chair and his book.

Selby had reached a point at which Lovecraft's Antarctic explorer was shredding his notebooks, leaving a trail of fragments by which he hoped to find his way back to the surface once he had penetrated to the heart of the ancient mystery— never thinking about what might follow that trail in the other direction, what long-buried monstrosity might fling itself slobbering into the daylight.

Perhaps all quests were like that, Selby mused. As you ran off looking for your magic sword, your Holy Grail, your elixir of immortality, you never took time to think about what might be following your breadcrumbs back to the place you left behind.

By the time Selby's towels were ready to come out of the dryer, Lovecraft's hapless narrator was stumbling through lightless tunnels, frantic with terror, as giant penguins squawked and shrieked behind him, driven by something carnivorous and vile. Selby folded his towels, stacked them in the basket with his socks and underwear, then dropped his paperback on top. Hefting the basket, he headed for the elevator.

Selby pushed at his apartment door with a grimace. *Again, I forgot to lock it. I'm going to have to get a spring lock.* The door swung open, and Selby stepped inside.

Time stopped.

Selby's heart seemed to seize up, then stuttered back into motion with an almost audible clatter of gears and flywheels.

He stumbled backward into the hall, checking the number next to the door, convinced that he had walked into the wrong apartment—but no. This was his address, his apartment.

His place. His refuge. His home.

He stepped back inside, setting his clothes basket down inside the door.

Besides the photo of his father, a dozen other pictures had hung on his wall in simple black frames and white mats. *Had* hung. Now, they lay scattered across the floor, the frames warped, the glass not just shattered but ground underfoot. His desk had been flipped onto its side, dumping pens and notebooks and the gooseneck lamp into a pile like the scree of a recent landslide. His laptop lay against the wall, the case cracked. The invader had stomped on his phone, leaving a mass of fragments held together by sinews of plastic.

Across the room, the bedsheets bore great slashes that showed the surface of the mattress beneath, while the foam stuffing of the pillows mounded here and there like snow.

In the kitchen, the glass face of his microwave had been shattered, and dishes and silverware littered the countertops and the floor.

Booted feet had stepped on Pancake's food and water dishes, scattering kibble everywhere, but failed to damage the heavy metal bowls.

Pancake.

"Pancake? Where are you, boy?"

Selby's voice came out as a warble, soft and shaking, barely audible. "Pancake?" he repeated, more clearly. "Please be here. Please be okay." He dropped to his knees next to the bed, gasping at the pain in his much-abused left knee. "Are you under there?"

A high, wavering growl answered him, and Selby felt part of his life slip back into place. He was sobbing now, and his chest hurt.

"Hey, there, my friend. Are you all right?"

The cat's eye glinted in the shadows. He stretched but made no move to emerge from his refuge.

"All right. Whenever you're ready."

Selby hauled himself back to his feet and continued his survey.

The bathroom had suffered less because there was less to vandalize. The invader had poured shampoo on the floor and emptied a bottle of painkillers into the sink. A bath towel was crammed into the toilet. In the closet, his clothes had all been dragged off the hangers and shelves and trampled.

Back in the living room, he saw that the vandal had singled out one item for special attention. The photograph of his father, the one he had just had repaired, had been reduced to a litter of crumpled fragments the size of postage stamps.

The trail through the dark tunnels that leads the monsters back.

"That *bitch*," Selby spat. "She's gone too far." He picked through the scraps of his father's picture, his expression grim. An eye, a hand, the side of the mouth, part of the child's face … He let the fragments flutter to the floor.

"Sir?"

Selby whirled around at the voice, then staggered and fell against the bookshelf as his knee failed to keep up with the sudden movement. A uniformed police officer stepped forward.

"Do you need an ambulance, sir?"

Selby waved away the offer. "No. I'll be fine. Just … my knees aren't what they used to be." He straightened. "Where did you come from?"

"Your neighbor called about half an hour ago and said she

heard sounds of violence coming from your apartment. She said you were out. She told us you had had a break-in a couple of weeks back."

Half an hour ago. While Selby was in the laundry room chuckling over Lovecraft's predictable horrors, this was going on upstairs.

"Yes. I didn't report it at the time, and that was stupid, but there wasn't so much damage on that occasion."

"Looks like they were more thorough this time," the officer said.

"Yes, it does."

Another police officer appeared in the doorway, an older man, and stood looking around, his hands propped on the gear strapped to his belt. The first officer waved Selby over to his comfortable chair. "Why don't you sit down, sir. I need to ask you a few questions." As Selby nodded and organized himself, she stepped aside, murmuring into a device clipped to her collar, which hissed and popped in return. She took the earpiece out of her ear and turned back to Selby.

He indicated the desk chair. "Please, make yourself comfortable," he said. "Watch for broken glass."

Selby's interview with the police took about an hour, almost certainly more time than the vandalism itself had required. They asked questions and took notes, recording everything. They took pictures of the damage. There was one amusing moment when one of them approached the bed, and Pancake released a thin, falsetto growl, startling everyone.

By the time the two officers left, they had cajoled Selby into allowing them to call Roy and Reggie for him. Reggie expressed her outrage in colorful language and told the officer that she was on her way.

"Maybe you should stay with your friends for a day or two," the first officer suggested after Reggie had disconnected.

Selby shook his head. "No. This is my home."

She nodded. She had been working this beat for three months, this neighborhood chockablock with crazy old people, all kinds of mummies and misfits, and she had learned to accept their peculiarities. "I understand. Please call us if anything else happens or if you feel something else might happen."

Selby agreed, glancing over at his smashed cell phone lying on the floor next to the desk.

"I will. Thank you."

At one o'clock, Reggie showed up with cleaning supplies, Chinese takeout, and a grim expression.

"Jackass downstairs thought I was somebody's maid. Let me right in."

Selby grimaced. "We do seem to have a security problem here."

"Are you going to be all right?"

"Yes. I'm very angry, though."

"I can imagine. Do you know who did it?"

Reggie cleared a space on the counter for the food, and they ate as they talked.

"Not so I could accuse anyone of anything in court," Selby said, "but I believe I know, yes."

"The same guy that came to our house?"

Selby thought about that. "I was thinking more of Ruth, but her husband—yes, he was probably holding a grudge after spending a couple of days in jail with bruised testicles."

"Are you in danger?"

This was a good question, to which Selby had no good answers. "I don't think so. They've attacked me physically before but never accomplished much. This is about terrorizing me, not about hurting me."

"The one often shades into the other before you know it," Reggie pointed out.

"I realize that, but I'm not as helpless as I was when all this started."

Reggie frowned slightly but didn't pursue the subject further. Selby himself wasn't altogether sure what he meant by that remark.

"I don't guess there's anything I can say or do that will convince you to come over to our place tonight."

"No. I … Thank you, Reggie, but I have to be here. I refuse to give up *one fucking inch!*"

Reggie stepped back, blinking at Selby's sudden vehemence, that glaring profanity.

"Sorry," Selby said quickly, his ears glowing pink. "I'm still a little tense."

Reggie took in his contrite expression and laughed. "You're entitled, this once. Come on, let's get this place put back together."

. . .

Fiona's Baby Diary:
Looks like I have to decide what to do about Thanksgiving this year. Last year, we did it at the farm with Ruth and Mitch and the two Mexican guys they had working for them, but this year, they're staying in the city right through to the end of the month, or maybe even longer. I asked about the Mexican guys, where they'd be having Thanksgiving, but Ruth said Mitch had given them a week off so they could spend it with family somewhere out near Carnes Valley. Preston's does a big Thanksgiving dinner, with all the tables pushed together and people waiting on themselves. We don't usually go there because it's so expensive, but we might go crazy just this once. It'll be a chance for Bingo to be around some people other than just us and Ruth and Mitch, and everybody says it's a lot of fun. All very Norman Rockwell!

CHAPTER TWENTY

Selby's insurance company replaced his cell phone, computer, and microwave and wrote him a check for smaller items.

The Highlander's security contractors offered condolences and sympathy, along with a carefully crafted tapestry of excuses which quickly unraveled in the face of Selby's quiet persistence. Eventually, the company agreed to provide him with a link to security camera video files covering two hours on either side of the break-in. The footage was copy-protected, but Selby was able to record the contents of his screen on his new laptop as the video played in the web browser. He saved the files to his cloud storage.

Although metal and glass picture frames had been destroyed beyond repair, most of his photos were salvageable—all but one.

A week went by, then another, and Selby repaired his life. He visited the Tavern for lunch, weathering Roy's anxiety about his state of mind until their relationship finally slipped quietly back into its deep, comfortable groove. Barry Ratliffe spent an afternoon at Selby's desk showing him how to configure and use the monstrous new smartphone his friends bullied him into buying. Ratliffe seemed larger and more intrusive in Selby's little apartment than even the police and the man who delivered and installed the new microwave, but Pancake took to him on sight, and Selby had to admit that he had his uses.

Thanksgiving came and went. Selby chose not to spend the

day with Roy and Reggie this year. Instead, he stood behind a long table and served gravy and stuffing to unhoused people at a shelter where he knew Juliet Mosley sometimes volunteered, interacting one-on-one with more strangers than he had ever encountered at one go. After the event was over, he blushed and ducked his way through a round of thank-yous and handshakes and went home to curl up in bed with Pancake, crying gently, until suppertime.

Selby heard nothing from Laylah or Doma nor from any of Doma's various minions, which was probably just as well. He enclosed his outrage, walling it off. He didn't want his anger to scorch everyone around him, but he had no intention of letting it burn out entirely before he had found an opportunity to use it.

By December, Selby was ready to make his first move. He isolated an assortment of stills from the security video, and on the second Sunday after the vandalism, he emailed the pictures to the offices of Unified Global Logistics Consulting.

By Wednesday, there had been no response to Selby's emails to UGLC. He was not surprised. It would take time for the messages to be routed to Ruth—he had sent them to the generic "info" address—and still more time for her to frame a response. He could be patient.

His apartment was back to normal. His photographs were back on the walls in new frames nearly identical to the old ones. Garabedian—gratified that his advice had proven so timely—had printed and framed the picture of Selby's father from the digital scan. Now, that image, too, had been returned to its accustomed place. Selby had to admit that the new pillows were a considerable improvement over the old ones, and putting his closet to rights had encouraged him to set aside an assortment of items for charity, things that he had worn so rarely that he hardly recognized them as his own, clearing precious shelf space. Selby still hadn't quite gotten the hang of the new microwave, and he viewed his fancy smartphone as a harbinger of the end of civilization as we know it, but otherwise, he found that he could get through a day without being forcibly reminded of the attack on his sanctum.

Selby's knee recovered from his encounters with Doma and her acolytes. It was still a chalky old joint that had seen a lot of wear and tear over a lot of years, but it was working fine, thank you, and Selby snapped at his doctor for suggesting that a replacement might be in order, startling them both. To prove that the knee was still worth keeping, Selby strolled—carefully—down to the Tavern for lunch after his visit to the doctor.

Today, Roy was wearing a royal blue catsuit of some thick, rubbery material, zippered down the back. Selby wondered how in the world she managed in the bathroom. Oval windows over each hip showed an area of bare skin, just where the hipbones protruded, while another window opened over what would have been cleavage in a person with prominent breasts; on Roy, this showed an oval of tight, hairless chest. Selby had never seen any part of Roy's skin besides her face and hands, and he blushed when he sat down.

"You look like yourself again," Roy said, grinning.

Selby's blush deepened, but he returned the grin. "I've mostly recovered, I think." This wasn't entirely true, as the hot little coal of anger toward Doma and Ruth Coates and their minions still burned bright, but Roy didn't need to hear about all that.

"I'm glad to hear it. Things are pretty much back to normal around our place, too." Roy slid Selby's beer across the bar and tapped his sandwich order into the tablet. "Reggie misses the new crows, but I think the babies are glad to be seeing the back of them. They were rowdy critters."

A couple came in from the street, blinking in the transition from the unexpected autumn sunshine to the pleasant dimness, and Roy hurried over to usher them to a table.

After Selby's dream conversation with Laylah in *The Day the Earth Stood Still*, the new crows at Roy and Reggie's had begun wandering further and further afield, staying away for one day, then two. Finally, they left early one morning and did not come back. Reggie, who had grumbled about the undisciplined and apparently untrainable creatures throughout their stay, was disconsolate at their departure. Selby supposed that Laylah had found occupation for them elsewhere. After a few days, Reggie resigned herself to the disappointment and got on with her life.

"Have you talked to our friend Ratliffe?" Roy asked as she poured glasses of tea for the young couple.

"Not since he helped me with my phone," Selby replied.

Roy narrowed her eyes at him, peacock-blue eyeshadow making her look like a giant, peering insect. "He's a nice guy. I think he's left a lot of his friends behind over the years, just like you, and probably appreciates finding somebody interesting to hang out with."

Selby's eyes went wide and round, and Roy laughed. "Relax, Coates. I'm not trying to fix you up. He has a girlfriend named Sheila, who works at the university. I'm just saying it's always good to get outside your own head now and then."

Selby nodded, blushing again, and Roy slipped out from behind the bar to deliver drinks.

In the aftermath of the vandalism of his apartment, Selby had known that his business with Ruth Coates—and indirectly, with Doma herself—was by no means concluded. The threat of further attacks still hung over him, and he wasn't as inclined to wait around for the hammer to fall as he might once have been.

If Selby was a pawn, Sullivan was a king, slinking across the far end of the board behind a screen of lesser pieces, playing no active role but still the center around which the game was being played. Until Selby knew where his father was, *who* he was, his life was going to be in disorder. Ruth Coates had information Selby needed. Selby had to convince her to share it.

What he would do with that knowledge if—when—he had it was still not clear.

Meanwhile, he worried about the people around him.

His sandwich arrived, and Selby focused on the food. He had been eating the same sandwich once or twice a week for a couple of years now. Was it time to broaden his horizons? Tempeh and avocado and mashed chickpeas were nutritious and predictable, but was that enough?

Roy spotted his expression and shot him a quizzical look. Selby laughed.

"Deep thoughts," he said.

Roy grinned. "Don't fall in."

Selby blushed and ate his sandwich, careful not to get crumbs on the bar.

After lunch, Selby didn't go straight home but instead walked the neighborhood. He had no particular destination in mind; he felt the need to reaffirm the ground beneath his feet. All the weirdness had made him forget where his strengths lay.

Aside from the five years he and his mother spent in the poky little apartment over Uncle Marty and Aunt Martha's garage, Selby had lived in Buckley his entire life, always somewhere in the Fallwood district. This was a sprawling neighborhood of immigrants and artists, rebels and refugees, occupying a zone that stretched from downtown to the river and from the industrial dystopia of Van Baar on the west to the exclusive gated enclaves of Bluff Park to the east. Zeus displayed his impressive musculature atop the PP&L building on Fallwood's southern boundary, gazing across the highway flyover toward the towers of downtown, standing guard over a domain that consisted of eccentric apartment blocks, tree-shaded single-family homes, and Depression-era shops and office buildings, snuggled promiscuously with the occasional 1990s blank-faced mini-skyscraper, or now and then a mid-century-modern house, all concrete slabs and plate glass. There were a few streets of once-glamorous mansions, now broken into apartments or occupied by feral packs of college students dividing the rent ten ways, the stately lawns patchy and wild, the graceful structures still clinging to a stoic dignity in spite of their fallen state. In Selby's eyes, Fallwood was every city, everywhere, throughout many lifetimes, all compressed down into a few square miles on the banks of the Pautasquot River.

Unable to drive because of his poor vision, Selby had always walked everywhere he could, in all weathers. There was hardly a tree or a street sign he had not brushed against at one time or another, a flowerbed he hadn't admired, a curb he hadn't tripped over. The map of Fallwood was written on Selby's face, and its dust was incorporated into his bones.

He sat down on a low fieldstone retaining wall that held a clipped lawn in place three feet above the level of the sidewalk. The building at the center of that two acres of grass had been built in 1994 after the demolition of a rambling, early 1960s apartment building that had itself been erected over the ruins of a church dating back to 1932. The church had replaced the town mansion of a minor shipping magnate whose home burned to the ground two days after he himself died in a fire at what was then the Carville Docks on the river a few miles to the north. The wall Selby was sitting on was all that remained from the days when Buckley's urban well-to-do arrived on Saturday afternoons in their DeSotos and their Cadillacs to drink bootleg liquor and dance, up there on that modest hill where today a firm of high-end corporate lawyers plied their trade. Expensive and impractical European luxury cars now squatted in complacent rows in the rigidly-landscaped parking lot where, once upon a time, Alastair McNair's celebrated collection of orchids filled two wrought-iron-and-glass greenhouses.

All this history, all these lives: rich and poor, past and

present; they all lived on in Selby.

Did Sullivan Coates feel something of this? Is this why, as he drifted from one existence to another, one decade at a time, he never traveled far from this beating heart? How long had he been on his journey? Was Selby's father a creature like the Colonel's old flunky Cudhill, somehow enduring endlessly, unchanged while the world evolved around him?

Selby could feel Chioke Okorie's possessive, territorial rage still burning inside him, along with Ruth Coates's single-minded dedication to her cause. Like Fallwood itself, Selby was becoming a patchwork of ideas and personalities, waiting to be stitched together into a useful whole.

The thread he needed to sew the pieces together was Sullivan Coates.

As Selby toiled up Tower Lane toward his apartment—his knee had proven less cooperative than he had hoped, and he was limping again—Selby was surprised to find the Colonel thrashing around in the shrubbery that screened the retired dictator's strange little house from the street.

"Is everything all right, Colonel?"

The grim old man glared at him. Selby was startled to see that he clutched a machete in one gnarled paw, and he took a step backward into the street.

"No, Mr. Coates, it is not. Something has bitten my Bolívar. The veterinarian suspects a rat. I am wondering if rats are living out here in all this jungle." He gave a clump of bush honeysuckle a vindictive whack with the machete.

"More likely in your basement," Selby said. He walked up to the iron gate and looked around, remaining well out of reach of the machete. "They like to be indoors. Do you have a storage shed or anything out back?"

"No. Only the house. There is a basement, but I have never been inside it. It reminds me of … similar places. Places I have been before that I don't care to think about." The Colonel shook his head and sighed. "My apologies. I am somewhat—what is the word?—distraught. Bolívar, like his master, is no longer young. I fear the day that I must live without his company."

Selby thought about Pancake and nodded.

"I've always heard that the best way to deal with rats is to deny them food. Or get a snake."

"Snakes, I have," the Colonel said. "My property is the last outpost of nature in the neighborhood. All the animals have taken refuge here. Last summer, I found a snake in my bathtub and a squirrel in my pantry. The winter before last, Bolívar and I were terrorized by a raccoon that climbed down the old chimney."

In all the years that Selby and the Colonel had lived within half a mile of each other, Selby had never really gotten to know the old man. It was only after his own life became so strange that he made the effort to see the Colonel as a human being. *He's interesting to talk to*, he thought. *All this time and I never bothered to find that out. What was it my mother called me? 'A supercilious prick'? Maybe she has a point.*

"You have accumulated a lot of stories in your day," Selby said aloud. "You should write your memoirs."

The Colonel laughed, resting the machete across his shoulder.

"Only after all these years have my enemies finally forgotten me. I would not wish to remind them that I am still here and that I still remember everything I have seen and done. Even in your own government, certain men lie awake nights worrying that I will do just that thing." He hefted the machete and looked at it. "No. I will tell you my stories, and we will laugh, and perhaps that will be the end of it. Speaking of stories, have you had further adventures with your strange young men?" He waggled his fingers over his mouth.

"No, but their friends are becoming a nuisance."

"There was a time when I could have addressed that problem on your behalf," the Colonel said, "but those times are gone. Tell me, if you will, Mr. Coates: do you have family?"

"My mother and her sister."

"Your father is no more?"

Selby made a face. "I don't know. This has become an important question lately. He left us when I was ten years old."

"And you have had no contact in all this time?"

"No. I haven't really thought about him much. Until lately."

The Colonel nodded. "Then he might be alive, and he might not?"

"I'm fairly certain he's alive. But that's about all I'm certain of. What about you? Brothers or sisters?"

"I have a sister. She lives in California. She thinks I died in 1989."

"You've never tried to contact her?"

The Colonel shrugged. "To what end? We are strangers now, and I am a stranger chained to a terrible past. She would not thank me for returning from the dead."

Selby nodded, his ears warm. "I guess that would be complicated. Were you ever married, if you don't mind my asking?"

"I don't mind. Yes, I was married, briefly, back before I became important. After a year, the woman ran away with a Cuban military advisor and went to live in Havana. He treated her very badly afterward."

"I'm sorry."

He grinned. "Not as sorry as he was. When I became President, he came to my country as part of a diplomatic mission. I had him garroted in a whorehouse, and his body dumped from a helicopter over the Gulf of Mexico."

"And your wife? Ex-wife?"

"I assume she found someone new. She was foolish, but hers was a practical foolishness. She was always a survivor."

"I'm surprised you never remarried. Presidents always have

wives."

"There is truth in that, my friend." He raised his machete in a kind of salute. "A wife may be an important ally. The men have the weapons, but the women know where the bodies are buried."

A considerably subdued Bolívar appeared in the open door-way, a plastic cone around his neck and one hind leg wrapped in a bandage. He looked at Selby and made a peculiar noise that combined a whimper with a snarl.

"Ah. My friend says it is time for his dinner." He bowed to Selby. "A good evening to you, friend Coates."

"And to you, Colonel."

Selby put a frozen quiche in the oven and set the timer, then settled into his comfortable chair with the telephone. Like a child left untended all day long, the sinister little device had been busy in his absence. A dozen voicemail messages, three text messages that were clearly not intended for him, and sev-eral email notifications blinked and beeped and chirped for his attention. The majority of the traffic was spam, or scams, or robocalls, companies trying to sell him a new roof, or landscap-ing services, or burial insurance—two of those—but there was one voicemail from his mother.

"Selby. Call me."

Frowning, Selby touched the green telephone receiver icon. On the fifth ring, someone picked it up.

"What is it?"

"Aunt Martha? Selby here. May I speak to Naomi?"

"Oh, it's you. I think she's out by the pool."

"She called while I was out."

"The whole point of a cell phone is that you can carry it around with you. That way, your loved ones don't have to wait all day to talk to you, and you don't have to annoy other people looking for them when you finally deign to respond."

"On the other hand, leaving the phone at home means I don't have to talk to unpleasant people when I've got better things to do," Selby said.

"Touché, you little shitbag. Hang on, I think I hear your mother stumbling through the door."

After a round of shuffling and murmuring, Naomi Coates came on the line.

"Hello, Selby. Sorry you had to go through Morticia to get to me."

"That's okay. I'll probably be like her one day. When I'm very, very old."

"Don't even joke about it," Naomi said.

"You called earlier?"

"Yes. I thought of something. You were asking questions about Sullivan when you were here."

"I know you don't like that, but—"

"*Speaking.*"

"Sorry. I thought you had reached the end of a sentence."

"Don't you know a dramatic pause when you hear one? Anyway, after you left, I got to thinking about something I'm pretty sure I've never mentioned to you before."

Selby didn't say anything, waiting.

"Don't you want to know what it is?"

Selby sighed. "Yes. Go ahead."

Naomi didn't say anything for a long moment. Selby started to speak, then caught himself. His mother chuckled and continued.

"I've always given you the impression that Sullivan just up and went one day."

"Isn't that what happened?"

"Not exactly. Your father didn't really *disappear*," Naomi said."Not all at once, anyway. It was more like he … faded. He was always a bad one for going away for a few hours or even a day or a night, not at the shop, not at home, just gone. I assumed it was other women, but those were stupid times. When your husband didn't come home, you always assumed it was other women, and you always assumed he'd come back when he felt like it. A wife didn't have a lot of options."

She made an impatient noise, and Selby could picture her shaking her head, her lips tight.

"Well, during the last couple of years, the absences got longer and longer. Sometimes a day, sometimes a weekend. Toward the end, he'd be gone for a week at a time."

"I remember that," Selby said. "Business trips. You were always angry, but I thought you were mad at me."

The silence was longer this time. "It wasn't you, Selby. It was never you. I hate that I let you think it was. No, I was frustrated. I didn't know what to do about your father. He would come home from these walkabouts of his all fuddled and lost. For a while, I thought he was doing drugs—this was the sixties, after all—but it was more like he was forgetting who he was, bit by bit, a little more every time. One day, he forgot that he ran a bookstore. Another time, he came home and called me 'Liz' for two days."

Liz, Selby thought. *Elizabeth Harwell. Ruth's mother.*

"I remember the softball game," he said.

"When you were … What? Nine? I remember that day, too. It was the summer before you turned ten, the last summer your father spent with us."

"I couldn't have cared less about softball, but I was so excited to be spending the whole day with Dad. I don't remember when it all started getting weird, but I remember him looking at me at one point and asking me how old I was. I froze."

"By that time, he was slipping up like that a lot."

"He remembered my name, but he didn't know how old I was. He didn't remember the time I broke my wrist or the time I got into a fight in school and got my head handed to me. He didn't remember arguing with the Campbells next door about the old man burning trash behind his apartment and filling our place up with smoke. It was as if I were some random kid he had ended up sitting next to, and he was making conversation, asking questions about my life."

"You came home in tears. Sullivan was baffled and upset; he wasn't at all clear what he had done to upset you. And you didn't want to tell me."

"I was afraid you'd get mad."

"I did. Just not in front of you. It took me a week to get the story out of you. I confronted him about it one day when you were playing outside, but he didn't remember any of it. He'd forgotten about having forgotten.

"By the time he left and didn't come back, he had been leaving off and on for months. It was like the last time it finally stuck. The other life got to be the real one. I never saw him again."

CHAPTER TWENTY-ONE

Selby was sleeping more soundly with his new pillows. When the dream began, it took him a few moments to figure out where he was.

"Selby. We need to talk, dear."

A petite, pretty blonde woman was sitting in front of him, all in demure gray. On the wall above her head, a large crow clung to a perch contrived of a few sticks. The bird was utterly motionless; as Selby found his focus, he realized the creature was stuffed.

"What ...?"

An owl spread its wings in one corner of the claustrophobic little room, and here and there, other examples of the taxidermist's art reared and snarled, trapped for eternity in a single moment. Caught between the two halves of a single heartbeat. Selby focused on the woman before him, and everything fell into place.

"Laylah. You're Janet Leigh, as Marion Crane. Which means you've cast me as Norman Bates," he said. "*Psycho*. I've never imagined myself as a homicidal maniac."

"I have to use what I find," the blonde woman said, managing to sound both polite and weary at the same time. "Your mind is a strange place, Selby dear."

"You do realize that Marion Crane dies horribly three-quarters of the way through the film," Selby said.

The woman looked at him, appraising him.

"You've changed," she said after a minute, ignoring his remark.

Selby blinked. His mother had said the same thing.

"*No*. I wish people would stop telling me that. I am who I've always been." His voice wavered. "I can't … I can't lose myself in all this insanity, become someone else just because the world around me is being ridiculous. I'm *me*. Just like I've always been."

Laylah/Marion looked at him for a long moment, with something that might almost have been sympathy flickering around the edges of her expression. After a time she merely nodded, dismissing the subject.

"None of that matters, Selby. The goal of all this was for you to find Sullivan Coates, something I am powerless to do. You've figured this out by now, or I wouldn't be able to say it. The aim of our Sister is to prevent that. You see that, as well."

"Yes."

"Your ventures into what you call the Empty Room are disrupting the possible outcomes, introducing new variables, variables that neither I nor our Sister can account for in our planning. The possible timelines are a tangle. You've complicated things beyond comprehension."

Selby looked at her, eyes wide, unconsciously mirroring the attitude of the stuffed owl looking over his shoulder. "You've never talked like this before. Your voice is Marion Crane, but your words are out of character."

"Foolish Selby. What does that matter?"

"I don't know, but I suspect that it does matter," Selby said. "The situation is evolving. You're evolving."

The pretty blonde stared but said nothing. Selby guessed that he had led the conversation somewhere Laylah was unable to follow.

"Can you protect me and mine from Doma?" he asked.

She looked down at her hands. She was holding a sandwich,

Selby realized with childlike delight. This was the scene in the parlor prior to Marion Crane's death. The accuracy was remarkable.

"No," Laylah/Marion said, finally. She put the sandwich back on the plate. "Not to any meaningful extent. I can do many things, but as you have deduced, I have little impact on your physical plane. That's why I need you."

"A pawn."

"An agent," she corrected sharply. "To counter the various catspaws employed by the other side."

"Why me? Doma's acolytes have unusual abilities. I'm just me." Selby kept his tone casual, but he sensed that he was veering close to the center of everything that had happened, that was happening.

"You are your father's son." Laylah/Marion took a deep breath, and Selby became aware of the scent of cedar and smoke. She shook her head. "These birds," she said, waving a graceful hand toward the exhibits. "Such a barbaric custom, preserving the poor creatures like this."

"They'll last forever," Selby said. This sudden change of topic meant something; he was sure of it. But how to cut through the allegories, the obscure parables?

Laylah/Marion looked up at the stuffed crow, her mouth tight. "Like mummies. A counterfeit of life. Mere appearances preserved forever while the true self remains broken and bereft, locked away like the fragments of a shattered diamond."

The room twitched, folding in on itself. Marion Crane cried out in frustration, and everything snapped back to normal.

She said too much, Selby thought. *Something important. 'Broken pieces?' 'Locked away?'*

The scent of spices and burning candles intensified. "Events are moving," she said, articulating each word carefully. "Things are happening. Try to keep your head, and to remember that a puzzle may solve itself once the pieces are all assembled in one place."

Time stopped.

When the clock resumed its ticking, Marion Crane was gone, and dream-Selby was alone among the birds, dead and immortal on their perches. He picked up the sandwich—egg salad—and chewed on it thoughtfully, looking at the birds.

The sound of birdsong shattered the dream. *Stuffed birds don't sing, Norman.*

Not only were the birds singing, but they were doing it very loudly. Selby dragged himself out of sleep, irritable and confused, shreds of the dream fluttering away from his head. The birdsong was coming from his desk; he stumbled over to investigate, looking for wildlife, but found only his phone, chirping and tweeting from its place on the left-rear corner of the desk.

"Hello?"

"Coates, this is Reggie. Listen to me. Listen to all my words because I need you to stay focused."

"What?"

"Roy fell in the alley behind the Tavern last night after she closed up. She hit her head. She's going to be fine, but she wants to see you."

"Roy's hurt?"

"All right, good job. We've come that far. Yes, Roy's hurt. She wants to talk to you. She's a little doped up, but she'll be all right. I'm hoping to take her home this evening." She told Selby which hospital and gave him the room number. "You have that?"

Selby repeated the information in a wavering little-old-man voice.

"Pull yourself together and get down here. But promise me something first. Can you do that? Can you make me a promise?"

"I'm not sure." Why was she talking to him as though he

were a child? "It will have to depend on whether the promise you want is actually—"

"Never mind. Just don't be all falling apart when you get here. Okay? You're a grown man, and I'm sure you can put on a happy face."

They both knew that Selby was no more capable of hiding what he was thinking or feeling than a three-year-old.

"I will. I'll be right there."

After what seemed like hours, Selby's bus finally decanted him at a stop several hundred yards from the main entrance to the Jackson-Green-Methodist Medical Center. He hurried across the intervening distance; he was distracted enough to walk straight across the prim front lawn instead of staying on the sidewalks, as per the signs.

Roy was in a double room; the other bed was, mercifully, unoccupied. Selby slipped inside as though he might visit without being noticed, but Roy smiled when she saw him.

"What? Did you jog all the way across town? Stop and catch your breath," she said in a faint voice. "I don't want you falling over on me. You'll steal all the attention."

Selby approached the bed, his face twisted by the pressure of unshed tears.

"Your makeup is all smudged," he said.

Roy laughed. "Oh. My. Fucking. God. I love you, Coates."

Selby blushed and looked at Reggie, who shook her head. "It's okay. She's a little loopy. They gave her something to relax her. That never ends well. She'll be singing 'I Will Survive' any minute."

Someone had tried to wipe away Roy's makeup but had done a piss-poor job, leaving smears of lavender eyeshadow over her eyes and lipstick on only one side of her mouth. ER nurses had chopped away a big chunk of her hair, and she was wearing an ugly elastic cap over what was left. Selby looked around for a wet-wipe or something, but he didn't know where anything was. He had forgotten to bring a handkerchief. Did Roy's mother ever clean her up as a child by licking a handkerchief?

"You with us, Coates?"

"Sorry. A little rattled." Selby took several deep breaths. "How did this happen?"

"I stepped in one of those potholes in the alley and fell flat on my ass. If I'd been wearing the right shoes, I'd have never hit the ground."

"You're still not getting those damned Manolo Blahniks. I don't care how many times you fall down; we're not paying a thousand dollars for three dollars' worth of leather and some Bangladeshi slave labor." Reggie turned to Selby. "Thank God for that honking big natural, though. When her head hit the curb, all that hair cushioned the blow."

"You've been coming and going through that alley for years," Selby objected. "It's well lit, plus you know every one of those potholes. You could walk from the Tavern to the parking lot blindfolded."

Nobody spoke for a moment, and Selby didn't miss the glance that passed between Roy and her wife. He blew out his cheeks, his ears pink.

"Oh. Let me guess. You were startled. Somebody stepped out of nowhere and spooked you. Nerdy guys with their mouths all sewn up? Or a woman made out of moths?"

"The nerdy guys. This wasn't your fault, Coates."

"Of course it's my fault! You know it is! This would never have happened to you if it weren't for me!" Selby tried to calm down. *I promised not to get upset.*

Roy smiled. "Sweetie, it ain't like that. Shit happens. Your shit is our shit. Ours is yours. We carry the shit bucket up the hill together. Don't make things worse by getting all twisted up over it. Do you hear me?"

Selby nodded. Reggie stepped over and put her arm around his waist.

"Listen, Coates. She'll be fine. She may look like a Disney princess, but she's tough as nails under all that spandex. I've been under there. I know."

Roy sighed. "Doc says I have a concussion. Knocked me out for a few minutes. They're keeping me tonight so's they can make sure my brain doesn't swell up or whatever." She chuckled. "Bigger brain. Could be an improvement."

"Call me tonight," Reggie told Selby. "Or I'll call you. As soon as I get her home."

"Fuckin' Manolo Blahniks," Roy said. "I bet they don't even have 'em in my size."

Reggie chuckled. "I think she's going to take a nap now. She wanted to stay awake long enough to see you."

Selby's face was wet. Reggie pulled a tissue out of a box next to the bed. He flinched as he saw the tissue approach.

"Oh. There they are," he said. "I didn't see them."

Reggie handed him the tissue and patted his cheek.

"Don't worry. I didn't spit on it or anything."

Selby chuckled, wiping his eyes. "My mother used to do that. It's really disgusting."

"Mine, too." She looked back at the bed, but Roy had fallen asleep. The two of them stood and watched the patient breathe for a few minutes, then Reggie turned to Selby.

"Go home. I'll call you, keep you up to date."

"Do you need help with the Tavern?"

"Dear God in Heaven. Selby Coates tending bar? The mind reels. No, that won't be necessary, but thanks. Joboss and his mother will be taking over for a few days. We've got it covered."

"Anything I can do …"

"I know, baby."

He looked at Roy lying in the strange bed, her makeup ruined, her hair chopped and disordered. *I did that to her*, he thought.

"Everything is going to be fine, Coates. You hear me?"

"I … Yes. Of course." He allowed Reggie to give him a careful hug, and then he turned and headed for home.

Pancake accurately assessed his master's mood and hastened to climb up onto the bookcase and sit staring out at the pigeons, pretending Selby wasn't there.

The bus ride home had been an unproductive whirl of recriminations and criticism, all leveled at himself. He was calmer now but still distressed.

Barry Ratliffe didn't answer his phone, and Selby hung up with a scowl after four rings. *Of course*, he thought, *midday on a Thursday. School is in session.* He redialed and waited.

"Hello. You've reached Barry's phone, but Barry is doing something else right now. If you're feeling optimistic, leave a name and number, and I may get back to you. Don't bother leaving a message because I never listen to those anyway."

Chirp.

"Ratliffe. Barry. Whichever you prefer. This is Selby Coates. Call me, please."

With a sense of deep dissatisfaction, Selby disconnected. Voicemail. Who thought that was a good idea?

The other conversations he needed to have weren't going to be possible. He was far too upset to access the Empty Room, and he had no other way to communicate with Laylah or Doma. They probably didn't have voicemail in whatever ghastly spiritual underworld they occupied when they weren't causing trouble in this one.

But that was not entirely true: he did have one link to Doma. A line of communication that didn't rely on reading the entrails of a sheep or inhaling hallucinogenic volcanic gases. He put his jacket back on and hustled out the door. He had put off the inevitable far too long already.

Pancake continued to watch the pigeons. Half a mile away, the father of the gods displayed his thunderbolts and his majestic backside in the shadowless light of a milk glass sky.

Bus service in the Intermodal District was designed to connect the area as a whole with the rest of the city, not to facilitate travel within it. After no fewer than three transfers—to cover a distance of hardly more than four miles—Selby found himself at a bus stop three blocks from the offices of Unified Global Logistics Consulting. He looked around, getting his bearings, then zipped up his jacket and walked.

Everything here looked like Ruth Coates: expensive packaging over a grim, industrial-grade product. After the first block, even the sidewalk withered away, forcing Selby to tramp along in the grit and litter of the shoulder, flinching at every passing car.

The Empty Room had opened during the bus ride, and Selby had hefted the great smoking boulder of his frustration into the space to prevent the door from closing again. Whispers sent agitated tendrils out into his mind, then snatched them back, singed. The emptiness surged and swirled with apprehension and anticipation, like the crowd at an apartment-house fire. He sensed Laylah and Doma, fragrant smoke and icy fog, but neither made any attempt to connect with him.

The parking lot at the UGLC building was about half full. Selby wondered how many people worked there and what they did all day. Office space in the Intermodal was pricey, so they had to be making money. It was hard for Selby to think of Ruth Coates as a human being, a person with a life and a career. In his mind, she was a cardboard cutout, a predictable villain in the drama they shared. What induced a successful corporate executive to stitch her mouth shut from time to time and play toady to a creature like Doma?

But then, he thought, one could ask how he himself had ended up doing Laylah's bidding. Perhaps Ruth Coates had also undergone some pivotal event, a moment when her life became balanced on the point of a pin, a moment when she made a choice that changed her and her world forever. Anyway, at least Doma existed. Laylah was nothing more than a voice, an animating principle stalking through Selby's dreams wearing the faces of long-dead B-grade movie actors.

The tattooed guard, Jason, was not on duty, but the other one —James? No, Joe—was sitting behind the desk while a young Black woman in the same uniform stood leafing through items on a clipboard.

Joe looked up with a canned greeting loaded up behind his teeth, ready to launch, and then he recognized the visitor.

"Mr. Coates. I'm sorry, but Ms. Coates has instructed us not to allow you into the building, sir."

"How unfortunate. I thought she and I were friends."

The other guard looked up sharply at Selby's tone. Her name badge read "Lainie". She moved to say something—

The Empty Room breathed, and time's arrow froze in flight. *Stuck in the middle of a heartbeat*, Selby thought.

"Selby, dear."

The smell of sandalwood and cloves and burning wax rose around the three of them, and Selby's eyes grew round. He looked around, but there was nobody in the lobby but him and the two guards.

"What do you want, Laylah?" He was being rude, and he would almost certainly feel bad about that later, but right now he had no patience for diplomacy. Everything felt brittle, as though the air around him might shatter at a glance.

"What are you about to do?"

There was something so absurd about Laylah's question that Selby lost his breath for a moment, and then the words burst out of him uncontrolled, startling him with their vehemence.

"Do? What am I about to do? I have no idea! You've told me nothing! Given me no tools to defend myself with! You set me an impossible task and then went about making it as difficult as possible. You placed my friends in danger! What do you expect me to do? And, for that matter, *why*? Who is my father, and what does he have to do with the likes of you? Whatever else he was, he was a human being, a person I loved. But you? You're a phantom. A voice. Wheedling and threatening." He paused for breath, fighting back his frustration. Joe and Lainie watched this outburst with slow, bland indifference.

"I loved your father, too," Laylah's voice said, the words slipping into the momentary silence like the smoke of a candle rising into a warm night.

Laylah was only a voice and a scent. Joe and Lainie had disconnected, as though Selby's presence in front of them, arguing with a disembodied voice that only he could hear, was a story someone was telling them, a story they didn't find all that interesting. They were wrapped in an apathy so deep they might as well have been asleep.

"Were you one of his wives? His women?"

"Oh, Selby. 'One of his wives?' I was his sister, Selby, his dearest, his companion through lifetimes. We were two parts of one beautiful thing. He was taken from me, shattered and scattered, while I was reduced to … What did you call me? A phantom. A voice."

Selby braced against the guards' kiosk, trying to take some of the weight off his knee. Joe glanced down at Selby's hand, where it gripped the edge of the counter, then back up at his face, his expression polite, a little bored.

"You couldn't tell me any of this before now?" Selby snapped.

"Something has happened. You've crossed some threshold. I can't pretend to understand it all, but you've connected with that part of your father that is in you. I don't know how long this moment will last, but until the infinite possibilities collapse back into one, I'm free to speak."

"My father is one of you? You and Doma?"

"And others. All different, all one. All forever."

Selby shut everything out and breathed. *In and out. In and out.* He counted the breaths, slowing them down, pulling in the good air, pushing out the bad, clearing the scent of incense and candles from his sinuses.

He turned to the guards. "Who is with my—"

Not my sister. I never had a sister.

"Who is with Ms. Coates?"

Joe shrugged. "Her husband, I think. There might have been a couple of other people." Joe could not have been less interested in what might or might not be going on in Ms. Coates's office.

In and out. In and out.

"Thank you, Joe."

Selby turned and walked back outside, leaving Laylah's hovering presence behind. He walked around the corner of the building and into the courtyard.

Presumably, he knew the names of the trees, since in his dream Jason had been able to identify them, but on a conscious level, Selby knew them only as small trees wearing leaves in pretty colors, even this late in the year. He walked into the park-like space until he found a concrete bench, a narrow slab suspended across two shorter slabs. Selby had never seen a more unwelcoming piece of furniture.

If Ruth Coates were a park bench, this would be it, he thought.

He eased down onto the bench and closed his eyes. A chilly, damp breeze blew across his cheek, cooling his hot ears.

His knee hurt. Maybe Doctor Lehman was right, and it was time to think about a replacement. He hated the idea of having some part of his body taken away forever, replaced with a coun terfeit, a lifeless thing of metal and plastic.

Change, he thought. *I don't like changes that can't be easily undone.*

He had to confront Ruth Coates and, through her, Doma. The attack on Roy was a step too far, even more than the vandalism of his apartment. Even if they did not intend to hurt her, they frightened her, and she was hurt as a consequence. Selby could have died under that bus in front of the Herald-Star—maybe he was supposed to have—but someone threw him a lifeline, and he took it. That didn't mean he had to allow the consequences of that decision to hurt other people.

He looked up at the broad, blank windows of the building. Ruth was there, and her husband. Doma's presence hung over the whole place like a layer of cold air, pregnant with ice. Watching and waiting.

"How far are you willing to go to keep Sullivan Coates hidden from me?" he murmured. "There are rules to this game, but I don't know what they are. Is there a line you can't cross?"

Doma had been pushing him toward a confrontation. Clearly, she was not afraid of the outcome.

With a shock, Selby realized that he wasn't, either. He was too tired. There was nothing she could do to him that time wasn't going to do soon enough.

He climbed to his feet and looked around the courtyard. In his dream, the place had seemed so much more alive. The real thing was just a bit of stage decoration, calculated and inert. A wave of sadness passed through him: pity for the little trees, trapped in their brick borders, isolated from each other, cut off from the living, breathing forests that their ancestors were once a part of. Nothing now but ornaments.

So lonely.

Selby adjusted his collar and checked to make sure his shoes were tied and his fly was zipped. Then he headed inside to beard the lioness in her den.

CHAPTER TWENTY-TWO

"Mr. Ratliffe? Barry Ratliffe?"

Ratliffe frowned and shifted the phone to his other ear.

"Yes? What can I do for you?"

"We haven't met. My name is Régine Bernard."

The woman had only the faintest trace of an accent except on the surname: *Behr-nahrd*. Ratliffe knew instantly that this was someone connected to his new friend. His very *odd* new friend.

"Yes?"

"You've met my wife, Roy Freeborn."

I knew it. "Yes, ma'am. You're friends with Selby Coates."

"Yes. I'm calling about Selby. Have you seen him today?"

"No, but he called earlier and asked me to call him back. I was in class and missed the call. When I tried to call him back, I didn't get an answer. Somebody needs to help him set up his voicemail, by the way."

"Good luck with that. Listen, Roy was in an accident last night. She ended up in the ER with a concussion. Selby is very upset."

"Is she going to be okay?"

"Yes, she'll be fine. I'm worried about Selby, though. I tried to call him a little while ago with an update, and he didn't answer his phone."

"Does he screen his calls?"

"No, he just doesn't realize he's getting them. He never remembers to carry the phone with him when he goes out."

"He's had a lot on his mind."

"You have no idea. Do you know where he might have gone? I don't suppose he said anything to you."

"No. I haven't talked to him since I helped him set up his phone." Ratliffe thought for a moment. "Ms. Bernard—"

"Reggie, please."

"Reggie. Roy's accident. Was there anything out of the ordinary about it?"

"Like creepy guys with their mouths sewn up, walking up on her in a dark alley? Yeah. There was that."

Ratliffe made a face. He looked up at the clock.

"I'll be getting out of here in fifteen minutes. I might have an idea where he's gone. I'll go look for him."

Reggie exhaled, a long, loud breath. "Thank you, Mr. Ratliffe—"

"Just Ratliffe."

"Ratliffe. Thank you. Will you call me when you find him?"

"You bet."

Ratliffe disconnected and looked around. His last class of the day had shambled out half an hour ago. In a perfect world, he'd be spending the next half hour or so grading papers.

In a perfect world, Ratliffe thought, stuffing the test papers into his briefcase, Selby Coates would look like Beyoncé and would have no problems more serious than finding a balding, middle-aged schoolteacher to take to the Grammys.

He pulled on his jacket and headed for the parking deck.

. . .

Joe and Lainie looked up when Selby came back through the front doors of the UGLC building. Joe started to speak, frowning, but a great wave of soundless whispers rolled over the guard station, wrapping its occupants in comfortable, feather-soft apathy. After a long moment, all the guard did was shrug. Selby limped past the desk and pushed the button for the elevator while the guards went back to paging through a super-market tabloid and commenting in soft, slow voices on the outrages they discovered there.

Selby felt calm in spite of all the recent aggravation, but the spectators in the Empty Room were anxious, agitated. What had Naomi said about the rustlings that accompanied Selby's birth? That sound in a theater just before the play, after everybody has settled down and put their art-appreciation faces on, but before the lights go down.

The interior of the elevator had mirrors covering one side. Selby resolutely turned away from the mirror and instead stared at a stylized map of the world that purported to show the reach of UGLC's operations. It was the same map that covered one wall of Ruth Coates's office; this one was shrunk down to the point where all the dots and arrows were just squiggles, devoid of meaning. Across the bottom of the map ran the slogan, "Unified Global Logistics Consulting: We Find a Way!"

The elevator jiggled to a stop, and the door slid open on two corridors running at right angles to each other. Selby's destination was the second door on the left, halfway down the right-hand corridor. He opened the door and stepped inside.

"My goodness," Selby said after a deep breath. "This is quite the reunion."

Ruth Coates stood behind her desk, facing him, her back to the view over the courtyard. Selby guessed that she didn't know the names of the lonely little trees either.

"You're not welcome here, Mr. Coates. You need to leave now," she said.

"An old man like you won't enjoy getting tossed out on his butt," added a short, stocky man dressed for outdoors standing to one side of the desk. The white lettering on his red cap read, "Beefy Boy's BBQ."

"Mitchell Coffey, I presume," Selby said. "I'm pleased to

finally meet you. I hope your time in jail hasn't soured your *joie de vivre*."

Two tall, thin young men dressed like Mormon missionaries stood in front of the sofa, under the giant map. They contributed nothing to the conversation because their lips were sewn shut. Selby looked at them, then looked away, his ears hot.

A fifth figure stood with her back to the room, staring out the window into the cold light. She wore an exquisitely tailored white pantsuit and low-heeled white shoes. Her hair, also white, was braided and coiled into a snowy crown atop her head. The skin that showed on the nape of her neck above her collar was as smooth and pale as milk.

"This is unexpected," Selby said. "A surprise visit from the boss?" His voice was less steady than he would have liked, but he stood in front of the door without fidgeting, and he was surprised to find that he still wasn't afraid.

Well, maybe a little, he thought.

"You hurt my friend," he said, turning to the nerdy boys. As one, they raised their right hands, and Selby felt the silence close in. He thought of Roy lying in that hospital bed, and his anger found focus.

"No," he said, his voice steady now. "Not this time. I've been figuring some things out since the last time we ran into each other."

The whispering in the Empty Room had grown to the churning of distant surf. Selby reached into the midst of the silent noise and brought back a handful of nothing. He tossed the nothing in the direction of the acolytes, and both men flinched, then jerked back, eyes wide. The gathering silence dissipated with a bone-rattling crack, and Ruth Coates hissed a curse. The acolytes clutched at their heads, making little muffled cries as the filament binding their mouths snapped in multiple places to dangle uselessly like the whiskers of a bottom-feeding fish.

Selby turned to Mitchell Coffey.

"Stop it!" Ruth Coates grated. She was pressing a buzzer on her desk, over and over. "Get the hell out of my office!"

Coffey looked at his wife, uncertain what to do in the absence of explicit orders. His hands, thick-fingered and strong, clenched and unclenched at his sides.

The hands that wrecked my apartment, destroyed my things Selby thought.

"Mr. Coffey. Your wife has, no doubt, told you about the security camera footage I have of you coming and going at my apartment building."

"So? You can't prove I did anything."

Selby stared at him, his ears pink, his eyes round and innocent.

"I'm not interested in proving anything, Mr. Coffey."

Coffey stepped forward, but he flinched after only a single step. He shook his head, his face screwed up in perplexity. Slapping at his ears, he looked at his wife, then at Selby.

"What the fuck?"

"*Stop it, Coates*," Ruth said again.

"He's experiencing the silence that you people inflicted on me. I saved a little of it. I don't really know how I did that, but… There it is. Seems a shame to let it go to waste."

Selby looked around the room. The acolytes were mewling and sobbing, dabbing at their mouths with tissues from a box on the coffee table in front of the long sofa. Mitchell Coffey was shaking his head like a bear tormented by hornets. Ruth Coates stood glaring at him with the same hard expression as ever—but was that a hint of fear creeping around her upper lip, the corners of her eyes? The white woman at the window continued to study the clouds and the passing crows and the tops of the ornamental trees shuddering in the wintry breeze.

This, then, was how it felt to be the one on top.

He should have been elated. After all, wasn't this the fulfillment of a fantasy for a man who had always been the one being stepped on? These people had done bad things to him and the people he cared about. Owen didn't deserve to be frightened into a seizure. Roy didn't deserve to be in a hospital bed, her makeup ruined, her glamorous armor cracked. Selby should have felt like a hero. An avenger.

But no. What he actually felt was *sad*.

Just ... sad.

They're not evil, he thought, looking at Ruth Coates's face. *Only stupid.*

In a way, Ruth really was Selby's sister, even without shared blood. Like him, she was somebody who was never pretty enough, never smart enough, who never wore the right clothes, read the right books, listened to the right music ... The sort of person who didn't get invited to things, not because people thought bad things about her, but because they simply didn't think about her at all. Ruth wore power and authority the way Roy wore her Emma Peel catsuits, and the way Selby wrapped himself in wordy introversion: as a defense, as a way to be real, to be strong, to be visible. To not be overlooked. Selby understood that all too well.

To his disgust, Selby found himself crying. His anger cooled, decomposing into something rank and stale. He reached into his mind and pulled and pushed at the door to the empty room until the whispers fell silent.

Mitchell Coffey let out a noisy breath, his expression baffled and relieved. The acolytes held hands on the sofa, weeping quietly.

"So. Now what?" Selby asked no one in particular.

Not everyone loves power, came a cold voice in Selby's head. *Your father also saw it as a curse.*

Doma turned to face him. Her face, as always, was a mask, expressionless and lovely, disfigured by the stitches across her lips.

"I give up," Selby said quietly. "I surrender. Whatever. You can keep my father. Knowing who he is, who I am, is not that important if it hurts people."

Doma bowed her head the tiniest fraction.

We've come too far for that, Selby Coates. Besides, you made a bargain with our Sister.

An invisible giant closed its fist around Selby's ribs and squeezed. Selby gasped, but he didn't cry out. A thread of stubbornness still held, and he refused to give her the satisfaction.

A new key was born, a new ark to contain all that was best and most sacred of our Brother, against the time of his restoration and the end of our shared ordeal. Once your father's new son had shown himself to be healthy and strong, you should have left this life behind.

Doma turned to gaze out at the landscape. A trio of crows flew past the window, wheeled, then descended into the courtyard. A moment later, they rose and continued on their way, disappearing from view around the corner of the building.

There can ever only be one. Our Sister intervened, and you survived past your appointed time. Now, there are two, and no way to know which is the one that matters and which can be safely discarded.

She turned to look at Selby again.

Are you the one we need? The one who has the potential to bring our Brother, the being you call your father, back to us? Whole and perfect?

The invisible grip tightened further, and Selby closed his eyes. The whispers, offended at having been shut away, refused to open their door to him.

Or are you just an empty box, the gift it might have contained long since passed on for safe keeping to someone else?

He felt wetness on his lip; his nose was bleeding.

Our Sister hoped to speed events to their conclusion. Instead, she sowed chaos.

"So you involve us helpless little mortals in your stupid

games, then beat up on us for not being what you want us to be," Selby panted through gritted teeth. "Aren't you noble."

Doma's bland expression sharpened the tiniest bit, her eyes focusing on his face for an instant. Selby wondered if this was, for her, a sign of emotion.

I had to force you to act, to wake up. To awaken your father's legacy inside you. To see who you were. Who you might be. I succeeded, but even now, I still can't be sure.

The fist gave a nasty jerk, and Selby's vision closed to a window the size of a coin, centered on the pale Botticelli face.

You are nothing. A hundred like you, a thousand, have been born, lived their petty, meaningless lives, and died, each in turn passing the burden to the next. Posturing apes.

She stared at him for several heartbeats, and then the giant opened its hand.

Our Sister is wrong. The time for redemption has not yet come.

Selby fell to his knees, grunting with the pain of the impact, and his glasses fell off.

Go. Do what you think you must. The future is smoke, and you are useless to us.

Selby fumbled his glasses back onto his face and struggled to his feet. Doma stared at him as if he were a bug or an unexpected water stain on the carpet. They stood like that for what seemed like hours until finally, the pale woman turned and walked through the plate glass window as if it didn't exist. Outside, a sudden dense whirl of white rode the turbulent air for a moment, then dispersed.

The first snow of the season had begun.

Selby looked around the office, his blood still loud in his ears. Ruth Coates stood, tottering, then fell back into her chair to glare at him. Mitchell Coffey went to her side and squatted next to the chair to hold her hand. The acolytes had fled, leaving the office door open.

Selby touched his lip and grimaced. He hobbled over to the tasteful sofa and snatched a handful of tissues from the tasteful dispenser on the tasteful coffee table. He looked at the map as he dabbed and snuffled, mopping up blood.

The map was painted onto an enormous sheet of metal. Magnetic markers were scattered across the surface, resembling nothing so much as the little game pieces that belonged to the Parcheesi set Selby had owned as a child. Red, blue, yellow, green. Singapore, Los Angeles, Tokyo, Buenos Aires …

Selby plucked another handful of tissues and stepped closer to the map, pinching his nostrils carefully. An inset showed a close-up view of the Five Counties. Port Sebastian was marked in blue, as was Buckley. Forming the third vertex of a tight little equilateral triangle, a lone white marker sat below those two. Selby stepped back, scanning the map. There were no other white markers anywhere.

He looked back at Ruth and Coffey, but they seemed to have forgotten about him.

Selby picked the white marker off the map, looked at what was beneath it, and then allowed it to clack back into place.

Taking some more tissues, he turned and limped out of the office.

Down in the lobby, Selby found Barry Ratliffe at the guard's kiosk, his face grim, leaning over the counter, nose to nose with Joe. He saw Selby and straightened.

"Coates! What the fuck, man?"

"Ratliffe. Barry. Whatever. What are you doing here?" An oceanic weariness had settled onto Selby in the elevator. Now, he felt as though he walked through water up to his chest.

"Looking for you. Reggie was worried. What happened to your face?"

"It's only a nosebleed. Is Roy okay?"

"On her way home this evening."

Selby nodded, breathing through his mouth. In and out. In and out. A drop of blood ran into his mouth, and he grimaced at the taste. He touched his lip and glared down at the smear of red on his fingertip.

"How do you know when you're having a stroke?"

"Do you think you're having a stroke?"

"I have no idea. That's my point. How would I know?"

"You'd probably be on the floor shitting yourself or something like that," Ratliffe said.

"Oh. That's disgusting. I'm not doing that." He grimaced at the mass of blood-stained tissues in his hand and looked around. "Where is the wastebasket?"

Joe and Lainie listened to the conversation without interest. Selby pried the door of the Empty Room open just far enough to return animation and personality to the guards, and they both blinked, looking confused and a little angry.

"I'll have to ask you to leave the building, Mr. Coates," Joe said, picking up the thread of the narrative from the last point at which anything had made sense.

"Of course," Selby replied. He stumbled, and Ratliffe took hold of his elbow. "I'm all right," Selby assured him. "Just tired. And my knee hurts. And I'm hungry."

"Let's get out of here. We'll go get a pizza or something. Get you cleaned up."

Selby dumped the tissues on the counter and allowed Ratliffe to walk him out the front door.

"Not pizza. Those takeout places are always so squalid."

. . .

Fiona's Baby Diary:
We took Bingo to Luna's for lunch today. What a mess! Nobody seemed to mind, though. Everybody just loved him. Father and son shared a piece of key lime pie with whipped cream. They might as well have put the pie on the floor and rolled in it. By the time they were done, Bongo had whipped cream all over his

shirt and even in his hair, and I won't even say what the baby looked like. The waitress was INCREDIBLY helpful. It was easy to see that she's got a massive crush on Bongo. But who doesn't?

CHAPTER TWENTY-THREE

Selby and Ratliffe ate soup and grilled cheese sandwiches at a chain restaurant while Selby explained the events of the day as well as he was able. Ratliffe accepted everything—both what Selby said and what he didn't—without argument.

"I wish you had let me know what you had in mind," the schoolteacher said.

"I called," Selby protested.

"Your message said to call you. You didn't say you were on your way to rain down the wrath of God on your enemies."

"I didn't—that's not what I—"

"Figure of speech. It's okay, man. You did what you had to do. I like Roy, too."

The snow continued all night.

Selby awoke before dawn and spent a quiet hour in front of the window drinking coffee and looking out at Zeus posing in his spotlights, the snow piling up around his naked brass feet.

I'll bet he wishes he had more than a fig leaf on right now, Selby thought.

Pancake slithered off the bed to circle Selby's ankles, his tail held up like a flag.

"Gods and monsters, Pancake. It all seemed so simple before. Is this Dr. Pretorius' new world?"

Pancake stretched and yawned and went to sit by his food

dish, staring off into eternity.

Selby nodded. "You're probably right. I'm overthinking it." He fed the cat and poured himself more coffee.

The light had risen enough that he could see a dabble of white among the trees and rooftops below his aerie, as though the artist had dipped a sponge in the paint and dotted it just there, and there, and a little bit across there.

What had Selby achieved yesterday? Maybe not the wrath of God, but he had definitely upset a number of people. Doma had implied that she was done with him. Did this mean an end to her and her servants harassing Selby and his friends? That would certainly make the trip worthwhile.

Don't forget the map. The white marker.

Sullivan Coates. A name from Selby's past. Just a name.

A thought struck him. What was his father's name, really? Surely an immortal being who had the likes of Laylah and Doma babysitting him could boast a more distinctive label than "Sullivan Coates." What was he? What were they? The Colonel had been right. For all Selby knew, there were whole colonies of immortal Lotharios and ice maidens and women who walked in dreams, living among the just-plain-folks, hidden in plain sight.

Gods and monsters. Naomi knew, he thought, as the sky lightened to the color of milk. She knew Sullivan wasn't what she thought he was when she married him. No wonder she had such a hard time keeping it together.

Not only Naomi. Elizabeth Harwell and her daughter. All the others. What did Doma say? A hundred, a thousand. All those families. All those women, so in love, caught up in Sullivan Coates's irresistible charisma. All allowed to bask in Sullivan's joy. All doomed to disappointment, to grief.

How many other little boys and girls woke up and looked around one day to discover that the father they had loved so unconditionally for their entire lives had simply evaporated as if he had never existed?

He was my father, and I worshiped him, and he wasn't even real.

The snow had ceased to fall for the moment, but every passing breeze brought down a fluffy drift from the roof to whirl past the window. The overcast looked pregnant, heavy with more snow, waiting to deliver.

Am I real?

Selby finished his coffee just as Zeus's spotlights clicked off for the day, leaving the old god naked and gray under the milky sky.

The snow fell for a week, sometimes coming down so hard that visibility was limited to a few confusing yards in any direction, and Zeus' spotlights came on in the middle of the afternoon, their sensors befuddled by the darkness. At other times, there were only a few flakes here and there, as fitful, disorganized breezes swept the fallen snow off windowsills or shook it down from the branches of trees. Rough snowmen proliferated in lawns and parks, diminutive and gritty, like fairytale dwarves up from the mines, white with rockdust.

Selby walked every day, wearing insulated snow boots and two pairs of socks. He hated the cold and gray of winter, but he found this early snow enchanting, even as passing cars and pedestrians turned it into dirty slush. All the familiar streets and alleys were new, heaped with gray and white lace, as though a herd of newly minted brides had galloped through on the way to their honeymoons, shedding their virginity as they ran.

A girl's dreams, Naomi had said.

Doma and her people had disappeared from view. Ruth Coates was presumably hunkered down, dividing her time between her career and her devotion to her Goddess, waiting for new instructions, a new target for her endless, anxious spite. The acolytes … What would have happened to them? Were they stripped of their power, their connection to the silence, when the bindings fell from their mouths? Were they now just ordinary men, young and foolish, struggling to find a new identity for themselves, a new way to say, "This is who I am?"

Laylah, also, had remained out of sight. Selby's dreams were sometimes turbulent, sometimes anxious, sometimes even steamy, but not once, while the snow fell, was his sleep visited by the scent of desert spices or the gaze of willow-green eyes.

On Saturday, the snow took a break, and Selby met Barry Ratliffe at the Tavern for lunch.

Selby arrived early and startled Roy by asking for a menu.

"A menu?" She stood gaping at him across the bar, her new, shorter hairstyle emphasizing her eyes in her long, narrow face. Her eye shadow was the clear blue of the Bombay Sapphire gin she gave the Botox Babes when all they wanted were gin and tonics but were afraid to be boring.

"A menu. A laminated card that lists the food items you have available?"

"Don't make me come across this bar at you," Roy said, handing him a menu. "When did you learn sarcasm?"

Selby's ears glowed. "I've always had it. It never seemed appropriate. Things have been different lately."

"Evolve or die, right? Isn't that what you always say?"

"That's what I always say, yes."

"Do you believe it?"

"Sometimes."

Apart from shorter hair, Roy appeared none the worse for her experience with the acolytes. She had, Selby noted, begun expanding her wardrobe beyond spy-movie catsuits. Today, she was wearing navy blue tights and a puffy baby-blue sweater, a cloud of drifting filaments that shivered in every breeze and with every movement. She wore a tiny mother-of-pearl comb in her hair. He found the change unsettling.

Selby was startled by a slap on the back. He was sure he

didn't know anybody who slapped people on the back.

"Hey, man. How's the dragon-hunting business?"

Ratliffe.

The schoolteacher's khaki pants were wet to the knees, and the knitted cap covering his balding head made him look more than ever like Scotty, Douglas Spencer's snarky journalist in *The Thing from Another World*, from 1951. Selby had always liked Scotty, apart from his speech at the end of the movie, which Selby thought descended too obviously into Cold War propagandizing. He responded to Ratliffe's backslap with a pink-faced nod. The schoolteacher slid onto the stool next to Selby's and accepted a menu from Roy with a smile.

"No new dragons, please," Selby said. "I want to finish up with the ones I have and go back to being boring old Selby Coates."

"May be harder than you think, Frodo. Seeing as how you've been to Mordor and all."

Selby nodded, flustered, and studied his menu carefully.

Two of the architects from across the way blew in from the cold in a flurry of duck boots and down-filled coats. They climbed out of their coats and caps, stomping slush all over the mat, then draped their things over the backs of their chairs, the remaining snow melting into a puddle on the floor. The back-slapper was missing; only the anxious one and the quiet one sat down to order burgers and beer. Selby wanted badly to go mop up the water before they tracked it into mud.

With a grim sigh, he turned to Ratliffe.

"What do you know about the town of Vale?"

Ratliffe shrugged, continuing to look at the menu. "Used to be '*The* Vale,' but they shortened it ten or twelve years ago. Dinky place, about four, five thousand people—too small to justify the extra three letters, I guess. I went up there a couple of times back when I was a paramedic on that beat."

"It's near where Ruth Coates had her accident."

Ratliffe put the menu down. "Yeah. Vale would have been the closest town. You figure that's where she was coming from —or going to—when she had her fender-bender?"

Selby told the schoolteacher about the map on Ruth Coates's office wall.

"That seems a bit thin," Ratliffe said. "How can you be sure the marker on the map was for Vale?"

"What else is near there?"

"There's Camden."

"That's eighteen miles away, on the other side of the Maryville Road. And Mary's Gap is thirty-six miles away. I checked the distances online."

Roy brought iced tea, and Ratliffe took a sip. Selby waited.

The schoolteacher put down his glass. "All right. Even if that's what the marker means—that your dad is living in Vale— why does Ruth Coates have it marked on her map? It's not like she's going to forget where she has him tucked away."

"Because that's who she is," Selby said. "She's like me. She needs everything organized and neatly pinned down. If she's marking other locations of importance, then she has to mark that one, too."

Ratliffe nodded slowly, chewing this over.

Roy took their food orders, raising elegant eyebrows in surprise at Selby's choice.

"You're sure?" she said.

Selby nodded, blushing. "Yes, please."

"It could be one of us next," The anxious architect said, too loudly, slapping the table. His friend shushed him.

"He brought this on himself," the quiet architect said. "He let himself get distracted by all the bullshit office politics and quit paying attention to his work."

The other man subsided, unappeased, and Selby looked over at Ratliffe.

"I may need your help again," he said carefully.

"Good," Ratliffe said. He crunched an ice cube, spitting half of it back into the glass and laughing when he saw Selby's expression. "Sorry. Bad habit."

"Not as bad as me being judgmental about it," Selby said. "Anyway, I'd like to go to Vale and look around. I need a driver."

"And bodyguard?"

"No. Definitely not. If we think there is the slightest danger to either of us, we turn around and run away."

Ratliffe laughed again. "I like the way your mind works. I've got some time off for Christmas break. From the eighteenth all the way to the end of the month."

"You don't mind?"

Ratliffe smiled, but he didn't laugh this time. "No, I don't mind. Since Laura passed away, I've been slipping into a kind of trance. Eat, sleep, go to work, walk the dog. A few weeks ago, I realized that I had started leaving dishes in the sink, not making the bed. Shit Laura would have hated, but she wasn't there, so screw her opinion, right?" He crunched another ice cube, his attention turned inward.

After a moment, he went on. "Since that dream, the one with the little girl and your monkey, since I met you and got involved in your weirdness, I've cleaned up my act. I'm washing the dishes and making the bed. I'm even dating somebody once in a blue moon, when my schedule and hers match up. I'm looking at things again, ordinary things, thinking about all the crazy shit that might be hiding just below the surface. It's … well, it's making me pay attention again. I owe you for that."

Tongue-tied, Selby blushed and rotated his beer mug a hundred and eighty degrees clockwise, then a hundred and eighty degrees counterclockwise.

Just in time, the little bell rang, and Roy delivered sandwiches to the two men.

"I feel as though I'm watching the end of an era," she said, looking at Selby's plate.

"Why do you say that?" Selby asked, his ears still pink.

"A veggie burger! Three years, a couple of times a week, you've never eaten anything but the tempeh and avocado. Who are you, and what have you done with Selby Coates? We don't serve pod people here."

Selby blushed and looked down at his food. "The other Selby is around here somewhere." He looked up at Roy with round, innocent eyes. "It seemed like the right time to consider a change. Evolve or die."

"Just don't get carried away," she said. "If you start coming in here and ordering bacon burgers and single-malt scotch, we'll have to have a talk."

"Under those circumstances, that would probably be a good idea."

One of the architects held up an empty mug, and Roy nodded and excused herself.

"So," Ratliffe said, "when are you thinking of visiting Vale?" He took a bite of his sandwich while Selby organized his food to his satisfaction, arranging the plate properly, moving his beer mug to its correct location.

"How long does it take to get there?"

Ratliffe shrugged, chewing. "Depends on the weather, this time of year," he said around a mouthful of food. "Couple of hours, each way, I'd say."

Selby took a cautious bite of his sandwich, chewed it carefully, swallowed. Roy watched from the end of the bar, grinning, then went to seat a pair of older women twittering and giggling as they stomped dirty snow off their shoes.

"We could do it during the week of the eighteenth," Selby said. "Whatever day works best for you."

"Wednesday, then," Ratliffe said promptly. "What's that, the twentieth? Interesting things always happen on Wednesdays. Go early, come back before dark?"

"That would be perfect." Selby blushed over his veggie burger. "Thank you. I'm not used to asking for help with things. I ... well, just thank you."

Ratliffe smiled and turned his attention to his own food.

Shimmering like a cloud of blue snow, Roy welcomed a dour quartet of bank tellers from up the street. The elderly ladies tossed back Manhattans and giggled. The architects drank beer and plotted the overthrow of the tyrant of the fifth floor.

On the way back up the hill to his apartment, Selby found the Colonel in front of his house, using a broom to clear a path through the snow from his front door all the way out to the middle of the street. He had cleared away much of the underbrush separating the house from the road, and the tall, narrow façade looked naked and uneasy, like a bearded man appearing clean-shaven for the first time in years. The front door stood ajar, and the Colonel had swept the snow to either side of a path just wide enough for a man to walk.

"Bolívar does not like going in the snow and wet," the old man explained.

"Why does he need to go all the way out into the street?"

"To shit, of course," the Colonel replied.

"In the street? I assume you clean up after him," Selby said, knowing perfectly well how unlikely that was. The Colonel merely chuckled.

"Have you had any more troubles with your strange young men?" the old man asked, zigzagging his finger over his mouth.

"I think they are retiring," Selby said.

"Good. There is a special place in hell for a man who kicks a little dog," said the ex-dictator alleged to have ordered the deaths of more than 75,000 people over a period of eighteen months in the mid-1980s. He stood leaning on the broom, a deranged shepherd propped up on his staff. "There is a new President in my country," he said, changing the subject.

"Elected, or …?"

The Colonel chuckled. "There are any number of ways a man may take power in my homeland. They are, for the most part, interchangeable. The new President's Minister of Justice is a fat man named Gregor Kadiel."

"You believe him to be Grigorio Cudhill."

"Of course I do. I've seen his images on the news."

"Nobody else sees the resemblance?"

"Everyone sees it, nobody believes it. Aside from my little collection here, I doubt you would find a photograph of the man anywhere. For generations, he has held positions that have allowed him to destroy records, to direct the public conversation, to hide himself. To rewrite history to his convenience. As I once did."

Bolívar came to the door to bare his fangs at Selby.

"Why doesn't Cudhill take the next step?"

"Become President, you mean?" The Colonel shrugged. "As I learned, to my very great annoyance, power is a curse."

Selby blinked. According to Doma, this was Sullivan Coates' philosophy, as well. The repeated parallels between the Colonel's crazy theory and Selby's own experiences were disturbing.

The Colonel went on: "Cudhill—Kadiel, now—has held on for many lifetimes of an ordinary man, through every change, every revolution. His power never diminishes because it is a quiet power, a power that everyone uses but nobody sees. He is the man behind the curtain, not the man on the throne. He is invisible, surrounded by more attractive targets."

If Sullivan Coates was someone—something—similar to Doma and Laylah, he seemed to have integrated himself into humanity far more effectively than they had. Laylah was a green-eyed visitor in dreams. Doma was exotic, visibly inhuman. Others, like Cudhill/Kadiel, were more human. This implied that Selby's father might also have been something other than human, able to hide in plain sight.

The Colonel picked up his broom and glanced back at the dog whining and snarling on the doorstep.

"You seem less inclined to disbelieve this time," he said, turning his clouded eyes back to Selby.

Selby took a deep breath and nodded. "'I've seen some strange and terrible things,'" he quoted.

The Colonel laughed and flung his broom onto his shoulder like a rifle.

"Perhaps we're more alike than you realize," he said. With a grotesque wink, he turned and allowed the little dog to lead him back into the house.

Selby *huff*ed at the implications of that idea and continued up the hill at a more brisk pace. He hoped the grocery store had a few cupcakes left.

CHAPTER TWENTY-FOUR

Selby finished the after-dinner cleanup, wiping down the counters and prying all the knobs off the stove to scrub them in the sink. Pancake sat on the bookcase in front of the window with his back to the snow-bleached night outside. He watched Selby work as though assessing the quality of his services and wondering whether it would be worthwhile to advertise for a younger replacement. Maybe somebody who didn't make so many odd noises when he moved.

Kitchen duties done, Selby changed into his sweats and t-shirt and turned off the lights. He stood for a time at the window in the dark, scratching Pancake behind the ears and gazing out at Zeus.

Snow had piled up on the lee side of Zeus' pedestal, creating a soft, white skirt that reached all the way up to the old brass god's ankles on that side. When the spotlights came on, the light diffused through the mass, softening the glow, giving the scene a fairytale luminosity. In the old days, the incandescent spotlights would melt the snow in minutes, but the LEDs would keep their veil of snow for some time before finally burning through it. Selby approved of the change.

In a little less than two weeks, Selby would visit Vale in the company of Barry Ratliffe. He would find his father, or he wouldn't. He was not entirely clear as to what his next move would be in either case.

Baby steps, he thought. *Deal with one thing at a time.*

He looked around the apartment, illuminated only by the PP&L building across the way, which was always lit up like a Christmas tree at night. He held out his hands to the faint glow, looking at the network of veins standing out just under the skin. Those veins worried him sometimes. They seemed so exposed, so fragile. A bump, a nick, a scrape, and one of them could be laid open. Blood everywhere. Maybe death. At the very least, a big mess for someone to have to clean up.

He tucked his hands under his armpits for a moment, breathing in, breathing out, then climbed into bed and turned out the light. Selby Coates slept on his new pillows, and dreamed.

. . .

The hardwood floors gleamed, and the brocades shimmered. The lighting came from a dozen sources scattered throughout the room, flattering the woman who stood next to the fireplace, smiling faintly.

Dream-Selby felt a flush of pleasure.

"Alice Krige, as Alma Mobley," he said. "*Ghost Story*. I remember when that movie first came out. Toward the end of the seventies, I think. No, maybe it was the beginning of the eighties. I was so young. I thought she was the most beautiful woman I had ever seen. A certain tension around the mouth, a tightness across the cheekbones. No one ever played the part of a dead person with such presence."

Laylah nodded once, acknowledging the compliment, then dismissing it. "You believe you've found your father," she said. She turned and repositioned a ceramic figurine on the mantelpiece, a shepherd boy with two lambs, then picked up a piece of jewelry—an earring, Selby saw—that was lying next to it.

"I think I have a lead," Selby said. "I'm following up on it in a couple of weeks."

Laylah-as-Alice-as-Alma turned to look at him through narrowed eyes, toying with the earring negligently, gracefully, with the fingertips of both hands. Tiny dangling strips of silver shimmered in the warm light. "What are your plans?"

"I would have hoped you'd tell me that," Selby said. "After all, you're the one who launched me on this track. I've been doing your work since you … since I left the hospital."

Laylah/Alma inhaled through her nose and looked away. "My work. I can tell you nothing you don't already know—which is, itself, something you already know. What will you do in Vale?"

Selby shrugged. "Look around, ask questions. It's a small town; somebody will have heard of him."

"And then?"

Selby looked at her. *She really is lovely*, he thought. Her dress was silk, of the palest pink, trimmed with lace at the sleeves and collar. The light brown hair was covered by a hat shaped like a bell, with a stiff scrap of veil descending just to the bridge of her nose. The expression on her face was suspended: not frozen, but held in careful stasis.

Controlled. Like Ruth when she wanted to look like Doma, Selby thought.

"And then?" she persisted.

"And then?" he echoed. "I don't know."

"Will you seek him out?" Her face tightened as if in pain as she spoke but returned to its calm intensity as soon as the words had left her lips.

"Maybe. Maybe not. I need to see him. Is he an old man? Ninety, a hundred years old? Drooling by the fire, shriveled and childish? Or is he the man I knew fifty years ago, young and handsome still? If that's the case, as I am beginning to suspect it is, *what is he*?"

"He is a man that you and I both have loved, in our own times and our own ways," she said. "You know this."

"My seeing him is important, but you can't tell me why. You can't even hint at the reason," Selby said.

"No. I can't. You know this, too."

Standoff. They looked at each other. She watched Selby with a cool intensity, waiting. Selby knew he was missing something, some clue, some opportunity, a question he could ask and that she could answer. Laylah was a lock begging to be opened, but he didn't have the key.

The strange and beautiful woman laid the earring out on the palm of one hand, arranging its parts with the delicate fingertips of the other. Her expression was thoughtful as she studied the bit of jewelry, but Selby could sense an undercurrent of intense anxiety.

"Find him," she said, softly. The air hummed with unspoken significance.

I'm missing something major, Selby thought. *Something critical. Life and death?*

"If I find him," he said, choosing his words one by one, "and if I meet him, face to face … Will I survive that experience? Will he?"

She stared at the earring for a moment longer, stroking it flat, then flung it into the fireplace with a wild gesture. Selby flinched back as the lovely features warped and crawled, becoming the face of a long-dead corpse.

"Will any of us?" the apparition cried. "*Will any of us?*"

. . .

Vale was an old-fashioned town, around four thousand people, all told, with a wide main street and a business district that began and ended abruptly, as though an invisible wall prevented the shops and on-street parking from spilling out into the residential neighborhoods that surrounded them. Ratliffe pulled into an empty parking space—most of them were empty—and turned off the car.

"I don't even know where to start," Selby said. "In the movies, there's always a pub or something, with surly locals and a chatty bartender who's from someplace else and doesn't mind being indiscreet with his information."

Ratliffe chuckled. "I wouldn't count on that, but I imagine an eatery is usually a good place to start. The one across the street has hanging ferns in the windows. That'll be a fancy place where the staff doesn't gossip. This place"—he indicated the slightly shabby shopfront directly in front of them—"will be more relaxed. We'll try that first, then see if there's a real estate agent who likes to chat."

Signage advertised "Fresh Coffee All Day" and "Luna's Pies and Muffins! You Know You Want Some!" A course of white ceramic tile ran along the base of the wall, and condensation hazed the plate glass windows.

"Another cliché," Selby said as they climbed out of the car. "There will either be a hard-bitten older woman, thin, with a sharp, impatient way of talking and a repertoire of sharp retorts, or a young, buxom blonde, possibly chewing gum, definitely reading a magazine."

The little diner was completely deserted apart from a young man of about twenty, wearing white earbuds, his curly red hair pulled back behind an elastic headband, standing behind the counter stacking white ceramic coffee mugs.

"My information is out of date," Selby said.

They moved to the counter, and the waiter greeted them politely, if without any great enthusiasm. Ratliffe ordered coffee for them both.

"Just made a pot," the boy said, putting down cups. "I drink the stuff all day, so it doesn't sit around and get stale."

"Anything to eat?" Ratliffe asked. "We've been driving a while."

The waiter poured coffee and gestured with the pot toward a display of pie and muffins.

"Lunch is over, so the kitchen's closed, but we've got pie."

"Pie is good," Selby said, eagerness coloring his voice. "Is that coconut meringue?"

The boy nodded. "Yep. Made right here in town."

"I'd like a piece of that, please."

Ratliffe ordered a chocolate chip muffin, and the three men chatted about the weather for a few minutes as the waiter laid out plates and napkins and forks, then dished up pie and a muffin.

"This is good," Selby said after a bite. "Baked locally, you said?"

"Yep. My mom. We have a small dairy operation right outside the city limits, plus this place." The boy gestured. "About half the population lives on the farms."

"What do they grow on the farms around here?" Ratliffe asked.

"Organic stuff. Beef, some dairy, veggies … peanuts are getting to be a thing, and there's a place that processes peanut oil, sells it to restaurants in the city. Everything goes to pricey specialty stores."

"Any in Buckley?" Selby asked. "That's where we're from."

"Some there, but the big business is in Port Sebastian. What brings you gents all the way out here?"

Ratliffe shrugged. "Just scouting around. I sell real estate in Buckley. Markets are tight in the city, so I like to get out and see what's happening in the outback. A lot of rich folks like the idea of buying a small farm somewhere for retirement or whatever."

"Yeah, we get a few of those."

Selby blushed at Ratliffe's obvious lie but said nothing.

"I think I've got a cousin in this town," Ratliffe continued. "Coates? Sullivan Coates?"

The boy shook his head, one hip propped against the edge of the counter.

"Could be, I guess, but that name doesn't ring a bell. Coates. Coates?" His left index finger tapped on the counter in time to whatever was playing on his earbuds. "We do have a Colt. Sully Colt. Just moved in a couple of years ago, him and his wife. They used to come in here two or three times a week, but I think she had a baby last year, so they don't get out as much these days."

"Does Colt work for a big company on the river?" Selby asked. "Something in shipping?"

"I believe he does. Whatever he does, he does it from home, but I think he said once that his money all came from hauling stuff from China to California and back again."

"Does he live in town or on a farm?" Ratliffe asked.

"Half and half," the boy said, topping up their coffee. "They bought Mary Mathis's farm. My sister sold them a washer and dryer when they moved in. Their place is right on the city limits, so it's almost town."

"I wonder if he's the same guy?" Ratliffe said. "The names are similar. He might have changed his name to piss off my uncle. They didn't get along worth crap."

"You never know," the boy said, losing interest.

Selby finished his pie, concentrating on his plate. He had never been able to lie convincingly, and even just listening to Ratliffe do it so effortlessly was making his head hurt. Still, the other man had extracted a remarkable amount of information in a matter of minutes. Selby wondered if that might be a skill that a person could learn or if the ability to be a plausible liar had to be inborn.

Ratliffe asked the waiter for the address of the local realtor, and the two men made their way back out onto the street.

"You do that remarkably well," Selby said as he pulled on his hat and gloves.

"Do what?"

"Make up … things. Identities, cover stories."

Ratliffe laughed. "I don't watch a lot of old movies, but I do soak up some television. You can learn a lot watching crime shows."

Selby laughed, looking down at his hands. "All I learned from watching television as a child was how to put down were-wolves and when to worry about the dietary habits of the Baron who owns the castle you're staying in."

They started walking. Now and then, a car, or more often a pickup truck, sailed by, its tires hissing in the slush on the street. Pedestrians moved from shop to shop, bundled up like Arctic explorers, offering the two men a nod as they passed.

"You're very quiet," Ratliffe said after they had traveled a couple of blocks. "You doing okay?"

"I'm fine. Nothing happened for so long; now everything's happening all at once. I feel a little off-balance." He made a frustrated noise. "It would have taken me days to get the information you picked up from that waiter in minutes."

Ratliffe shrugged. "Different skill sets. I'm glad my ability to lie with a straight face has turned out to be so useful."

"Me, too."

Selby didn't tell the other man about the activity inside his head, the surging and seething among the whispers in the Empty Room. Things were moving, taking interest, rising through oceans of thought to taste the waters of Selby's life. It was becoming hard to focus, hard to stay present.

They had reached the end of downtown, a cross street that separated the two-story brick buildings of the business district from the houses and trees of a residential neighborhood with surgical finality. Ratliffe stood and looked around for a moment, then led the way partway down the block to the right.

A sign extended discreetly over the sidewalk with the words "Edwards Realty" written in gold over an obvious imitation of the "ER" monogram of the late British monarch. The plate glass windows were covered with photos and descriptions of properties in the area.

"Hello there! Glad somebody could make it out on a day

like this!" A tiny, sharp-eyed woman of about fifty-five looked up from a table covered with a laminated map as Selby and Ratliffe pushed through the front door, stamping slush from their shoes on the big coir mat. "I'm Jackie Edwards. What can I do for you?" The realtor had a Louise Brooks bob and very red lipstick that matched her eyeglasses,

Ratliffe stepped forward and shook the hand she offered, then Selby followed suit, hanging back a little, not sure what to do or how to do it. He looked at Ratliffe.

"I'm Barry, and this is my friend Selby," Ratliffe said. "We live in Buckley, but we're scouting around for some property in this area for a place to retire to. A friend told us about a farm that was on the market some time back that she thought would be perfect. We were hoping it was still available, or at least something like it."

Selby blinked, and his ears turned pink. Ratliffe's tone, his body language, everything had shifted, changed gears. He sounded like a different person. Was this another aspect of lying to people convincingly that Selby had never understood? Live and learn.

"Can you tell me which farm it is?" Edwards asked, stepping back and indicating the map.

Ratliffe nodded. "Ruth said it belonged to somebody named Mathis. A widow, I think?"

Selby's face went hot. *Ruth*?

Edwards nodded. "Ruth? Is your friend Ruth Coates?"

Ratliffe nodded. "You know her? She and Selby are related. A pair of Coateses."

The realtor laughed. "Always such a small world. Ruth and her husband were involved in the purchase of the Mathis property, as a matter of fact. Something to do with the company she works for. They have the neighboring farm."

"So the Mathis place is off the table? I can't believe she didn't tell me." Ratliffe's dejection was a little overdone, in

Selby's opinion, but impressive nonetheless.

"They bought it about a year and a half ago."

"Oh. We talked about this … I don't know … two Christmases ago?" Ratliffe looked at Selby, who stared back round-eyed.

"Um. Something like that," he ventured after a blank moment.

"We do have a place not far from there," Edwards suggested, looking back and forth between them.

Ratliffe and Selby crowded around the map, and the realtor circled a place with the butt end of a dry-erase marker. "This is the Mathis property," she said. She tracked away from it a short distance and circled two other locations. "And Ruth Coates' farm is here. This one here is the Ringer property. It's been on the market for about three months. The house is a fixer-upper, but I'm sure you gentlemen would enjoy getting it knocked into shape."

Ratliffe nodded. "Close enough to town to be convenient, but far enough away to offer some privacy." He nudged Selby. "What do you think?"

"I … It sounds … it sounds interesting," Selby said, blushing.

Edwards smiled. "The house is unlocked. You could drive out and look at it—although I'm not sure how much you can see in this weather."

"I think that's what we'll do," Ratliffe said. "It's a shame about the other place, though. I should have touched base with Ruth and Mitchell. Thank you so much for your help."

CHAPTER TWENTY-FIVE

They were walking back to the car when Selby finally spoke up.

"You led her to think we were a couple," he said.

Ratliffe shrugged. "Gay couples are great for fixing up underperforming real estate. They have a lot of disposable income, not a lot of kids. House-proud. I imagine we'd be just what she's looking for with some of these places around here." He elbowed Selby. "You played your part beautifully."

"You're making a lot of generalizations, don't you think? Gay couples and real estate?"

Ratliffe stopped and turned to look at Selby. "Statistics. I read *USA Today* sometimes and look at the pie charts. Are you offended?"

Selby opened his mouth to say something, then closed it again. A moment later, he shook his head. "No. I'm not offended. I guess it caught me off guard."

They resumed walking. "Remind me never to commit a crime with you," Ratliffe said. "You don't think on your feet very well."

Selby chuckled, surprising himself. "I've never really thought about it, but you're right. If we have to rob any banks, you'd better not tell me what we're doing until we've made our getaway."

They walked back to the car, looking into shop windows and down side streets.

"How did you know to drop Ruth's name like that?"

Ratliffe chuckled. "Just a guess. There are lots of Ruths in the world. I figured if she bit, then we'd know, and if she didn't, no big deal."

"Brilliant. You got so much information so quickly."

"Not being able to lie is a handicap in a situation like this. Maybe you should practice some little white lies or something and see if you can build up a tolerance."

Selby shook his head. "I blush too easily."

"There is that."

Ratliffe brushed snow off the windshield with his gloved hand, and then the two men climbed into the car.

"So, how do you feel?" Ratliffe asked as they headed out into the countryside. "Really feel? If you don't mind my asking."

"Scared. Excited. Apprehensive. Confused. Need any more?"

"No, those should do it. What do you expect to find? At this Mathis place?"

Selby blew out his cheeks. "Unless we've gone off on a wild goose chase, I hope to find my father. Sullivan Coates."

"Sully Colt."

"Sully Colt. Either a very old man with a surprisingly youthful libido or a man whose apparent age is half mine."

Ratliffe nodded. "I'm not really processing that," he said. "All this supernatural shit is not the way my universe works."

"Mine either, until the bus ran over me. Now, I don't seem to have any choice."

"Will he know you?"

Selby made a sound, an involuntary groan, and Ratliffe glanced over at him. "You don't have to answer that."

"No, it hurts to think about it. How *can* he recognize me? He hasn't laid eyes on me in more than half a century. If he's old, he probably doesn't even remember that I exist. If he's young, then he'll see an old man, somebody old enough to be *his* father. I don't know how to deal with that."

"Jesus. I see what you mean. Do you regret coming out here? We could always go back to the highway and go home."

"No. I can't leave this hanging. I have to know. I have to get Laylah and Doma out of my life, one way or another. I have to put the ghosts to rest. Or at least find them someone else to annoy."

Ratliffe nodded, his eyes on the road ahead. The snow was a powder sifting down from the white sky, blowing in every little breeze, not really sticking to anything, just forming fluffy little dunes. Selby thought the fields and unplowed driveways looked like meringue.

"That was excellent pie," he said, and Ratliffe laughed.

A mile or so from town, Ratliffe slowed, looking at the numbers on the mailboxes.

"This one," he said after a few minutes. He pulled over to the side of the road. "Okay, boss. What's our story?"

Selby shook his head. "I don't know. We shouldn't block the driveway, and I'd rather no one saw us—at least until we know the lay of the land—so the car should stay here. I'll walk up to the house." The driveway curved around to disappear behind a small stand of pine trees. "I assume it's not far."

The two men climbed out of the car. The driveway might have been a river of milk running through the trees. It was obvious that no one had driven it since the snow began.

"You don't need to come with me," Selby said. "You can wait in the car where it's warm."

"And you can eat shit and howl at the moon," Ratliffe said. "I want to see what's going to happen."

"What's going to happen is, I'm going to walk up the drive and look at the house. I might even knock on the door." Selby looked up the driveway, trying to get a glimpse of the house at the other end. "I'm not sure what comes after that."

"All the more reason to have backup on hand. Look, I won't go all the way up to the house unless you need me to. I'll hang back out of sight and just watch and listen."

"I don't like involving you any further than I have to."

Ratliffe scoffed. "Tell that to your buddy in the basement back at the Herald-Star, or your friend Roy, or the old fascist with the dog. Your private business has spilled out into the world, Coates. I didn't get involved because I needed a strange new friend who knows a godawful lot about some godawful movies that were made before I was out of diapers. I got involved in this because I needed an adventure, a reason to get out of bed every morning. So here we are. Now we really are friends —at least I think so—and I need to see the adventure through to the thrilling conclusion, for your sake and for mine. Plus, you're an accident waiting to happen. I don't want something to happen to you that I might have prevented."

Selby fidgeted, and Ratliffe laughed.

"Your face is going to stick like that if you're not careful," he said.

"All right, fine. Just stay out of sight. I want to look at the house without them seeing us."

"This is me, being invisible."

The driveway took the shape of a gentle S curve, trending away to the right. When the two men followed it around the pine trees, Selby stopped.

"What is it?" Ratliffe asked softly.

"Listen."

Voices carried on the snow and the fitful breeze. Laughter. An infant's shrieks.

"Something's happening," Selby said, starting forward. "There's a child screaming."

Ratliffe grabbed his arm. "Wait. That kid's not screaming. It's *laughing*. That's a toddler being entertained."

"Are you sure?"

"Yeah. I'm sure." Ratliffe released his arm, patting it gently as he did so. "I've got three sisters, all with kids. I've heard a few babies."

Adult laughter alternated with the child's shrill enthusiasm.

"More than one grownup," Selby said.

"Sounds like they're having a good time."

Selby nodded. "It does." His chest was heavy, dense, full of rocks. "They're having … They're having *fun*." The Empty Room was in turmoil, the whispers rushing out into Selby's consciousness, then retreating to their refuge. Selby felt as though he was watching himself from a great distance, over the heads of an anxious crowd.

The two men resumed walking, very slowly this time, peering ahead through the falling snow. Ratliffe kept back a few yards, allowing Selby to move ahead.

A last clump of shrubbery screened the house. Selby crept up to where he could see past the long leaves of rhododendrons burdened with snow.

The house was neat, not large, a doll's house in white clapboard, two stories tall. Blue shutters framed the windows, and a narrow porch ran across the front, three steps up. A lawn and winter-bare flowerbeds blurred into the fields and woods that surrounded the property, any definite boundary hidden by the snow.

A woman stood on the porch, laughing. She held her arms tight to her torso, conserving warmth. Selby couldn't see anything but her face; everything else was covered by a fluffy shawl wrapped around her shoulders and pulled up over her hair. Her cheeks were red, a little chapped, and her mouth was wide and expressive.

She was watching a man and a baby.

A man and a baby, playing in the snow.

The baby was no more than a year old. He, she—no, he, Selby was certain the baby was a boy—was wearing a snowsuit that turned him into a blue mass, a cylinder with a giggling face at one end.

An adult, a man, bareheaded in the snow, was flying the baby around the yard. Laughing. Laughing as though he and that child had just invented happiness, and they wanted to see all the ways it could be worked.

They were playing "airplanes." Selby knew this was what they called it because he had once been flown around in the snow the same way.

By the same man.

Sullivan Coates—now Sully Colt—looked to be about thirty. He was not tall, but Selby knew he would always seem taller than he was. His hair was a red-blond tangle, dusted with snow. His teeth were very white, and his eyes were very blue. He needed a haircut.

Breathe. In and out. In and out.

Selby could sense Ratliffe standing behind him. What would have happened if he had been out here alone? Would he have stood behind the rhododendrons until he froze to death? Staring, feeling …? He didn't know what he was feeling.

He's beautiful, isn't he.

The voice was colder than the snow gathering on Selby's shoulders and spotting his glasses so that he had to keep wiping them.

"No. Yes." The man was not beautiful like a model or a movie star. Photos would show a generic, healthy, thirty-year-old male. Attractive, but not someone you'd look at twice. But in person, watching his mouth, his eyes, the way he laughed, he *was* beautiful, beautiful like someone who was once the center of the world and had been gone a long time, leaving a hole.

This is his life, Doma's bland, icy voice told him, echoing inside his skull. *For now.*

Selby looked over to his left and saw Doma and Laylah standing in the driveway. Laylah was still in the form of Alma

Mobley, staring at the man and child with a hunger that no flesh-and-blood body could have supported.

"What's the baby's name?" Selby asked.

Alexander, came the reply. *They'll call him Sandy. Like you, he'll be fair-haired. Like you, he has his father's eyes.*

"Free him," Laylah said, her teeth gritted, her face rigid with concentration.

"They'll hear you," Selby warned.

They are unaware of us.

"Free him," Laylah said again, still not looking away from the man and child. "This is why you were born, why I brought you back from the threshold of death. It is your destiny to be the instrument of our Brother's release."

She still talks like a character in a comic book, Selby thought, the observation giving him perspective, keeping him from drowning. *She's in pain. She's breaking the rules, being here, talking to me while I'm awake.*

"The Empty Room," he said. "All the missing bits of him are there, aren't they? Floating around with all that other stuff. Everything he needs to … to what? To become one man again? With only one life? No more fading in and out?"

Doma bowed her head briefly. Her hair was unbound, and tiny breezes lifted it so that Selby couldn't see where the hair ended and the snow began. She was wearing gray and white: dove-gray jeans tucked into white boots, a heavy white poncho. She might have been made of snow.

The parts are there. You are the template, the blueprint, that guides the recovery.

Selby counted his breaths, watching the man and child, the laughing woman. In a few years, he knew, Sully Colt would begin to wander, to disappear—for days, at first, then weeks, leaving a baffled wife and a hurt child behind. One day, he would be gone, and only the bafflement and the hurt would remain. This moment would become a confusing memory. Nostalgia.

What a wonderful word, Selby thought. *The Greeks understood*. Nostos, *homecoming, and* algos, *pain. Coming home to the hurt.*

He breathed, in and out, clinging desperately to himself, his identity, his reality. All the while, the undertow from the Empty Room tugged at him. Vast, formless intellects rose to the surface to sniff at his desires, his fears, his loneliness.

The baby giggle-screamed, and his father squeezed him, pressing their noses together while they laughed into each other's laughter. *So much love,* Selby thought. *So much love,* he remembered.

"What will happen to him when his identity is returned to him?"

He will rejoin his Brothers and Sisters. He will be whole.

"And this woman? This child?"

Doma said nothing, and Selby turned to face her. "Tell me."

Her eyes were frosted quicksilver, cold, cold.

They will get on with their lives. Without him. In time, they will age, and they will die. As you will. As you all do. As he cannot.

A crow called from somewhere across the field behind the house and was answered from the depths of the trees.

Laylah turned to face him. He saw that her hands were trembling. "None of this matters. Dear Selby. *None of this matters.* This is not who he was ever meant to be. This existence is punishment. A punishment you can bring to an end, at long last."

Selby turned to Doma, frowning.

"I'm not the first."

No.

"What happened to the others?"

Doma looked at Laylah, then at the family.

They failed.

Selby scoffed. "That's it? 'They failed'? Surely, we've gotten past the 'vague hints and allusions' stage by now."

The times were wrong. The circumstances were wrong. The key no longer fit the lock.

"And if I fail?"

Doma focused her chill, passionless regard on the man and child.

There will be another time, another key.

Selby's tears were freezing onto his lashes. If he could go back into the past and warn Naomi Goodwin that the man she found so irresistible was not what he seemed … What then? Would she thank him for his intervention? Would this woman choose to give up this moment to spare herself future pain? A pain shared by so many, for so long.

Sandy, he thought. *If I fall by the wayside, he's the next candidate. That's how this works. Generation after generation until somebody finally gets it right.*

"Go," Laylah said, her face shifting. She became Patricia Neal, then Marion Crane, slender ankles disappearing into the snow. "Now. Greet your father. After all this time, isn't that what you want? Will you ever tire of all this useless chatter? Go talk to him." Maleva raised a withered arm, clattering with bracelets, to point at the house, commanding.

Selby looked at her, his thoughts jumbled together with the Empty Room. He was finding it hard to keep track of which was which.·

Laylah was right.·

And it was all wrong.·

Sully had brought Sandy up to the porch, and the parents were talking to him, the three of them so close together that when Selby took off his glasses to wipe them, there seemed to be only one organism on the porch, one shape, one being.

The crows called again, one to another and back again, and the snow intensified. For a moment, Doma became nothing more than gray eyes and dark stitching, screened by the falling snow, while Laylah shifted again, becoming a small girl in a black sweater clutching a sock monkey to her chest.

"I was that baby," Selby said, speaking softly, speaking only to himself. "That child. I was so happy with him. Even when things got strange, there toward the end, I was happy. I didn't know how to show it. I didn't know how to share my happiness with my mother, with him, with other kids, but I was happy. Everyone doesn't get that, do they? That kind of joy. Even briefly." He glanced back at Ratliffe, who stood quietly, snow gathering on his shoulders and on top of his knitted cap, then at Laylah and Doma. He looked at the group on the porch.

"He's happy. My father."

Of course, Doma said, gazing not at the house but at Selby. *It is his nature.*

Selby met her eyes.

The world seemed to breathe—in and out, in and out. The milk glass goddess nodded slightly.

Everything paused for a moment.

Doma's silver gaze held Selby's faded blue as she dissolved away, breaking apart into a swirl of snow that rode the breeze away across the fields and woods.

Laylah whipped around to stare at him, her eyes wild, a child's hands clutching Daisy with a manic strength. With a strange, inhuman cry, she turned back to the house and dropped to her knees, her head sagging.

Selby watched her for a moment, almost blinded by freezing tears, then he turned and looked back to where Ratliffe waited.

"We can't just leave her there," Ratliffe protested. "She's only a child."

"I doubt if she was ever a child," Selby said in a broken voice. "She never had that."

When he turned back, the little girl with the willow-green eyes and the insanely happy sock monkey had vanished, and a murder of crows flew across the fields, disappearing into the white haze of the snow.

Still carrying his son, Sully Colt followed his wife into the house. When the door closed, a lacy curtain of white slipped off the roof and down onto the front steps.

CHAPTER TWENTY-SIX

The mid-April sunshine was anemic but recovering day by day.

The ancients had sacrificed their livestock, their captive enemies, sometimes even their own children, to hasten the process, blood offerings to feed the god, to bring him back to the fullness of health. Today's offerings were less grisly. Down below, far across the grass, shirtless young men played soccer while their girlfriends lounged on blankets in shorts and tank tops, cheering them on with words and with the implied promise of more substantial rewards later. The breeze was still cold enough to numb Selby's ears, but the kids on the grass were made of sterner stuff, offering their goose-pimpled flesh as a bribe to lure summer back into the sky.

Selby approved of the new rituals.

Winter had come early and stayed late, bringing cold and sleep and an unwelcome understanding of the inevitability of change, but now the sun was finally making a trial appearance, testing the equipment, making sure all the parts still worked.

Selby sat back on the bench at the halfway point of Two-Mile Trail and let the sunlight soak into him. All his parts still worked, but some were showing signs of wear and tear. He was scheduled for cataract surgery in five weeks and a knee replacement in September. He spent far too much of his time these days imagining all the things that could go wrong with either procedure, but he had put things off long enough.

Evolve or die, he thought.

A woman appeared at the edge of the woods, where the trail emerged from the trees. She was tall, wearing a long charcoal-gray dress trimmed with rows of fuzzy black balls the size of grapes. Her hair was dark, pulled into a bun and covered by a hat, a confusing thing in gray felt and black tulle, with little dangling bits of what Selby supposed was jet. The woman wore a shawl, and her boots were black patent leather, buttoned up the sides.

"Deborah Paget in *The Haunted Palace*," Selby said as she reached the top of the hill. "It suits you."

Laylah smiled. "Thank you. I do like the hat. May I join you?"

He gestured at the bench next to him. "Of course. I'm … I'm pleased to see you." He was surprised to find that he meant that.

She settled gracefully, pulling the long dress aside and arranging her shawl—gray satin trimmed with black feathers—more comfortably around her shoulders, her black handbag in her lap.

"How is it that I *am* seeing you?" Selby asked. "Am I asleep?"

"Dozing. The spring sunshine seems to have a soporific effect."

He nodded. "It's been a long winter."

"Yes, it has. How are your friends?" Laylah asked politely.

"Everyone's fine. Roy has bleached her hair. She looks like a dandelion gone to seed. She and Reggie have a new crow, an albino. They call him Doma."

"Oh, my."

"The name was my idea," Selby said.

"Our Sister will probably be flattered."

"As if anybody could tell. Anyway, the Colonel has asked me to help him write his memoirs. He's still a monster, but he's led a fascinating life, and I look forward to working on the project." Selby paused, looking over at the woman on the bench next to him. If she knew that working with the Colonel might well bring Selby into contact with another of her kind, she showed no reaction to that knowledge.

He continued. "Ratliffe and I get together for lunch two or three times a month. Sometimes, he brings his girlfriend."

Laylah smiled. "A chaperone?"

Selby blushed, looking down at his hands. "Probably. I'm so irresistible."

Laylah laughed, the laugh Selby remembered from their first meeting, there in the hospital as he lay more dead than alive. He had wanted to laugh with her then but couldn't. This time, he could and did.

Selby looked at her, one furtive glance, then out over the landscape. Early wildflowers dotted the grass: henbit, bitter-cress, hepatica, patches of ground ivy humming with bees. Trout lilies glittered yellow in the shadows at the foot of the rockpile, and further away, among the cultivated beds, daffodils shimmered as fitful breezes stirred them. A heron stalked the weedy edge of the pond, hunting the spring peepers, and crows called and quarreled at the edge of the woods.

I won't beg, Selby promised himself. He blew out his cheeks. *But I might as well get right to it.*

"Are you here to take back your gift?" he asked aloud, speaking slowly, carefully.

"My gift?" She held out her hand and looked at it, admiring an emerald ring she found there. Drawing out the moment.

"My life."

Finally, she turned her eyes to his, and he remembered how alien she was, no matter how familiar her disguise.

"My dear Selby. You may keep your life, such as it is. I'm disappointed in your failure to keep your end of our bargain, but you're only human, after all. Humans are, at best, unreliable."

"Then … it was an empty threat? This notion that if I failed to track Sullivan down for you, you'd let me die?"

"An empty threat? No. I could end your life right now. But what would be the point? I'm not going to be vindictive toward a tool that proved inadequate for the intended task. I'll just put it aside and look for another." Laylah smiled. "It was important that you believe that your survival was in peril, or you would never have left the suffocating comfort of your petty little life to do what I wanted done."

She still talks like a comic book villain, Selby thought. He took off his glasses and cleaned them, his movements fussy and precise. His emotions were so bewildering at that moment that they seemed to belong to someone else.

"So," he said, putting his glasses back on, "if you're not here to throw me back under the bus, figuratively speaking, to what do I owe the pleasure of your visit? Last time I saw you …" He faltered. "That was a very complicated situation. I'm sorry I disappointed you."

Laylah smiled into the middle distance. Crows flapped across from the woods to land on the grass a few yards away. She opened her bag and pulled out half a sandwich wrapped in a sheet of Bates Motel letterhead. She tore the sandwich into chunks and tossed them to the birds, who leaped and pirouetted, devouring the treats with *churrs* of satisfaction before marching back and forth through the grass, preening and posing.

"To have waited so long, and to see the prize snatched away like that … I won't deny that it was difficult." She watched the crows, and Selby watched her. Finally, she said, "You did what you had to do, and I will do what I have to do."

"Which is what, if I may ask?" Selby asked, his apprehension returning in a rush.

"I will wait," she said after a minute. "I will wait."

She crumpled the paper and put it back into her bag. "I will wait another mortal lifetime, until after you're gone and someone else carries the key. I've waited a thousand mortal lifetimes, and I've been disappointed a thousand times. One day that will change. Just not now."

"I'm sorry," Selby said again. "Our relationship, yours and mine, hasn't exactly been sunshine and roses, but I never wanted to cause you pain. I know I owe you. It's just that … My father. He was so happy. Even if it can't last, I couldn't take that away from him, away from his child. The few years they have together … To have that time." He paused, struggling to find the words. "That was me, once. That baby. That joy."

Breathe. In and out. In and out.

"He was so happy," he repeated.

Laylah nodded, resigned, calm. "I know. He has always been happy. He will always be happy. That is why we love him as we do." She gathered her shawl and rose to her feet. "I promised you gifts to replace your cupcake," she said, looking down at him.

"I had forgotten that. DeQuinn's cupcake."

"This thing you carry, that is a part of you and us at the same time, what you call the Empty Room. It is more than a receptacle for the shards of our Brother's soul; it's who you are. You will have time to explore it, perhaps to learn to use it responsibly, before the time comes to pass it on to the next custodian. Try not to unleash the Apocalypse or drive yourself mad."

"Thank you," Selby said, his ears hot. "I'll do my best."

Crows squalled to each other as they flew overhead, and Selby awoke, startled and blinking, his butt numb and his knee aching. He looked around.

Alone.

He took a deep breath and sat up straight on the bench, a small man under a vast blue sky, basking in the spring sunshine. There was a scent of cedar and cloves and soft candles in the air.

Alive.

"Thank you," he said again.

. . .

Fiona's Baby Diary:
Ruth has been sick, but she's feeling better now. She and Mitch are talking about her retiring soon and going back to being a farmer's wife. I think it'll be an adjustment, but it might be good for her. Maybe I'm just being selfish. I'd love to have Ruth right down the road 24/7. She's like a grandmother and fairy god-mother all rolled into one. (A GRUMPY fairy godmother, but still!) When spring gets here, Bingo is going to spend a few days at the farm while Bongo and I get reacquainted. Ruth still can't get used to calling the baby Bingo. She's called him by his full name for forever, but lately she's finally loosened up enough to call him "Sandy."

I hope these days last forever.

# # #

REFERENCES

Selby Coates refers to a number of movies and books during the course of this narrative. The following is an alphabetical list of the works mentioned. Films are listed by title, year of release, director, and distributor. Printed works are listed by title and type, author's name, and publisher.

- **The Abominable Doctor Phibes**, 1971 film, Robert Fuest, Am. Int'l Pictures
- **Attack of the Crab Monsters**, 1957 film, Roger Corman, Allied Artists Pictures
- **At the Mountains of Madness**, 1936 novella, HP Lovecraft, Astounding Stories
- **The Beast From 20,000 Fathoms**, 1953 film, Eugène Lourié, Warner Bros.
- **The Birds**, 1963 film, Alfred Hitchcock, Universal Pictures
- **The Black Scorpion**, 1957 film, Edward Ludwig, Warner Bros.
- **Black Sunday**, 1960 film, Mario Bava, American Int'l Pictures
- **The Bride of Frankenstein**, 1935 film, James Whale, Universal Pictures
- **The Brides of Dracula**, 1960 film, Terence Fisher, Universal-International
- **The Deadly Mantis**, 1957 film, Nathan H. Juran, Universal-International
- **Devil Girl from Mars**, 1954 film, David MacDonald, British Lion Films

- **Dracula's Daughter**, 1936 film, Lambert Hillyer, Universal Pictures
- **Ghost Story**, 1981 film, John Irvin, Universal Pictures
- **The Gorgon**, 1964 film, Terence Fisher, Hammer Films
- **The Hunchback of Notre Dame**, 1831 novel, Victor Hugo, Gosselin
- **The Lord of the Rings**, 1954-1955 novel, J. R. R. Tolkien, Allen & Unwin
- **The Mummy**, 1932 film, Karl Freund, Universal Pictures
- **The Mystery of the Wax Museum**, 1933 film, Michael Curtiz, Warner Bros.
- **Psycho**, 1960 film, Alfred Hitchcock, Paramount Pictures
- **The Raven**, 1963 film, Roger Corman, American International Pictures
- **The Shadow Over Innsmouth**, 1936 novella, HP Lovecraft, Visionary Pub. Co.
- **SpongeBob SquarePants**, 1999-Present, animated TV program, Stephen Hillenburg, Nickelodeon
- **Tarantula!**, 1955 film, Jack Arnold, Universal-International
- **Them!**, 1954 film, David Weisbart, Warner Bros. (only an indirect reference)
- **The Thing from Another World**, 1951 film, Christian Nyby, RKO Radio Pictures
- **Village of the Damned**, 1960 film, Wolf Rilla, MGM/Loew's
- **The Wasp Woman**, 1959 film, Roger Corman, Allied Artists
- **Whatever Happened to Baby Jane?**, 1962 film, Robert Aldrich, Warner Bros.
- **The Wolf Man**, 1941 film, George Waggner, Universal Pictures

ACKNOWLEDGMENTS

If I've learned one thing about writing a novel, it's that you don't do it alone. Many thanks to the folks who made this all possible: Denele Campbell, Anne Burgos, and Keiren Westwood for editing and moral suppport; Mary and Steve Anderson, Jackie Holcomb, Ann Malkie, and Sally Williams, for being my test subjects and providing essential feedback; my mother, for teaching me the language; and always John, for keeping me sane.

Cover by David Lee Holcomb
Cupcake photo by WNstock on *shutterstock.com*
Crow photo by Ralphs_Fotos on *pixabay.com*
Crow silhouettes by Vexturo on *shutterstock.com*

DAVID LEE HOLCOMB

www.ingramcontent.com/pod-product-compliance
Lightning Source LLC
Chambersburg PA
CBHW071543110726
47908CB00007B/1978